Undead Redhead

Buried. Made up grotesquely. Still wearing that horrid fuchsia bridesmaid's dress and matching killer heels.

And then there were the stitches, in an all-too telling "Y" from shoulder to shoulder and on down her sternum. She could see them when she pulled the front of her dress out an inch or two. The crazy eyes. Not to mention the undeniable stench of slightly rotting (although presumably nicely embalmed) flesh.

How on earth was this possible? Reanimated? Organs removed and stuffed back in haphazardly? Hooked up to a pump and gutted of blood?

Zombified?

Sharon's stomach rumbled alarmingly. At first, she had a surge of hope. Maybe her plumbing *was* all still hooked up the way it should be. The next moment, she had a decidedly darker thought as the organ in question growled loudly for a second time.

Zombified? And zombies ate…

"*REALLY* not good," she said.

CELEBRATING 10 YEARS OF UNDEAD MAGIC!

Praise for Jen Frankel's Undead Redhead

Jen Frankel does a wonderful job at delving into the psyche of a repressed main character who acquires personal liberty while being the living dead. It's a refreshing, lively, and entertaining story… The cast is diverse and interesting… a gang of deadbeat friends, a crack lady, Morgoni the cryptoparapsychocriminologist (say that ten times fast), an Internet stalking identity thief, and the ever precocious and adorable Waglet… This is a nicely written book; fun, silly, and intelligent too… It's an easy read, but I wouldn't advise reading it too fast or you might miss moments of subtle humour.

Kit Daven, *The Xinisi Trilogy*

Who knew a zombie could be vegan?! That's just one twist on movie version zombies in Jen Frankel's book Undead Redhead… Wonderful story, full of humour and great characters. If you like any type of zombie, this is a great story for you.

Lee A. Farruga, The Geeky Godmother

Frankel is good at creating credibly absurd scenes. The climactic scene in the novel, which brings many of the main characters in the story together in a television studio, wraps up storylines in a satisfying humorous way. To her credit, Frankel is trying to do something fresh with a currently overexposed sub-genre. Those who are expecting a zombie apocalypse will be disappointed by Undead Redhead. However, those who are looking for a fun, original take on the zombie sub-genre will find a very rewarding book.

Ira Nayman, *Amazing Stories Magazine*

This story is less about zombies and more about learning self-love, self-acceptance and gaining confidence…The characters in this story are funny, quirky and memorable as Frankel masterfully weaves together the subplots and various narrative viewpoints into a tense but satisfying showdown.

Vanessa Ricci-Thode, *After the Dragon Raid*

This is not your typical horror tale… (T)he protagonist is in fact a redhead who has indeed come back from the dead as a zombie. There happens to be one slight problem with her reanimation: Sharon, the redhead, is (was) a vegan… Not only does she have to now adjust to being a very sentient, yet mildly rotting zombie, but she also to has to find an atypical undead regimen to satiate her growing hunger… I would recommend this book to light horror fans (no gore alerts here!), those who enjoy some romance, as well as those who like comedic and ironic situations in their stories. **I rate this book 4 out of 4 stars.**

**rssllue, Beardmaster of Bookshelves
Onlinebookclub.org official review**

4.5/5 stars. This was a delightful read. Funny and resonant of modern society in all its North American wackiness. I loved the satire in the story, sentimentally for the redhead in the pink bridesmaids dress (been there), but more intellectually for the fun poked at the pomp of weddings, the irrationality of internet sensations, the opportunism of the media, and the way humans can interact in crazy, unfeeling ways. All that said, the characters were realistic, and some were caring, compassionate people.

Ann Dulhanty, *The Spiders Edge*

Undead Redhead

A novel about love after death

a Xeno Productions publication
Contact: XenoProductions
info@jenfrankel.com
www.jenfrankel.com

10th Anniversary Edition copyright © 2014, 2024 by Jen Frankel & XenoProductions
ISBN: 978-1497356849

Table of Contents

to the notion of love after death –

and always, to more humanity in this life

Undead Redhead

Finis

1.

It was the darkness that woke her. Strange, that. It wasn't the noise of the vehicle shutting down, or the tick tick tick of the engine as it cooled. It was the darkness.

She had never slept a night in her life without some kind of light on. Fear of the dark was a fact of existence for her, really. There was a parade of night-lights throughout her past that would have rivaled the unintentional frog collection of someone who'd mentioned once that frogs were cute, and suffered for decades under a growing, groaning, ever-increasing assortment of amphibian figurines, cozies, mugs, mouse pads, and stuffed animals.

Sharon Backovic didn't like the dark. She didn't like things that went bump in the night, or boyfriends who jumped out from behind bushes and laughed when she squealed, or even America's Funniest Home Videos, because too often they just seemed mean. She did like soft blankets with patterns on them in pastel green and yellow, and kittens up for adoption at the pet store, and well, who doesn't like sunshine and blue skies?

At first, she wasn't even sure she'd opened her eyes. There was no change in the inky blackness, no sign that her eyelids were up and not still shuttering her gaze. There was… there was nothing. Nothing, just dark.

If she hadn't immediately realized she must be dreaming and having the very kind of nightmare she slept with a night-light to avoid, she would have started screaming. As it was, she had just enough presence of mind (which was created in large part by worry that she'd disturb the neighbours if she *did* sound off like a siren) to squeeze her eyes back shut, telling herself firmly that *This is a dream, this is only a dream,* and try again.

But there was no change in the density of the blackness surrounding her, only the faint ticking of the motor which was finally able to intrude on her consciousness.

Consciousness. It couldn't actually be consciousness, not really. It *had* to be a dream.

And then, as her awareness increased and her senses spread beyond just her eyes and ears, she realized something almost as disturbing as the notion she'd fallen asleep somehow, somewhere, and woken in the pitch black.

That froze her, eyes still open, staring sightlessly into the dark. There was no way she was in her own bed, not in anyone's bed, not a bed at all per se. Definitely not a slightly saggy-in-the-middle bed owned by someone she knew (Dan? Darryl?) where if he wasn't in a particularly cuddly mood, she had to cling slightly to the outer edge of the mattress in order to stop herself from rolling into him all night. Nor was it her own warm, slightly remembered and wonderfully yielding queen-size bed, a gratefully-received post-grad present from her parents, festooned with extra pillows, throws, and a few choice stuffed animals (no frogs among them).

No, this was definitely not a bed. Her back was hard-up against what felt like the kind of padding they put on benches in public spaces like art galleries and museums to convince people not to linger too long. There was a smooth coolness to whatever covered the surface which was probably satin, definitely *not* a welcoming fabric. You put satin sheets on your bed only once before you realized that they're cold, slippery, and tend to make you feel more like a creature in an aquarium than sexy as all hell.

Then there was the feeling of *closeness*. She could feel, even without moving, the nearness of the sides of whatever she lay in. The sides of her shoulders were almost touching what could only be vertical slabs of padding covered in the same cool slickness.

Tentatively, almost afraid to find out, she lifted a hand from her side and raised it—only to encounter more padding a face-breadth's distance above her.

Now, she figured, she really should start to scream—but the time no longer seemed ideal. Waiting until you'd discovered the parameters of your situation before reacting was something that only small children could get away with (slip, skin the knee, stare at mummy whose mouth has opened in horror, look at knee, see blood, take huge gulp of air and… *SCREAM!*) No, an adult had to scream at the moment of impact, so to speak, had to complain *at* the moment the food arrives wrong, not two days later, had to tell the boyfriend he was pissing her off and not nearly as funny as he thought right at the moment he was mocking the way she half-snorted, half-guffawed during the movie and not, well, never.

So actual screaming was out. Panicking, something she could do discretely and silently, was *on*.

The undeniable conclusion she had reached, the culmination of sifting the evidence and following the logic God had given her, led her to one thought and one thought only. She was in a coffin. She had been buried alive.

2.

Neon fuchsia is a colour best reserved for accents on royal wedding "fascinators" or little girls' ribbons. Maybe, at a stretch, for a socialite's matched luggage, although only allowing for the adverse reactions of anyone with a weak stomach who might have to handle it.

It wasn't a colour Sharon had ever worn before, even with a happy attraction to other, less virulent shades of pink. Even neon fuchsia held a small, well, very small, place in her heart. Always provided, of course, she didn't have to *wear* it.

"Is it…" she said, raising her voice so that Dave would hear her in the next room, "does it… I don't know. I think it makes me look a little… green."

He said something, but not loud enough for her to hear. Sharon raised the dress again, then the shoes, then the dress. It had to be some kind of through-the-air chemical reaction between the red of her hair and the pink of the dress. Had to be. She could almost believe there was a crackle in the atmosphere when she brought it closer to her face.

"Dave?" she tried, a little louder this time. Neon fuchsia, dress, shoes, and, in all likelihood, accessories in the same hideously clashing shade.

Suddenly, through a break in either the television blaring from the living room or a momentary skip in the playing of her own thoughts, she heard Dave as clear as day. "I can't talk now," he said, and her heart skipped a little beat, just like her train of thought had.

"Dave?" she said. "Who's that?" That's why he hadn't heard her before; he was on the phone. Of course.

This time, his reply was clear and unambiguous. "No one, honey!"

Sharon-in-the-mirror frowned back at her, and the hand holding the hanger drooped. *No one?*

3.

Okay. In a coffin, and buried alive. Could be worse, right? She could be dead and buried in a coffin. She could be buried alive *not* in a coffin. Or just dead.

Alive meant that at least she wasn't dead, right? That was something.

And Sharon Backovic was nothing if not an optimist. She'd even put a good face on Dorri's choice of colour for the bridesmaids' dresses, and smiled with unabashed (if not entirely honest) delight when her friend had unveiled them with a flourish.

If she wasn't such an optimist, she'd have maybe remarked on the sly way that Dorri kept looking at her while rhapsodizing about how she'd always wanted a *really stunning pink* for her bridesmaids when she got married, instead of pretending she didn't notice. She might have said something like, "You know I look horrible in pink, especially bright pink, don't you, Dorri?" instead of clapping her hands in pretended delight like a trained sea lion. *Arf! Arf!*

But Sharon was a dyed-in-the-womb optimist. You had to be, born into a family where your parents' constant bickering formed the lullaby of your infancy, where their own self-involvement meant that the only thing you could ever do to catch their attention was to do something *really, really wrong, Sharon,* and then the attention you got was worse than being ignored. You had to stay positive when people told you it was *such a shame* when your parents not only split as soon as you were old enough to leave home, but virtually fled to opposite coasts, abandoning you in the middle *where you'll be happiest, dear* and then staying in touch only the bare minimum when offspring ear-bending was required (*yes, dear, I'm sure you're having lots of adventures. But really, I called to talk about me…*)

Sharon was unrepentant in her pursuit of happiness at unreasonable odds. Yes, maybe it kept her with Dave even when she wasn't entirely sure he even liked her much less ever demonstrated a real desire to pay any attention to her. Yes, maybe it got her a degree in English literature because no matter how boring it became by year three, there *had* to be an upside of slogging through the Dead White Male Canon, some kind of tangible reward for *sticking with it and never giving up.*

Yes, on her darker days, Sharon wasn't sure *anything* she'd done to stay positive was really worth it, whether playing referee for parents and siblings alike during what seemed like an endless parade of petty complaints and mortal slights or trying to be a dutiful girlfriend because, after all, according to everyone else, she was *so so lucky to be with Dave.* She couldn't say for certain, though, that it wasn't *exactly* the right response, and so she kept on. If being a Pollyanna was a somewhat mitigated reaction to strong stimulus, at least it was something she could live with. She had seen too many hissy-fits between adults before the age of ten to want to participate herself.

All this was *not,* however, going through Sharon's mind as she lay in the coffin. In fact, Sharon Backovic was at that moment currently quite unaware of her own names, neither Sharon nor Backovic, didn't remember her fraught childhood where the stuffed animals she'd received every Christmas and birthday until the age of twelve seemed almost a kind of "consolation prize" for surviving a little longer in the insanity, and not aware she'd been dating—up until her burial at least—a young man who was also a recent graduate from an English program, called David Jules Swinson.

Impressions and images floated through her beleaguered brain, but nothing was connecting like it should. In fact, she had a memory or two that *weren't* hers in addition to lacking the usual complement of the ones that were.

In one of these *not my memories*, Sharon bent over a circle drawn in the dirt. Her nails, which felt like they were hers but were on someone else's hands, had dirt caked blackly under them. Her hands (same deal, not her hands but seemingly attached to her) had dirt on them as well, but also a more troubling splatter of blood and what looked like the fluffy down of a chicken's feathers.

A barbecue? No, a camping trip? But if the former, why an open fire and not a grill? And if the latter, why the empty clearing; why was she alone out here with the... *Knife*!

Sharon's hands moved with a surety she definitely didn't feel. They made a cut on her thumb (*not her thumb?*) and moved a candle into the center of the circle to catch the drops that oozed, collected, fell. The knife was your standard *everyone has one in a kitchen drawer* cheaply-made steak knife, serrated blade no more than six inches long, with a battered wood handle that had seen a lot of washings and many better days. The candle was a standard-issue glass jar filled with wax bigger than a pint glass with the image of a saint in garish colours on the side. The blood, well, it was red and the thumb itched more than hurt.

This is not me, Sharon told herself, but it didn't help. While she fought the memory, tried to exorcise it out of her own head and back to whomever it belonged, it seemed inviolate. Only as she gave up, gave in, and tried to make the best of it did the memory lose its tangibility. Then, as she chased it, hoping to understand how it fit into her own life, it faded as quickly as it had come into the ether. Into the sticky darkness.

Then, a memory that felt more like it might be hers. A woman's voice, a little strident not with anger but as if its owner wanted to communicate just by her tone to *get this right, all of you.* Sharon had a sudden flash of sunlight, water, a cascade of sparkling droplets—sunshine on a fountain? And then, screams.

4.

Toward the front of the hearse carrying the coffin in which Sharon was making discoveries about her situation, a man stretched his toes. He reached them as far as space would permit forward into the space under the dashboard, then opened the car door and unfolded himself from the vehicle.

He took another moment to stretch before moving to the side of the hearse and opening a small door there. The space between the front seats and the coffin in the cargo space was full of the tools of a gravedigger's trade: shovels, picks, mattocks, and the folding frame used to mark off the boundaries of the grave before cutting the sod above it. He removed a shovel, stood it upright on its handle to check the blade for wear and imperfections, then gave a sigh worthy of Job before slamming the door closed and starting off toward the distant site where the backhoe waited for him.

In the coffin, Sharon started as the door slammed. The sound was too distinctive for her not to recognize it. In a coffin, and in a vehicle. Her mind would not go so far as to say the word "hearse," but it lurked, unexamined, in her troubled head. A terrible mistake had been made. She had been judged dead, somehow, some mysterious how, but it was not too late for someone to rescue her.

Her brain wasn't going a lot of reasonable places, not that Sharon was particularly aware of the lapses. A fog was surrounding her thoughts, thick and viscous. It was what had allowed her the momentary luxury of thinking at first that this was all a dream, and what now was avoiding the perhaps obvious conclusion that if she was in a coffin at all, everyone she knew could conceivably believe that she was indeed dead. In that case, of course, no one would be coming to save her, not ever. You didn't try to rescue a dead person from a coffin, even if the rumours of her death had been undeniably exaggerated.

Something about the bleakness of this future crept into the more conscious part of Sharon's mind, and started a little tickle of concern. If no one knew she was still alive, who would come to check on her? Presumably, if she was in a (hearse) vehicle of some kind, she was heading for or already at a graveyard or cemetery of some sort, and the next logical step would be (burial) something she didn't even want to think about.

Abruptly, the coffin rocked, just a minor degree or so off upright. What was that? Someone getting into the back of the (hearse) cargo area? Whatever sounds that might have accompanied whatever was happening were entirely muted by the walls around her, but she had an odd feeling that, just for a few moments (but then, who can tell time in the dark in a coffin?) she was no longer alone.

And then, a quieter, much quieter sound that she took to be the door closing again, this time with far more finesse. An almost… stealthy finesse, actually. And suddenly Sharon felt not only alone but bereft, as if there would never, ever be anyone to look at or talk to or laugh with ever again, and this was unbearable.

She reached a tentative hand up again to encounter the padding above her face. Did they lock coffins? It didn't seem likely, or at least, it was a bit of a wasted effort. I mean, no one (usually) would want to get *out* of one, and who would try to get *in,* knowing what they'd find inside?

Okay.

Determined, squashing the possibility of disappointment, Sharon placed both palms against the lid and pushed, trying to shift it off the bottom part of the (coffin) box.

Not okay. There was no sensation of movement in the heavy lid above, no shift, no give.

Sharon had a vague recollection then of some TV show or other where she'd seen a coffin's lid secured not with a lock but with thumbscrews. If that was how this lid was attached, there was absolutely no way she was getting out, alive or otherwise. The horror of this idea was so overwhelming that Sharon's brain, fuzzy as it was, pushing it away into the dark recesses of, well, of the satin-lined box in which she lay.

Which may or may not have absolutely for certain been a coffin.

5.

A beautiful day, the sun warm but not hot, the clouds covering enough of the blue, blue sky to provide a screen from the direct light which might have ruined the photos.

Sharon fidgeted, shifting her weight back and forth on the fuchsia shoes. They hadn't seemed that high when she'd walked from Dave's car to the church, but she could swear they'd got steadily higher throughout the service. The walk to the limo after the reception line outside the chapel had seemed miles long, not a mere few hundred feet.

And now, in this lovely little park by this lovely little fountain, as people milled about in their wedding finery, the heels could be seventeen inches high, two sizes too small, and made of molten steel for all the lauded "comfort" the wedding planner had insisted was the hallmark of this particular model. Sharon was a flats-girl primarily, her max heel height in the low-rise bracket, not in the stratosphere.

It was all very well for Dorri, of course, who never went anywhere without perfect makeup, exactly the right mix of vintage and latest couture, and her creamy cafe au lait skin glowing with health and an almost aggressive vitality. Her mix of Asian and Caucasian blood also gave her the almond eyes and perfectly bowed lips that apparently were enough to overcome any amount of civilization and turn all males into drooling cavemen.

Because Dorri was just so damned beautiful, Sharon had decided early on to *never envy her,* and in addition to *bear any of her bad behaviour patiently.* Dorri couldn't help that her beauty could make her a little arrogant or cool. It was because of the way people treated her that she could be a little self-absorbed. But you couldn't hate someone because of an accident of nature.

That's what Sharon told herself, at least. Some days were worse than others with Dorri, unfortunately, like when she discovered she'd been invited to a party only because six of Dorri's closer friends had won tickets to a concert out of town and weren't available. Or when Dorri got her to run around all day looking for *the perfect wedding topper,* sending dozens of pictures back on her iPhone and eating up an entire month's worth of data, until she was told *Oh, just come back to my place. I'll do it myself.*

But it was still a kind of enchanted thing that Dorri was her friend at all. She wasn't sure how it had happened. Dorri was *That Girl* at high school, the one the girls envied and the boys followed, tongues hanging out of their heads just like the tongues hung out of their Nikes.

Being asked to be one of Dorri's bridesmaids was an unsought and incredibly unexpected honour. Sharon knew just how unlikely it was to have been asked, but she was under no illusions that it made Dorri her new bestie. The fact was that the same six friends had won a trip to the Bahamas for the same weekend. They had give their *OMG, Dorri, we swear we'll make it up to you* apologies instead of participation (which amounted to paying for Dorri and her new husband to fly down to the Bahamas to meet them all expenses paid, with an extra week tacked on at the end for just them to properly celebrate their honeymoon).

However it had happened, though, Sharon had set her ambition on being *the best bridesmaid ever,* and she was damned if she was going to start wingeing about how much her feet hurt.

And she could hardly make a fuss about how the bridal photo shoot was about to start, and Dave had vanished.

6.

After a moment, in the cloying darkness, a new thought

occurred to Sharon. Instead of the kind of troubling ideas that had been pressing down on her since her return to consciousness, this one was vaguely comforting.

As it formed, a sense of hope started to rise in her. *What if,* it said, *that lid is just really, really heavy, and not fastened to the bottom at all?* It was worth another try, then, to lift it. True to nature, Sharon had found a reason against all odds to be optimistic.

She put her palms solidly against the satin, steeled herself, then pushed with all her might.

Nothing.

In any normal person, this should have been the moment when panic became inevitable. In Sharon, this was not the case. If you wanted to quantify it, you might be tempted to say that Sharon had a residual "one more try" reserve that exceeded the national average by a factor of two or three times.

So even now, entombed for the moment above ground but in grave (no pun intended) danger of making it a more subterranean and permanent place of residence, Sharon had not yet reached the moment of *giving up*.

Instead, she had a small tantrum.

It really wasn't fair—she might not have any particular memory of suffering under the inconstant and non-preferential friendship of Dorri Davenport neé Chu, and she might not have even the inkling of a suspicion that it was at Dorri's lavish wedding photo op where she first developed what could no longer be called just a vague sense that her boyfriend Dave was cheating on her.

But something must have lingered in her foggy brain that told her *Enough! I have had enough bad luck for one lifetime! It's my turn to get the prize!*

And she pushed again, not sideways this time, nor straight up, but up *and* sideways at the same time. Maybe she'd divined the truth—that although the lid of the casket wasn't locked, it did however feature a deep lip to keep it in place in case of accidental jostling on the way to its eternal rest— or maybe it was plain dumb luck. But the lid—gave. Just an inch or so, before slapping back down to its first position, but it was enough. Sharon bore down with her arms, put her feet (again with the high heels!) against the heavy cover, and pushed with all her might.

The lid slid aside, just enough to create a triangle of light at two of the corners. Heartened, quivering, she used her shoulders and arms to push away the lid from its seat on the rim of the casket, and sat up.

Sunlight streamed into the back of the hearse and into Sharon's aching eyes. The pressure of the dark on her poor eyeballs had been so great that its relief was palpable. She rubbed her eye sockets, and stared as her fists came away coated in goopy, thick makeup. This was enough to make her giggle. Even dead and buried, she couldn't remember not to rub her eyes and smear her mascara.

Sharon took a quick look around, but a new imperative was building inside her. *Get out, and get away,* it said. *If they see you, they'll just put you back in.*

However little or much sense this made, Sharon obeyed. She pushed herself out of the coffin, fuchsia heels first, into the small space left between the casket and the rear door of the vehicle. Automatically checking the place she'd vacated for anything she might have left behind, she was surprised to see a small silvery clutch, a really nice, dressy little bag in fact, and a wilted bouquet. She lifted both out of the coffin, placing the strap of the bag over her arm and the bouquet under it. Then, gingerly, she opened the back door.

Although there wasn't much in the way of organized thinking going on in her head, she did have a moment of curiosity: just why was a hearse supplied with a handle *INSIDE* the cargo space? Did a mourner sometimes ride with the corpse, or was Sharon's apparent situation more common than most people realized? For that matter, is that why the lid hadn't been fastened to the coffin? Just in case someone had made a terrible, terrible mistake?

But the freshness of the air and the enticement of the day pushed such musings aside. Sharon lowered herself on unsteady legs to the pavement below, turned to reseat the lid in its groove (*NEVER leave a mess like that for me again, Sharon!*) and ever so, ever so quietly closed the rear gate of the hearse.

7.

Sunlight glints on the water of the fountain. Everyone is lined up now, or almost everyone. The photographer hasn't remarked on anything because the bridal party is balanced. Of course, since exactly one bridesmaid and one groomsman are missing.

There's a squeal: Dorri of course. "Come *on,* you two. You're ruining my day!"

The photographer, still apparently clueless, gives the countdown: "All right, everyone. Say 'cheese' in one… two…"

Dave squeezes in beside Sharon, and takes her arm. On the other side of the grouping, she sees Monica do the same. "Hey, sweetie," he says, as if it's the most natural moment in the world. Somehow, despite the artificiality of the poses, the stiffness of everyone's posture, and the painted-on smiles, Dave's casual sincerity trumps everything she sees for *utterly, totally fake.*

Monica's apparent fascination with the photographer's gear and total lack of regard for either Sharon or Dave also strikes Sharon as about as convincing as two men in a horse costume would be in fooling a cowhand in the old west.

"Where were you?" Sharon hisses between jaws clenched in the brightest smile she's ever managed.

"Three!"

8.

Sharon made it up the wooded slope to the top where she could just see the hearse at its roadside berth. It hadn't been a moment too soon that she'd hidden herself in the trees; warned by approaching motors, she'd fled (well, maybe *stumbled* would be a better word. Those shoes didn't get any easier to walk in) into the only cover nearby.

Now, from the crest of the hill, she could see three cars parking, and about half a dozen people get out and move in appropriate solemnity to the long rectangle of astroturf which must cover her intended final resting place.

One of them, she saw, was Father Dawson, the priest who'd officiated at Dorri and Davin's wedding. He took his place at one end of the sod, and stood shifting his weight as if he had somewhere better to be.

The other few took seats on folding chairs (far too many set out for the meagre number of mourners) and two men, obviously cemetery employees, extracted the casket from the hearse on a trolley, rolling it to its place at the graveside.

Sharon squinted, trying to resolve the faces of the attendees, but it was no use. Between the haze that refused to exit her brain and the abuse her eyes had taken between alternating light and dark, she couldn't see anything clearly.

She couldn't hear anything either. Not only that, but she imagined time was running in a peculiar fashion. The interment service couldn't really have lasted such a short time, could it? It seemed like the priest had hardly opened his book before closing it again with a sharp snap—just about the only sound that travelled far enough to reach her —and returning to his car. The other mourners followed just as quickly, and all that remained were the two men who had been waiting patiently by a smallish crane to finish the burial.

That feeling of unfairness which had given her enough passion to push up the coffin lid surged back. Maybe Dorri was still on her honeymoon. It was hardly likely that either of her parents had come in from the coasts for her funeral, especially if there was even a chance in a multitude of hells that the other would attend. But where was Dave? Where was Monica? If a boyfriend and a best friend didn't show up for her, well, who the heck were those others?

Fortunately, Sharon didn't have quite enough consciousness to realize *who* was missing, just that someone important was.

Thunder interrupted her reverie.

The mourners below scattered faster toward their vehicles, then vanished over a rise in a burr of engine noise. No, more thunder, not car motors.

Sharon, aware at an almost instinctual, animal level that shelter was called for, stumbled away from the crest of the slope and down a winding cemetery road.

She saw a building just off the path, with carved columns and marble facing. It seemed odd, out of place. Or maybe that was her? In any case, it offered the chance of cover from the approaching storm.

But the front door was barred by a solid metal grate, and no matter how Sharon shook it (*not giving up now, are you, Sharon?*) it wouldn't budge. Chancing the soft grass in her heels, she stumbled off again, toward another small building.

It too was locked up tight, barred and shuttered. What kind of place was this? What were these (mausoleums) buildings?

A flash of lightning. There must have been more before, to complement the thunder rolls, but maybe she'd missed them in the riot of light and dark and moisture building in front of her poor, tortured eyes. Thunder, and lightning. She knew she was supposed to count—something. What, she didn't know, nor was she sure she remembered *how* to count.

A third of the buildings, this one squat and low, not really so much a little house as a miniature one, and this too unyielding to her efforts. She felt the first droplets on her arms and in the cleavage of her low-cut (fuchsia) dress. Fuchsia? That sparked memories. Why on earth was she dead and buried wearing fuchsia?

Forget for the moment that someone had done something major and decidedly *nasty* to that cleavage. Stitches? You'd think she'd remember getting stitches, especially in such a sensitive place. Sensitive, not because of the thinness of the skin (Sharon knew a tattoo *would* hurt especially badly in that particular area regardless of the fact that she'd never ever in a million years have one there herself, not that there was anything wrong with someone else doing it). Sensitive not because of the thinness of the skin, to return to before the digression, but because, well, Sharon didn't have a lot up there, and it stretched probability that she'd happily let someone fool with what little God gave her. Really!

The raindrops burned on her skin, like little hot pokers. Some hot rain! It didn't make sense—she was certain the air must be cold. It had been clear before, but the kind of clear you see on a day late in fall or very, very early in spring before the buds emerge from winter gestation. The trees were almost bare of leaves, so it *must* be cold out.

But the rain was hot, and this was a mystery she had no time for. What she needed, what the incredibly thick makeup caked to her face needed, was a place to hide out from the storm.

Shambling on, she thought for a moment she had caught a glimpse of a figure in the shadows near the treeline; the cemetery must be old to have such mature trees surrounding its (mausoleums) monuments. But the next second, the shape was gone and she convinced herself it was yet another trick of her aching eyeballs.

Suddenly, a flash of green caught in the corner of her. Teal? No, more toward green than blue, with a yellow roof. A tiny building stood at the edge of the woods, out of place as a nun on spring break, but welcome all the same. It didn't look big enough to hold more than her, but as long as that shape at the wooded verge was really a figment of her imagination and not a competitor for this particular niche, Sharon thought it would do very well.

She opened the door—easily this time, although it didn't surprise her as much as she had expected it might—and stepped inside.

A moment later, she was flinging herself out again, horrified, fingers pinching her nose shut.

"Oh my god, oh my god, oh my god," she breathed, although it came out more like, "Omaha, Omaha, Omaha."

Defeated, she tried to get herself close enough to the trees to steal some of their branches for cover (fat chance, with almost all the branches bare as spring breakers who *weren't* nuns) but not so close as to be in danger of a collateral lightning strike herself.

And there, by the trees at the edge of a cemetery, in the shadow of a mausoleum she could no longer think of as any kind of normal, live-human type of dwelling place, Sharon realized to her even greater horror that the stink she'd noted in the portapotty wasn't after all from the portapotty. It was coming from her.

"Omaha," she said.

Toxic

9.

**From the case files of V. X. Morgoni,
cryptoparapsychocriminologist**

It's been ten days since the last contact from the troll, or
rather FOUL MORLOCK whose screen-name should be
DONT_TRUST_ME instead of ILLUMINATED_SEEKER.
Repeated attempts at surveillance have gone unrewarded,
and so have the efforts of my euphemistically called
"Baldwin Street Irregulars." This calls into serious question
the validity of his work in the area of ectoplasmic
phenomena. How can I take seriously the conclusions of
anyone who would put his integrity at risk for nothing more
than the chance of…! I can't even say it. I admit I was
sucked in, but THIS ERROR SHALL NOT BE
REPEATED.

In any case, I am on my own again except for the aid of
Juan Carla, Dibber, and little Fawn. Reminder: payment for
the trio is due tomorrow. Consider offering choices from
80s comic collection up to value of contract. So many of
those in the lock-up I can pay them out for years if they're
willing to accept pop lit instead of cash.

Regarding the show, it seems that I am now flying solo
again in my duties as host, primary researcher, and on-the-
spot correspondent. Probably for the best. Fawn is getting
good at framing shots, and if her technique isn't superb,

hopefully the quality of the reporting will smooth over critiques of all but the greatest TROLLS.

Without Stupidhead, I have no further access to the Beta Kappa basement where the disturbances were allegedly noted. I will spend no more than another 48-120 hours on this project without some secondary source presenting itself. It would be criminal to allow his inconstancy to be a deterrent, especially if there is something to the story. But, as with so many other potential areas of investigation, perhaps this is just not the time nor the place that will get me the answers the public deserves to hear.

Reminder: no milk. Make sure to again tell that abysmally nicknamed flake Teeny that not all of us have fallen for the medical industrial conspiracy to hawk their satanic soy products.

Morgoni out.

10.

Sharon hadn't really even remembered the clutch around her elbow until the rain had finally stopped. The shower had been mercifully light, if not short in duration, and she found herself not so much a drowned cat as a liberally spritzed one.

Now, she sat on a stone bench just at the edge of the tree line where she'd taken shelter, going through what remained of her possessions.

First and most importantly, she'd found a driver's license in the name of "Sharon Backovic." She tried the name out a few times on wobby lips: Shhharon. Baaaacko-vich.

Backovick? She couldn't quite remember, although it seemed familiar in the way a place can be if you've recalled it more in your dreams than your actual memories.

So, Sharon Backo-something. Hard "C" or "CH," it didn't matter much at the moment, not until she had to introduce herself to someone, and stuck alone after the rain in a cemetery with nothing but an abandoned casket-crane in the distance, that wasn't an issue.

The lipstick wasn't a particularly useful discovery either. Judging by the way her eyes had left their impression, so to speak, on her hand, she wouldn't need any more makeup until at least the turn of the next century.

She emptied the rest of the clutch onto her lap. A keyring, with some kind of creature on it to which she assigned the name "Mewtoo." It was a Pokemon, her brain told her, and she was awfully good at *leveling them up*. File that for later. It obviously meant something, but at the moment, it was maybe just a little TMI. Too much insanity? Yes, that had to be it.

The keys must go to something important, and although there was no indication of what, with luck it would be somewhere to go that would protect her from the elements. Next time, at least.

A small selection of coins, and a couple of bills. A token or two for public transit, which seemed like a happy bonus

One small compact, with blush powder and a mirror in the lid.

A cellphone, dead. No charger.

Mascara. That was just more trouble waiting to happen!

That droopy bouquet: orange roses, baby's breath, and something white with lots and lots of petals she didn't have a name for.

Back to the mirror. Her brain still felt oozy, so maybe it was a good idea to check her face against the picture on the photo I.D. She raised the compact, and took a look.

"This is *not* good," she said, although maybe it wasn't all that bad either. Jury was well and truly out.

Except for the smeared mascara and the paleness of her flesh (had her veins always stood out quite so prominently? And so pinkly? And what were those blotches around her hairline that looked like someone had attacked her with a pink highlighter?) it was clearly her in the picture. That was a bit of a relief. She could get an address from the license too, which might clear up the key question (also, a *key* question), and solve the shelter dilemma for future bad weather.

The sun broke suddenly from behind the departing clouds, and Sharon peered closer into the reflection in the glass.

Yes, there was too much makeup on her face, but that didn't explain the strangeness of her eyes. The pupils seemed a little fixed, as if they no longer responded flexibly to changes in brightness. That would account for the difficulty she'd had going from the pristine darkness of the coffin to the light of day. A little dry, too. She blinked a couple of times, but nothing changed. Maybe it was some temporary thing, something to do with…

Just why *had* she been in the casket? Had someone really thought she was dead, or was there some other reason?

She was still having trouble making the necessary connections to parse a reason from the facts she'd managed to put together. *Dead, and on the way to being buried, only not* actually *dead...*

Sharon shivered. Was it possible she'd been buried *on purpose?*

But that didn't bear consideration, did it? How can you even begin to go down a road that starts with someone wanting you gone so badly they let everyone think you're dead until it's too late?

Sharon had the unearthly sensation that it wasn't above the bounds of possibility that yes, someone indeed had been playing a massive practical joke at her expense.

Really, it wasn't much worse than practical jokes her older brothers had played on her, vaguely remembered not so much as crappy treatment by siblings but as troubling flashes that resembled what might have flashed through her brain in a past life regression as a victim of the Inquisition (*NOOObody forgets the Spanish Inquisition!*).

And in the end, things had got out of hand, and she'd been taken to the cemetery instead of everyone standing around snickering until someone said, *hey, y'all, good joke, but! Sharon's alive, so get her out of that coffin before she starts to cry!* Maybe it was even Dorri! After all…

And the memory fled. Just a brief flash of Dorri very, *very* angry, as angry as she'd ever seen her, even madder than when the caterer had forgotten to bring the coconut dream cake for the sampling. Something about Dorri yelling, screaming really, her voice pitching up high enough to give dogs conniptions…

Somehow, out of all the chaos, a thought emerged triumphant, but not at all welcome. It happened about the time Sharon reached that point in her thinking and at the same time began looking through the detritus from the purse for nail polish, and realizing that particular impulse had been sparked by the way her nails had somehow become a horrible shade of yellow.

Buried. Made up grotesquely. Still wearing that horrid fuchsia bridesmaid's dress and matching killer heels. The wedding bouquet, something Dorri'd never have parted with willingly just for the sake of a joke (*Remember,* Dorri had said at the bridal shower, *whoever catches the bouquet GIVES IT BACK at the reception. Preferably with a nice little speech about how my future happiness is so much more important than any idiot tradition*). The coffin. The hearse. The funeral. Did priests participate in pranks? She couldn't see it.

And then there were the stitches, in an all-too telling "Y" from shoulder to shoulder and on down her sternum. She could see them when she pulled the front of her dress out an inch or two.

The crazy eyes. Not to mention the undeniable stench of slightly rotting (although presumably nicely embalmed) flesh.

How on earth was this possible? Reanimated? Organs removed and stuffed back in haphazardly? Hooked up to a pump and gutted of blood?

Zombified?

Sharon's stomach rumbled alarmingly. At first, she had a surge of hope. Maybe her plumbing *was* all still hooked up the way it should be.

The next moment, she had a decidedly darker thought as the organ in question growled loudly for a second time.

Zombified? And zombies ate…

"*REALLY* not good," she said, and slumped. The mascara tumbled off her lap and onto the damp grass, but she never even noticed.

11.

After every tragic death in this compassionate, modern world, a certain traditional monument is bound to be erected with the intention of providing the loved ones of the departed a way to celebrate a life cut short too soon, and to begin to heal.

That, of course, is the obligatory Facebook Memorial Page.

Custom dictates that if the death is particularly tragic or bizarre, the person who initially sets up said page should be a total stranger, or at the very least a sympathetic former stalker trying to deal with the shake-up of the obsession that has driven his or her life.

In Sharon's case, she had been entirely correct about her parents. Each had assumed the other would fly to Toronto to attend their daughter's service, so both (in the interest of familial peace, *and of course Sharon won't know either way*) had elected to skip the funeral. Instead, they'd each made identical phone calls to Sharon's two older brothers (Skip in South Africa and Harrison in Dubai) to tell them of the tragedy and make sure they wouldn't waste their time and hard-earned money making a useless trip back to Canada when there were certainly better ways they could use both.

Each parent also insisted that he or she *would* attend, and that the other half (the worse half, of course) of the splintered pair would almost certainly let their daughter down, *again*, and make some kind of lame excuse not to show up.

Since neither Skip nor Harrison had been in the country for a dozen years, the Backovics senior were fairly certain this prevarication would go unchallenged.

The only regret for either was that, upon hearing about Sharon's death, Mrs. Backovic (still swearing she was *just about* to return to her maiden name) called Skip first, and Mr. called Harry, so neither was able to claim victory in having made both the notifications first.

Neither of them, nor their elder offspring, had the least interest in setting up a Facebook Memorial Page for Sharon.

Her friends, such as they were, were curiously unmoved by her death, as you, gentle reader, might have surmised from the sparse turnout at the graveside. In point of fact, the attendees were: 1) Mr. Jacobson, the maintenance man from Sharon's apartment building, who had a big soft spot for her because she was so entirely, unfailingly polite and always apologized whenever she needed something fixed; 2) Carrie Richmond, whose dog Sharon walked regularly and who honestly believed she would never find another walker as willing to put her own plans aside to jump to Carrie's aid; 3) Steve from accounting who'd developed a fairly decent-sized crush on Sharon after reading her "Plenty of Fish" profile and recognizing her as a co-worker, but who yet had never been able to fit her into his rather busy dating life; 4) some lady who went to every funeral at that particular cemetery because it had recently been taken over by a large corporation and she was always looking for someone sympathetic to her belief that cemeteries should never be *treated like a goddamned Starbucks and run like a business by soulless men in suits*; 5) Elena Karpova, a slight acquaintance to whom Sharon often spoke at the bus stop who was eighty and feeling her own mortality a little too much these days and appreciated the schadenfreude of a much younger woman passing away so suddenly while she remained strong as a horse despite the slight stiffness of her knees during winter, and 6) Tina from Grade Six, who'd been Sharon's best friend for one not particularly memorable school year before she'd moved across town and discovered boys. She was still carrying an embarrassing load of guilt over that one, and attending Sharon's funeral seemed to be the last chance she'd ever have to assuage it.

None of them, either, set up the Facebook page.

12.

It was really amazing how few people stopped or stared as Sharon made her way down the street away from the graveyard. Could it be close to Hallowe'en? Did she look more like a homeless person than a (zombie) girl recently self-disinterred from the back of a hearse?

One way or another, Sharon caught only half a dozen startled glances as she made her way along, and some of that might be because not only was she still mega-clutzy on those stupid high heels, not only were the balls of her feet probably bruised black and blue by the repeated abuse, but she now had developed a blister around her right big toe.

Sharon didn't know a lot about zombies, since they were scary and not sweet and friendly and fun, but it was hard to live in the modern world without knowing the basics: A) they shambled; B) they groaned. And worst, and most troubling: C) they attacked people, and killed them.

She was brutally conscious of the irony: here she was, trying hard *not* to resemble the moaning, shambling zombie she undoubtably was (yes, let's just say it and get it out of the way), but the stupid high heels made her walk like, well, a walker. Without the incipient blister, she'd probably be able to march along and attract no notice whatsoever. After all, who would believe a total stranger passing in the street was a member of the ranks of the (to this point, in her experience at least) totally fictional walking dead and not just some dumb party girl on the third day of a bender?

Those crazy unmoving pupils gave her a decidedly dead look, but no one was really going to get close enough or look long enough to see that. She had a moment of glee realizing that David Bowie only had had half the frozen-iris-issues she had suddenly developed. *"Hey Bowie,"* she imagined herself saying when they met in the Afterlife, *"Didja get a load of THESE eyes?"*

Playing out that particular fantasy took her most of the way to a more deserted section of town and face-to-face (face to decaying skull?) with what she'd been trying to avoid.

"If I'm a zombie," she asked herself quietly, "do I have to eat brains?"

Sharon, being a sensitive person, didn't care much for zombie movies. There was only so much killing without character development she could take (which was her code for *these darn things really, REALLY scare me*) so her specific knowledge was limited to the most obvious tropes. Zombies were dead people. They rotted, and presumably smelled bad (no getting around that one, obviously). They didn't die unless you hacked their heads off, and sometimes not even then. And they attacked people, cracked open their skulls, and ate brains.

It was enough to make her feel slightly nauseous (was that another sign that her stomach was still attached as it was supposed to be?) and she paused for a moment to place her hands on her knees and lower her head to take a few deep breaths.

That was something perplexing too. If she was dead, why was she breathing at all? Or was she just *imagining* air going in and out of her lungs, some kind of post-traumatic wish-fulfillment, finding life where there was none?

As she raised her head back up, she noticed a bus stop across the road and half a block further on. At it stood a lone… woman? Boy? She wasn't totally sure, but the figure was solitary and seemed intent on the screen of a small video camera in its hands.

Easy enough to sneak up on someone so intent, so unwary of the danger… Sharon focused on the person's head: a dark watchcap pulled down hard, thick-framed glasses hooked over ears half hidden by black dreadlocks.

Yes, she was almost sure now it was a woman, probably not much older than herself. Sharon forced herself to imagine the brains inside that head, under the layers of cap and hair, and got an even stronger rush of nausea than before.

Her stomach growled again, even louder.

"Omaha," she muttered, and, trying to be silent if not steady, picked her way across the street.

The woman, she now saw, was wearing ill-fitting jeans, a

long-sleeved sweater, and over it a padded vest of the type hipsters and lumberjacks prefer. This woman was neither, she could tell, just some lonely, solitary oddball who (Dorri) would mock from here to her honeymoon and back. *Dorri.* Now there was a person who deserved to have her brains eaten, if she could even find them in that big, empty head of hers!

Startled at her own cruel thoughts, Sharon hopped up to the sidewalk and hugged the nearest empty storefront. Death was making her stridently uncharitable! With any luck, that would make this next—very distasteful but necessary—action a little easier.

She sidled closer, flinching when her toe came into contact with a discarded pop can, dislodging it into the road. The figure never moved, just continued staring down into the hands cradling the camcorder. She was wearing wool mittens with the fingers cut off, Sharon saw, something else Dorri probably would have ridiculed her for, despite their clear practicality.

Closer, and finally the other woman sensed or heard her coming. The heavy-framed glasses came up to the level, and the mouth, thin and pinched, twisted as if to begin a snarl.

Sharon diverted her gaze as quickly as she could, and pretended to be examining the schedule posted below the bus stop sign.

She could almost feel the wariness of the other, and at the same time the utter dismissal of her importance.

That was far too much like the way she'd been treated when she was alive, and it sparked a sense of rebellion in Sharon. *Ignore me, will you?* she told herself. *Not worth fleeing in terror from, am I?*

And with that, Sharon charged. Or at least took a few quick, shaky steps forward.

When the woman with the camera looked up with an intensity that could reduce steel to ash, and said, "Back off, freak."

Ignoring her stomach this time, Sharon fled.

13.

Somewhere far away, in another city in fact, in a big country to the south of Canada which, although a separate sovereign nation, exerted an unholy influence over her little sister to the north, a woman considered a package of hair dye.

"Southern Flame" did seem like the ideal shade to try out this time. It would go nicely over the purple that had faded to a mauvy puce, like a washed-out eggplant, and in addition would be a nice tribute to Sharon.

Ah, Sharon. Such a tragic, romantic death. Done to death at a wedding of all things, the purported happiest day in the life of a woman. And after catching the bouquet as well.

She'd watched the video on YouTube so many times she knew it by heart—the exact colour of blue in the sky, the way the clouds dotted its azure glory. The narrative, some poor woman playing with her dog in the park and going on about nothing in particular. The way the camera's attention moved from cute pooch to distant formal grouping by the fountain.

She closed her eyes and imagined the sequence of events

that followed. The video played itself out using the inside of her lids as a personal cinema.

First, the way camera-girl moved in on the wedding party assembled for photos by the cascading fountain, the whiteness of its flume in stark contrast with the bright green of the grass, the blackness of the men's formal wear, and those god-awful fuchsia bridesmaids' dresses. *Salad, dressing, and raw meat.*

Then, the bride in her wedding-cake gown moving off far enough to turn her back on the women in the party and make that fateful toss…

And the redhead with the long bright hair clashing so stridently with the neon pink of her dress catching it, raising it high above her head, triumphant until the blonde (*much more suited to the strength of the colour she also wore*) plowed right into her.

The fight that ensued, as the rest of the wedding guests crowded in, iPhones emerging from pockets and purses. The only one *not* taking pictures as far as she could see was the photographer who kept calmly packing up his equipment as if he really had seen it all before.

And the bride, finally realizing she was being memorialized on film (or at least in digitally encoded images) in exactly the way *no* bride wants her wedding remembered, charging at the girl holding the camera, who ducked behind a concrete embankment.

The videographer was by this time in hysterics—giggling that is, not upset by this turn of events. Who would be, at this stage? We watch reality TV to mock those more ridiculous than ourselves, and this was just that kind of voyeuristic opportunity.

During the brief interval during which the only thing captured by the lens was the bare concrete of the embankment, you knew that a more dire set of circumstances had developed on the fountain side. No, you didn't realize there was tragedy, but you did know something significant had happened. First, it was the screaming, then the enormous *SPLASH* as if at least one body had gone into the water. More than one had—as was clear when camera-girl emerged from the other side of the embankment.

The wedding guests were in a frenzy, glued to the screens of their cellular devices as they rushed to poolside, furiously snapping pictures and trying to figure out how to switch their cameras to capture video instead. She'd seen those videos as well, before they were pulled from YouTube and Vimeo or only posted heavily edited to hide the more gruesome aspects of what followed.

But this, the original, was her favourite by far, the one that truly captured the pathos of the situation without cheapening it. It was a stranger shooting the scene, one without any prior emotional involvement with the principals, and yet it seemed that she, this anonymous user who went by the name *chickitty2112*, was the most truly moved of all those who witnessed the events that day.

She could almost picture that poor, compassionate soul's face just from the sound of her voice as she narrated the horrors she was seeing. A girl, no more than university-aged, relaxed and probably casually dressed for an afternoon in the park, just an average, friendly, nice person who'd had no idea what to expect on such a bucolic day. She was a true innocent here, just a bystander swept unknowingly into the worst wedding disaster of recent history.

She'd watched the video so many times herself that she had discerned certain elements she was sure no one else had noticed. For example, despite the danger transpiring only a short distance away, the blonde bridesmaid seemed more furious than concerned. She'd obviously been hauled from the water by the tuxedoed young man nearby who held her hand as she stood on the rim of the fountain, defiant and ramrod-straight, managing the dignity and fury of an Amazon queen despite being dripping wet from head to foot.

Who were this attractive and devoted couple, so intent on each other that the fate of another went totally unnoticed?

The bride, in the arms of her groom, was inconsolable. Despite it being a fair distance from this couple, the microphone of the camera managed to pick up her sobs and her repeated, staccato insistence that *"They've ruined EVERYTHING!"*

And then, the camera swings back to the group by the fountain, still busily snapping and peering into their mobile screens. The girl behind the camera asks her companion who's followed her this far to guide her toward the edge of the water, to capture what's going on behind that fence of formally-clad bodies.

"Where's the other one?" she asks, not imagining the horror the answer will bring.

The *least* Sharon Backovic deserved as a tribute to her terrible, ironic end was a nice Facebook page to remember her by, and a box of "Southern Flame" hair dye.

14.

Sharon stumbled along, the pain of her blister and the blinding agony of her hunger combining to make her almost unaware of her direction. Twice, she veered into a wall, once into a post forehead-first. It was amazing, really, that a dead person could feel pain. The bump to her head seemed to trigger an older injury to the back of her scalp, a swift and emphatic referral of pain.

She paused in the circle from a streetlamp. It was almost dark, but it felt early. It must be almost winter, or barely past it. She felt the cold, but not nearly as much as she thought she should. Gingerly, she touched the area of her forehead where she'd banged it on the post, then moved her fingers around and to the back of her head.

The knot under the hair was huge, felt like a pulpy but solid lemon. Even a small orange. When had *that* happened? It must have been when she was alive, because it had clearly swollen, bled, and been swabbed and cleaned at some point before she'd awoken in the coffin. *Ouch!* The residual damage was plainly pretty severe, even to her untrained fingers.

Maybe she'd just discovered the cause of her own death.

Shaken, she retreated into an empty doorway. There, in the glass of a bevelled showcase window, she saw the empty look of shock on her face—what (a friend) someone had once called a "Van Damme look." Opening the clutch, she retrieved her lipstick and the compact with the mirror, and tried with quivering hand to put some more (expressly unneeded) colour into her lips.

Just as she'd pressed the makeup to her mouth, a couple, arm in arm, passed her little hidey-hole. The woman glanced toward the movement Sharon made, and started to smile.

But almost simultaneously, as if God really had it in for her, Sharon stumbled, her ankle buckling slightly under her, and the red lipstick painted a hideous slash across her lower face.

The woman shrieked, then her male companion, and they fled screaming into the night. Sharon, even more shocked at their response than she had been by her own stumble, chased after them, trying to get out the words to stop them and reassure them she wasn't *THAT* kind of zombie… at least, she hadn't succeeded in being that just yet.

But the couple easily outstripped her, and she continued along only in a kind of hopeless futility, shambling on the ankle that might actually now be twisted, miserable, comical in her smeared lipstick and glowing in her fuchsia dress. Her feelings were hurt, her nerves raw, and yet she understood only too well just what a bizarre image she must present. Even if you didn't know she was *actually* dead, her appearance was a horror-show.

As she went, she saw that she had not been alone on this little stretch of run-down street even before the appearance of the unlucky couple. Nearby, leaning against a pole, head buried in a comic book, was a delicate young black boy. He glanced up, then back down again just as quickly. The reaction reminded her of her own furtive approach to the woman with the dreads and the camcorder. He wasn't watching *her*, was he?

She took a few quick, limping steps forward, and his head came up sharply. There was a look of panic on his face, but not terror.

"Please…" said Sharon, hoping that maybe he could help return her to some sort of sanity after the craziness of her day.

But he stuffed the comic book into a pocket in a hastily made roll, and took off with the fleetness of the barely-pubescent, and was soon out of sight around a corner.

Sharon, miserable and rejected again, sank to the stoop of a nearby shop and began to dry-heave in anguished, staccato jerks.

40 - undead redhead

Homestuck

15.

In its first day of operation, the Sharon Backovic memorial page got two likes, both by young men from Iran. One of them sent a message as well to the administrator:

yu r very beutiful. I want to know yu more

Shaking her newly-minted red hair, she deleted it. Well, you take what you can, but another random Middle Eastern man looking for romance was nothing to write home about. Or back *to*, for that matter.

Obviously, the tragic plight of a lovely young woman was not capturing the attention of the Facebook generation. It was heinous, really. Freak-out worthy. Well, she was damned if she was going to let this story die without a fight.

Not to mention, it might be a damned good way to bring a little more attention to her blog. But that was what you had to expect if you were a tireless crusader for recognition of your own special, unique soul in a world of cheap media whores. A little bit of the whoredom was bound to rub off on you. And if you were woman enough to take that ball and run with it, who could put the blame on you?

She clicked over to the tab where the *Toronto Star* story on

Sharon's death was still open, as it had been every day since the tragedy. One column inch, buried on an inside page. *Heinous.* There had to be an angle. If people were so freakin' jaded that even this kind of thing wasn't enough to make a blip on their radar, well, that was as much of a crime as… well, anything really criminal. It was *heinous.*

She closed her eyes, and saw the end—only this time, along with the rest of the wedding guests, she was there too in a yellow chiffon mini dress that made her red hair look like the cherry on a cake. Alone of the throng, she wasn't being a dick and filming the whole thing. No, she was crying out for help, for justice, for *just a little assistance here! Put down those phones and help me! There's still time! We can save her!*

Was that the way to go? Instead of celebrating Sharon's life, why not attack the people that let her die? Why not go negative? I mean, there'd been no real followup online or in what she could track down of the print media in Sharon's hometown. And there'd apparently been no accountability. Did anyone question Toronto's civic engineers or whatever they had up there in Can-Can-Canada to make sure the public parks were safe? Did the bride even have a license to shoot there? I mean, there was probably no end of blame to go around.

It was time for a new blog, and a new identity. Forget Sharon Backovic, forget the waste of her life. From this moment on, *she* was The Undead Redhead, an avenging angel, returned from beyond the grave to call out those scumbags who'd let her down in life, the system that failed her, and the false friends who couldn't even take a moment out of their oh so busy days to like a Facebook page dedicated to her.

Time to up the ante.

Seriously, two likes? That was bogus.

16.

Sharon, the original (and natural) redhead, stopped in front of the low-rise apartment building. She checked the I.D. in her hand. Yup, this was it.

It seemed familiar, if not entirely so. She took a few tentative steps up the walk, and it felt more right. A small smile crossed her face, maybe the first since she'd woken in her coffin. She was going home.

Or... Just as quickly as the optimism came, it ebbed away. What if she had a roommate who'd already replaced her? Would she be welcome? After all, everyone thought she was (dead) never coming back.

That stopped her, just as she was fumbling in her clutch for the keys.

That's when she saw the FOR RENT sign taped inside one of the big windows. For her apartment?

She backed away. She was dead. There was no going home.

Maybe at the very least she could sneak inside, walk the hall, see if she could recapture any more memories. Behind the building, she approached the back security door. A sign was taped to this door as well, and she choked in sorrow as she scanned it. *CONTENTS SALE* it said, above pictures of her old apartment, and this time she had a surge of true recognition.

There was her bed, the one her parents had given her shortly before the split, and beside it, a stack of pillows and folded bedlinen. Atop the stripped mattress, her desk lamp and the one from the bedside table. She choked back a sob as her finger traced the familiar items, memories flooding in: her IKEA angled desk. The low sofa she'd found on the street and paid Mr. Jacobson five bucks to help her carry into her place after soaking it in Dawn dish detergent and alcohol to make sure there were no bugs. Her coffee maker, the Keurig she only used on *very, very special occasions* because those K-cups were so bloody expensive. Her kitty-cat shower curtain, and the white wicker laundry hamper.

It was all so sad: all her things, no matter how much she loved them or took them for granted. Someone else would have them, or they would end up in a dump somewhere.

That gave her a glimmer of hope, or at least an idea with some potential. Backing away from the door, she scanned the area behind the building. Something beside the dumpster caught her eye, a large cardboard box with her old apartment number on it.

Bending to open it, she saw treasures. All the small items too personal or used to go into the sale were here. A public speaking trophy with her name on it from a competition in grade three. Letters from a pen-pal in Japan. Photos in an album with puppies on the front and back covers. A worn teddy bear with a missing eye. A small, fluffy "Hello Kitty" pillow.

Tenderly, she collected a few in her arms, then considered the tiny clutch looped over her arm. Until she had something else to carry things around in, until she had someplace where she could *be* as opposed to wandering around at the mercy of the weather, there was no point in trying to salvage memoirs of her old life.

Sighing, she replaced the items she'd taken out back in the box, carefully laying the teddy on top off everything and stroking his sparse fur before closing the box again.

Anger hit her then. Why shouldn't she have anything left? Why was this happening to her?

She kicked the box, and succeeded in connecting perfectly with the blister on her big toes.

"Ow!" she squealed, and sat down heavily on the curb by the dumpster, bruising her bum in the process. She burst into tears, and was surprised to find herself leaking at least a little from the corners of her strange, frozen eyes. She could cry. She was dead, but she could still cry, a bit at least.

She rubbed her sore bottom, and then took off the offending high heel to massage her big toe. There was a crumpled Kleenex in her clutch that she used to pad the end of the shoe before replacing it. Too bad none of her infinitely more comfy shoes (or even her floppy rabbit slippers) had made it out to the dumpster with the rest.

Then, she leaned back with her hands on the grass behind her, beside the dumpster in the back of her old apartment building, beside a box of all the treasures left in the world to her, and shook her head in perplexity. Her stomach growled, and she bent over in pain until the pangs passed.

"This is ridiculous," she said out loud, and a silent world seemed to agree.

*

17.

**From the case files of V. X. Morgoni,
cryptoparapsychocriminologist**

I have heard through the virtual grapevine that the FOUL
MORLOCK not only *did* in fact hook up with the girl with
blue hair and enormous ear-plugs (ugh!) he had been
engaging in cross-talk during at our last meeting, but has
posted a new *relationship status* vis a vis their on-going
coupling. Disgusting! That I ever took him for a serious
pursuer of truth is the burden of shame I must carry.

Re: the Irregulars—while no new photos have come to light
from the Kappa boys featuring orbs, Juan Carla was quite
right in believing others have some limited blackmail
potential. Maybe I'll be able to secure our entrance to their
basement for further paranormal investigation after all. On a
related topic, the trio was apparently quite happy to accept a
run of 1980s Thor comics in return for their recent services.
Dibber seems stupidly enchanted by *Moon Knight*, which is
great since they are totally worthless no matter what the
guide says.

A new lead, but one which I don't think will lead to any
story of real investigative value: I was waiting for the bus
last night, and was approached by a girl in a zombie get-up.
She seemed confused, possibly unmedicated schizoid.
Possibly delusional, since she gave no indication she knew
she was in public. Psych ward escapee? If so, where did the
makeup come from?

Except for the time of year, would have guessed drunken
sorority girl out partying, except even with the famous gross
fashion sense of that ilk, could not see how this particular

"dress" would fit that scenario. A hazing ritual gone bad? But again, not the right time of year.

Probably nothing of interest, but until I get more traction on the current investigation, or a new one opens up, I am reduced to vlogging about poor service and hygiene at local eating establishments. Not my favourite pastime, although I do accept the necessity of my societal participation as a media and cultural watchdog.

…just received a text from the Morlock. Apparently he and blue-hair girl are on the outs and he's renewed his interest in our work. My dilemma now is whether to simply ignore him, or deliberately destroy his reputation and credit rating online. Will sleep on it.

Can't make a firm decision while Teeny plays her garbage music in the next room. The choice I face now with her is whether to post a complaint to her Facebook page, or simply loosen the battery on her iPod again.

Morgoni out.

18.

Sharon, undead redhead extraordinaire, hungry and homeless, hugged herself. She'd been surprised at how little the cold seemed to affect her, but maybe it was all relative. If her own internal body temperature was nil, of course the environment around her would have little effect on her. It explained why the rain had felt hot, in fact. On cold skin, even a warm rain would be startling in contrast.

She wasn't entirely sure where she was currently, only that the area was more commercial than residential, and that business was bad. It must be late, because there were few people around. Would dawn bring solutions, or only more problems?

She heard laughter and voices approaching from around a corner, and ducked into an alley, disappearing down its length, around a dogleg, and into a dead end. Something struck her as familiar, despite the low light, and she realized it was a sign on the back door of a restaurant whose entrance must be on the main street. "Vegan Goodness: Wholesome Eating From The Earth," the sign proclaimed.

A vague flash of memory passed through her—sitting with a guy around her own age (Dan? Darryl?) who was picking at something on a plate. She herself was happy, joyful really, and seemed to be amused at the way he was eating.

"It's couscous," she heard herself say, *"not poison."* Her own laughter echoed in her head, far lighter than she would have believed herself capable of, at least not as the Redhead. Sharon Backovic, alive, could laugh and tease, gently and with affection. The Redhead could smile wryly at the memory and wonder at how lucky she'd been without knowing it.

This was her identity now. No more pretending she could still be Sharon. She was just the Redhead. Unless she somehow… but it wasn't worth thinking about.

The ache in her stomach was a constant now. She was going to have to do something about it, one way or another. The thought of cracking another living… well, of cracking someone's head open and eating their brains had not lost its repugnance for her. There had to be an alternative.

Oddly, the sign for the Vegan restaurant had made her feel more hungry, not less, and didn't carry the kind of nauseous reflex she had gotten used to when considering other, more homo sapiens-oriented foodstuffs. Was it possible she could actually eat human food, and not eat them *as* food instead?

It was worth a try.

She checked her money again. It was running out fast, and all she'd bought were a few more transit tokens and a big bottle of water which she'd drunk at breakneck speed after the crying jaunt behind her old walk-up. Yes, she could cry, but the outburst had left her seriously dehydrated. At least, that's the conclusion she'd come to when drinking a couple of litres of water had made her feel much better. Didn't cure the hunger, but did make her feel less… desiccated.

But the eating situation had to be taken care of, and probably sooner rather than later. She considered the nearby dumpster with more than a little disgust, and just a hint of longing.

19.

It wasn't any particular event in the life of Sharon Backovic that made her become a Vegan. It was more an inevitable progression from not wanting to eat nice moo-moos as a child, to meeting and falling in love with a wild turkey on a farm in grade school, and finally deciding at university that her allergy to milk and its derivatives was her body telling her to give up all animal products.

It surprised her how easy it was to make the transition. Everyone had told her it would be so hard, and she would have to deny herself everything that made life worth living.

But instead, it felt like she was constantly treating herself.

She loved her new diet (*regimen, not diet,* she'd tell people, *or just call it a life choice*) and felt like a queen when she sat down to rapini in olive oil with cashews and sundried tomatoes. Deprived? Hardly.

And if it decreased the already small number of diner invitations she received to near zero (once, she overheard Dorri saying to another friend, *"Well, of course it's too hard to have Sharon over. You can only have some many vegetables on the menu before Darren just WON'T EAT at all"*), so be it. And if she ended up with not one but six yoga mats donated to her by well-meaning acquaintances who couldn't imagine her being Vegan *without* taking up yoga, it was kindly meant.

She did start doing some tai chi in deference to the perception and quite enjoyed it, but the yoga mats stayed rolled in her closet and only came out when she painted her kitchen.

 Still, she was able to laugh at the common conception of Vegans as out-there (like, Pluto out-there) and it was the only subject she could get a little heated about, even if she always felt bad afterwards. Sharon Backovic was a blubberer, not a fighter. Get her too mad and she'd burst into tears over the insanity of arguing when you could talk things out like kind individuals who cared about beliefs but not to the point of cruelty.

That instinct probably explained the natural progression to Vegan-hood more than anything. When she read The Wizard of Oz as a child, Sharon identified most with the Tin Woodman, who was so tender-hearted he constantly checked where his feet landed so as not to inadvertently squish a bug or a flower in his path. That made perfect sense to her. Once you became aware of the damage you *could* do, wouldn't it take a pretty heartless person to not try to stop?

Her favourite restaurant after becoming Vegan was a little start-up in Kensington Market called "Vegan Goodness." Yes, the name was slightly clunky, and the owners just a little over-serious in a way that rather fed into the stereotype of Vegans as humourless and too socially conscious for being social. She'd once suggested they shorten the name to "Vegan Goodies," and was told by Maud, one half of the lesbian couple that ran the kitchen, that "goodies" would suggest they primarily served desserts, and they wanted no part of false advertising.

But Sharon could not fault the quality of the food, or the price (darned okay on her budget!) even if the portion-size wasn't all she could have wished for. It always seemed like she was just starting to enjoy her dinner when it was suddenly all gone.

And the implicit support of the staff just by continuing to make and serve a wholesome Vegan cuisine really went a long way to helping Sharon accept her own Vegan nature. It would have been impossible, for example, to have been Vegan in her parents' home without being subject to the ridicule of her brothers, the silent censure of her father, and the *never* silent criticism of her mother. Her determination to keep to a diet (*regimen*) free of animal products would either have collapsed within a week, or drowned her in a sea of depression. Maybe both.

Dave teased her about the six kinds of nut butter in her cupboard, but he also availed himself of all of them every time she made toast (Wonder Bread for him, something entirely different and far more delicious for her, even if he never seemed to believe it). And the avocado chocolate mousse she'd learned from a dairy-free blogger on the web seemed to disappear almost as fast as she could make it, even when he mocked it. When Dave got up in the middle of the night, she could swear he was only using having to pee as an excuse to raid the fridge for mid-night dessert.

At the heart of it all, though, Sharon loved animals. She loved every kind of animal you could name, and some you'd be stumped on. One year, she'd gotten obsessed with marsupials and other animals peculiar to Australia and had actually exceeded her bandwidth quota with her Internet provider in three days downloading documentaries on their lives. In her estimation, it was money well spent.

How can you really fault a girl for love, even if she oozed, dripped, and otherwise gushed it as liberally as pundits oozed scorn? The only problem was that no one seemed to appreciate just how loving Sharon was, and that what they might term *peculiarities* were, for her, just instances of demonstrating that affection.

Even Dave sometimes got enough of her adoration and pushed her off him. "Babe," he'd said, holding her at arm's length, "no more with the love, okay? It tires me out."

And she'd oblige, keeping her hands off him until he'd say with equal gravity, "Babe, is something wrong? You don't seem yourself," and she'd wonder just what she *should* do to be herself without crossing the line.

20.

The people at the soup kitchen were very nice, although The Redhead caught a couple of them exchanging glances when they thought she wasn't looking. That made her just uncomfortable enough to refuse the soup and instead to just take a random sandwich and another bottle of water, and leave the building.

Outside, she found a bench occupied at one end by a messed-up lady who seemed to be vibrating, as if the world was moving a heck of a lot faster in the air just around her. The Redhead might not have known much about crack addicts, but it was pretty clear to her that the lady was harmless, if not in the best shape.

She unwrapped the sandwich. It was the first real food she'd held in her hands since she'd awoken from her (death) sleep. The dumpster behind Vegan Goodness had been a bust, but she figured it might offer her at least a little shelter in the corner behind it if she returned there later, a place to wait out the busy day where more people might be startled or remark on her (deadness) appearance.

It wasn't that she was afraid of notice, but she hadn't exactly racked up the best kind of responses so far. After a few screams and a drunkard or two charging as if they believed she really *was* a zombie out for brains, she'd decided to cut the chances of being seen as a threat and keep to alleys, and night-time as much as possible.

Regarding her past life, the memories were still fractured and incomplete. She'd tracked down the old apartment by a combination of the I.D. she'd found in her purse and a bus shelter map, but that was a dead end, and no other leads had presented themselves to her. She *must* have a past, an identity from before her death and zombification, people who missed her, not to mention that guy with the "D" name who must be her—boyfriend?

Only, how did you spark remembrance in a brain belonging to a dead girl? It wasn't like she could ask anyone, and there weren't exactly a lot of familiar sights or scents surrounding her, triggering a revelation.

If only she could figure out where to go FROM the place she'd once lived; maybe then she could find the next crumb on a trail leading back to herself.

She bit into the sandwich, chewed and forced herself to swallow. Tuna. That was something she knew, and gave her a tiny surge. School? Public school. Sandwiches in an orange, insulated zip-up sack. Oreo cookies in a baggie. Apple juice in a tetra pack.

No, that was it. Nothing more.

And the bite of sandwich wasn't sitting right. She took another couple of bites in quick succession. Maybe she was *too* hungry, and so her body was reacting badly.

Nausea swamped her, nearly turning her vision black. She leaned to the side of the bench and threw up everything she'd just eaten.

She had a few sips of water, washing out her mouth, then a few more. Water good. Sandwich bad.

Despite the abuse, her stomach began rumbling again.

"What do you *want?*" The Redhead whispered to it.

The cracklady whipped her head around to face The Redhead. "Nothing," she said, apparently in response. She sounded offended.

The Redhead, embarrassed at being caught talking to herself, shrugged into herself a little more, carefully wrapped up the sandwich and set it on the bench between her and the other woman.

A moment later, despite the harshness of her previous salvo, the cracklady said in a more conversational tone, "So, whatcha on?"

The Redhead was confused. "The… the bench, for now. Tonight, probably the ground beside a dumpster."

"You're funny," said the cracklady, a smile showing yellowed but mostly present teeth. "I like that."

The Redhead tried a smile back. It didn't go too badly. They sat in silence for a few minutes, companionably, the cracklady because she didn't have enough money for a fix, and the Redhead because she wasn't sure, money or otherwise, she could figure out what to eat for food. She tried *not* to sneak peaks at the other woman's head. *Brains? Please, no.*

Finally, probably because the silence was a little heavier than conversation might be, the cracklady said, "If you ask me, life isn't all it's cracked up to be. Get it—crack?"

The Redhead sighed. Philosophy was at least a distraction from hunger. Better to contemplate her past mortality than the pate of the woman next to her. Brains? Could that really be what she was supposed to eat?

"I kinda miss it," she replied finally.

"Crack?"

"Life."

"Yeah," chuckled the cracklady. She seemed to think the

Redhead had made a joke.

"Because I'm dead," she clarified.

The cracklady chortled, making a bit of a snorting sound. "Tell me about it. Then I get some juice in me and I'm way too alive."

She wasn't getting it. Suddenly, the Redhead felt overwhelmed by the need to tell someone, anyone, even someone who probably wouldn't remember in an hour, much less repeat it to anyone who might know what to do about the whole crazy situation.

"No," she said, still trying to get through, "I'm actually dead. And rotting a little, I think."

"Tell me about it," said the cracklady, slapping the Redhead's knee. "Then I get some juice in me and I'm way too alive."

The Redhead started to feel a little frustrated. Should she mention the cracklady had just made the same joke twice?

Brains. Just how were you supposed to crack open someone's head? A little voice responded in the Redhead's mind: *Get it? Crack?* She shook her head.

The cracklady leaned over, concerned. "That's some nasty shit you're on, honey."

The Redhead looked down. A bit of skin had started to peel away from her forearm. Were the veins starting to look more bluish than pink? She scratched at the loose skin and it came away in a strip.

"Crap," she said quietly. Not just rotting, but falling apart.

The cracklady leaned closer, shook a finger. "Gotta stop picking or it'll just get worse."

"Yeah," said the Redhead, non-committal. Just how much worse could it really get at this point?

The cracklady leaned back into the bench, and they settled back into silence broken only by the cracklady's occasional coughing. Finally, the cracklady poked the Redhead in the shoulder, then poked at the sandwich.

"You gonna eat that?"

58 - undead redhead

Left Behind

21.

OMG Dorri Davenport just posted her redo wedding pix – gorg!

          WTF – didnt they do that b4???

yeah BUT. U know about the whole s.b. thing

          yeah, gross. Did you go to the funeral
ment to – had to wrk. U?

          Didnt know her 2 well, just thru d

u shouldnt say this about dead ppl but she was kinda lame

          omg, you are such a btch!

I know! So bad

          kinda true. Her bf was hot tho

tt. you herd about him n monica

          no, wft

hooked up at the wedding

          ns???

yeah. Good thing s died or she would of DIED lol ;)

        u are a TOTAL btch. But thats why I <3 u

:)

22.

The cracklady attacked the tuna sandwich with a vigor the Redhead envied.

"See," she said, mouth full, "that's why it's crack for me. No meth for these pearly whites! You didn't want this?"

"I did," said the Redhead. "I tried, but it wouldn't stay down."

A hopeful squirrel pranced up, rearing onto its pantalooned hind legs. "You getcher own!" said the cracklady sternly, but tossed it a chunk.

Everyone gets to eat but me, thought the Redhead, disconsolate.

"I hear ya, about the food," the cracklady said. "Sometimes nothing sits right, other days I could eat a horse and like it."

She folded the saran back around the sandwich and stuck it in a pocket. "Other days," she continued, "I got enough self-control to save some for later. This'll do me when I get back to the shelter."

That made the Redhead think about her own current domestic status. "I don't know where to go. I can't remember a lot."

"Homeless?" asked the cracklady. There was sympathy in her voice.

"They put my apartment up for rent. All my stuff got sold, or…" *put in the trash.* She couldn't quite say it out loud. How long before the box of her old possessions went to the dump? Maybe there was still time to… but that was foolish. Look forward, not back.

"That's tough," said the cracklady, patting her on the knee again. "You gotta watch out the bailiffs don't get to know you too good. Or if they do, that they like you, just know you're down on your luck."

That was a world the Redhead knew nothing about. She'd only been to court once, on a class trip. Evictions and cops and lawyers? All foreign. And what exactly did bailiffs do? Was she making herself a target by just sitting here with this lady whom she didn't even know? She looked around nervously.

"Do I… are they around? Do I have to watch out?"

"Not if you keep movin', hon," said the cracklady, tapping the side of her nose with a finger that was almost as pale as one of the Redhead's own. The Redhead's anxiety seemed to reach her finally, and she made a big show of changing the subject.

"Sssssoooooooo, you got an old man, hon?" When the Redhead didn't answer at once, she went on in a cajoling tone: "I had an old man once. He went to jail, and I ended up like this."

The Redhead nodded in sympathy, but a memory flashed at the same moment, strong if a little rough around the edges. Her eyes opened in surprise.

A walkway in front of a townhouse. Her view mostly blocked by a guy, the same one who'd joked with her in the Vegan restaurant, the "D" guy. David. Dave. She was almost sure that was it.

And then he kissed her.

The Redhead smiled, closed her eyes savouring the memory.

"Me too, I think," she said, eyes still shut. "A guy, I mean…"

The crack lady leaned toward her, lowered her voice conspiratorially. "You should find that man, hon. Short of crack, love's the best drug."

The Redhead opened her eyes, and with that, reality came back a little too harshly. "The way things have been going…" She trailed off.

"Don't listen to me, whadda I know?" Now the cracklady seemed to have caught the downer bug as well. Then, she rallied and tried again. "But if you got someone, you should at least give it a chance."

It was the first thing that had made sense to the Redhead in a long time. "Thank you," she said, only just holding herself back from shaking the cracklady's hand. They might have bonded, but there was a limit, after all. "Thank you, I will."

Shaking a few tuna sandwich crumbs off her dress, she got up off the bench and stumbled off.

The cracklady relaxed back into the slats of the bench. "Nice kid," she said to herself. "Bad taste in clothes, but nice kid."

Something wriggled on the bench where the Redhead had sat. Leaning to look, the cracklady saw a collection of small white shapes. *Maggots?* That girl was in worse shape than she'd thought.

23.

Red hair isn't really red of course, unless you're Raggedy Ann or Andy.

It's more of a rusty orange at its brightest and most Irish, gingery and startling. Strawberry blonde was a very inappropriate yet evocative name for the lighter variety, less orange and more reddy gold.

The darker shades weren't really reds at all, not as hair colour was charted, but just warm tones of brown. And then there were the totally artificial crimsons, carmines, and scarlets, not in the least bit colours that nature created but damned fun all the same.

She'd chosen "Southern Flame" because it seemed to combine the best of all worlds: the depth of the auburns, the burn of true redhead red, and the drama of the jewel tones never seen in the natural world of hair. It had gone on beautifully and hadn't needed any touching-up or a second treatment; because her hair had been bleached out entirely for the last colour, she was just putting tone over tone instead of replacing the natural pigment of her hair. Even covered the couple of (utterly unwelcome and FAR TOO SOON) gray hairs she'd noticed.

It made her feel—different. Better. More dangerous.
Stronger.

All that was missing, really, was the hook for the website.
She'd been racking her brains for exactly the right spin. You
couldn't launch a really powerful social media campaign
without having your message thought-out. That was the one
thing you didn't get a do-over for. Change your image,
change your mind, but the central narrative had to be there
from the first.

Tragedy. Anger. She could see the problem with her original
memorial page: it just wasn't sexy enough. The article had
vaguely mentioned a boyfriend, but hadn't seeded any
details she could make use of. There was no scandal
attached, just a nice girl who'd fallen into a fountain, hit her
head, and drowned while more than a dozen people looked
on.

That wasn't it either—the shame of a large wedding party
so involved in filming a disaster no one had bothered to stop
it from happening. It was one of the elements that had
struck her hardest at first, because of course she'd have
probably done the same. Still, not sexy. And the *last* thing
she wanted was to make any of THOSE losers the story.

She'd done some awesome selfies to use as graphics on the
new blog site, and the one of just her eyes was truly stellar.
She was going to use that as the banner. Yeah, she'd upped
the green of her eyes to apple-scented shampoo luminous,
but that's Hollywood, baby. No one could fault her for using
what God provided, right, and that including this sweet CS
suite some eager fanboy had stolen for her. Presented on a
cute, personalized 16 gig thumbdrive, no less. Good, good
boy.

She checked the mirror again. Yeah, she'd been doing that a

lot, but it was to recheck the hair, not to ogle herself. Well, maybe a little the second. But seriously, that colour was bad-ass. It took "natural redhead" to the future of hair—a real burnt orange with a serious intensity you only found on one redhead in a million. Hot, burning hot. Burn your eyes out hot.

Sharon's exact colour, in fact.

A tragedy, for sure, but one with all the makings of a great legend. Seriously. The intense burnt orange hair fanning out in the water. A glimpse of that god-awful fuchsia dress clashing hideously (but damn, that would make for good cinema!) A pale hand still clutching at the bouquet whose white baby's breath and camellias contrasted so gorgeously with the green fern stalks, and with the sparkling blue of the pool.

And the red, the true primary red, of that poor girl's blood as it ebbed out of that head wound the coroner had described as "a fist-sized knot, sadly in exactly the right spot to kill" at the inquest. She'd poured over the transcript of that. Lots of juice, made you cry.

Sharon, Sharon, Sharon. This was a good story. Hell, it was freakin' *great.* If she didn't run with it, she was a moron. And redheads are accused of many things, but stupidity sure ain't one.

And from this day forth, she was a serious redhead. With a mission. And a brilliant angle that no one had ever seen before. As soon as she figured out what it was.

*

24.

A beautiful clear evening. David/Dave's face framed by the townhouse behind him. His place? He'd invited her in, but she'd refused virtuously. She was tired, had to work in the morning.

But she'd lingered, and so had he, holding hands, wavering back and forth as if a decision was being made for them by their linked fingers. And then, ever so slowly, he'd bent forward, and kissed her.

The Redhead opened her eyes, the memory of the kiss still stinging her lips. Yep, same townhouse. Same walkway leading up to it. And here was exactly where she'd stood the first time Dave had kissed her.

In her head, she heard the cracklady's words of wisdom—or reasonable drug-addled facsimile. "You gotta go for it… As long as the guy's not a double murderer or anything. And hey, even then…"

Her tingly lips parted in a wide smile.

But he'd missed the funeral, right? And how long ago had that kiss been? Had things changed between them since that magic moment? Maybe they weren't on good terms any more. Maybe he'd even moved. Or just moved on.

Maybe this wasn't such a good idea. She'd try again when she'd had time to think about it more, or when some other memories returned to clarify the situation.

She turned to go. And ran straight into another woman.

A flash of instant recognition. "Oh my god—Monica. Hi!"

She chalked up the stare Monica gave in response to her greeting to surprise. But when the silence lingered, and continued…

"This is awkward," the Redhead said at last.

That seemed to be all that was needed to get a real answer from the girl who'd been her best friend. Monica started screaming, like the sirens of a six-alarm fire.

The door of the townhouse shot open. The Redhead heard it but was too busy flailing her hands defensively toward Monica to react to the new development at first. When she did turn to see who was approaching at a run from behind, she saw the man, literally, of her dreams—or at least of her recently recovered memory.

"Dave!" she said, her genuine pleasure making her fail to take into account the circumstances in which he believed she now existed. The confines of a cemetery, in other words.

Dave, back-pedalling to a frantic halt, took a breath, looked with wide-staring eyes between his former girlfriend and her former best friend, opened his mouth, and began shrieking to drown out Monica herself.

They think I'm dead, the Redhead reminded herself. *This is just natural. They'll stop screaming in a moment, and I'll explain…*

But they didn't. Lights went on in windows along the row of townhouses. A front door opened, and a neighbour leaned out. "Shut that bloody racket up or I'll call the cops!"

"Very, very awkward," said the Redhead to no one in particular. She backed out of the space between Dave and Monica, as if stepping away from a rabid dog. Two rabid dogs. Two people who believed they were seeing a ghost, when it was really just… well, a dead girl.

Okay, maybe it was a little much to hope for a return to calm anytime soon.

"Okay," she said. "…Uh, see you…"

She fled.

25.

Night. Trees. Underbrush.

She'd lost the path a while back, but that was good. If she wasn't on a path, no one would stumble across her.

How could she have been so ridiculously stupid? How could she have blithely wandered up to Dave's place without a plan and, more importantly, without a clue? Of course he thought—knew in fact—that she was dead. Even if he hadn't been at the burial, there was no way he'd missed out on her death. He was right there, probably trying to save her.

And Monica: okay, she had maybe grabbed the bouquet out of the Redhead's hands when Sharon had caught it fair and square. And that's the only reason they'd gone into the water…

This was good. More memories. The fountain. Right, in the park where Dorri had insisted the wedding photos *just have to take place.* That long walk in high heels across the grass, damp and spongy from rain earlier in the week, sinking backwards with every step. Of course it hadn't rained for the photos though. Not even God would dare rain on Dorri's wedding.

There was something else too, a little tickle of discontent she couldn't quite bring to the surface of her mind. What was it? Something about Monica, or Dave, or both of them.

And when had she actually died, and how? That mega-nasty lump on the back of her head would seem to be a pretty stunning clue, but it wasn't exactly time- and date-stamped.

Oh god, had it happened at the wedding shoot? Dorri would never, ever forgive her if it had.

And now what? She was alive, or rather she was dead but still around. She needed to eat, something, and she needed some place to live. And at some point, she needed to figure out if she still had, although dead, anything of her old life left.

She'd found a pile of peanuts before she'd chanced the woods that some animal-lover had obviously left for the local wildlife. Despite the ever-growing hunger, she hadn't been able to bring herself to try them. The memory of the failed tuna sandwich experience still loomed large.

But she had them, and maybe tomorrow she'd feel up to the experiment. If only *something* would go her way!

She must have fallen asleep, because she was aware of waking with a start sometime near dawn by the chattering of an irate squirrel. Opening her eyes, she saw him not three feet away, sitting up on his hind legs, tail twitching. Eyeing her peanuts.

"Go! Shoo!" she shouted, waving her hands. "Mine!"

Reduced to stealing nuts from a squirrel. Not what she'd expected from life. Or death, for that matter.

26.

From David J. Swinson x and Monica Gulyas x to all their friends

Yesterday evening, Monica and I had a very disturbing experience that we feel we need to share with all of you in hopes that someone has a reasonable explanation for what transpired.

As you know, my girlfriend of two years, Sharon Backovic x , recently and tragically passed away. Monica and I have appreciated your kind words and sensitivity as we start to build a life together after this terrible event.

Last night, however, Monica was terrorized in front of my house by someone who was either a total dead ringer for Sharon, or someone playing an incredibly cruel joke. If it was the former, we still can't believe that no harm was meant because the individual in question was made up to look like a zombie.

We were not attacked but felt like the situation could have gone that way if we had responded at all aggressively.

In the interest of the safety of our friends and to make sure that anyone else approached by this individual is not as unprepared as we were, we thought it was essential to let you know that someone out there is either pretending to be Sharon, or Sharon herself faked her own death for reason or reasons unknown. If the latter, Sharon, please get help. Monica and I still care about you, and we can't imagine what could have driven you to do this to your friends and family.

Please don't contact us if you see her, but call the police and report the incident to the proper authorities. Whoever this person is, she could be not only sick but dangerous.

Like · Comment · Share

👍 You and 43 other people like this.

>Hey guys, totally despicable. People are nuts!

>Find that sicko and give her a bitchslap for me! Sharon might not have been everyone's favourite person, but NO ONE should be mocked when they're dead.

>Except Hitler.
>Like · 👍 3

>Just wondering if anyone considered the possibility that it really IS Sharon and she didn't fake her death on purpose. Read an article online a

while back about false declarations
of death. Some people even wake
up on the dissection table!

Send me that link if you can. Would
like to have SOME kind of
reasonable explanation. Otherwise,
Zombie Sharon could be on the lose!

Loose. Oops.

27.

The Redhead had claimed another bench today, this one
near the public library. She felt strangely at home among the
other homeless, the uncontrolled schizophrenics, and the
just plain ornery who also seemed to congregate here.

She'd dumped the peanuts she'd found out of her clutch
onto the concrete arm of the bench after discovering that her
fingers weren't up to the task of cracking them open. She
could pick *up* the peanut, and even hold it, but she couldn't
judge the pressure she was putting on it. The first time, she
had crushed it to so much peanut dust; the second time
she'd been so afraid to do it again that it just wobbled there
between her thumb and two middle fingers, taunting her.

What she could and couldn't feel seemed to change minute
by minute. Sometimes she seemed to feel pain; other times,
she had realized one of her shoes had actually dropped off
half a block before and she hadn't even noticed until it
occurred to her that she was lopsided.

Same with the memories. They came and went, as
capriciously as any well-fed cat, taunting her more than

anything. It was infuriating—and with that thought, she snapped another peanut into oblivion.

Scrabbling in her purse for a tool to help, she found the cellphone. Its battery was dead, her plan certainly expired and impossible to renew without an address (or identity for that matter). Really, it was nothing more than a glorified rock now, just with fewer pointy edges than a caveman might have preferred.

She set another peanut on the concrete arm, and raised the cellphone.

As she did, a flyer stuck to the library's outdoor events board caught her eye. Leaving rudimentary tool invention for the moment, she got up and took a closer look.

FREE INTERNET ACCESS, it said. SIGN UP ON LINE OR JUST COME IN! ALL WELCOME.

Really. She smiled. Finally, a way to reach out and see what had changed—and what hadn't—since her apparent demise.

She removed the flyer from the board and folded it away into her clutch. Something positive, just like she'd wished for. Maybe this was going to be okay. She'd wanted a sign that she could reconnect with anything familiar, and here was the opportunity, staring her in the face.

Returning to the bench, feeling a heck of a good piece more positive, she brought the cellphone resolutely down on the peanut. It skittered away into the grass.

"Oh… sugar!" said the Redhead.

*

28.

**From the case files of V. X. Morgoni,
cryptoparapsychocriminologist**

Something strange on the local scene—don't know yet if it
is anything or just another false lead. Also not sure if it
relates to my own odd sighting of the cosplay zombie in
Kensington earlier in the week. If so, that would neither
assert or deny the truth of the situation but might put me in
the correct vicinity to investigate further.

Led to a series of tweets by Juan Carla who makes it her job
to follow the #Toronto hashtag robot retweeter that
nevertheless pulls up some good dirt from time to time.
From that, requested and received confirmation of
friendship on FB through one of my aliases and from there,
access to a very intriguing conversation about an apparent
"dead girl" who may or may not have become a zombie.

Expecting this to be a big disappointment, either a
deliberate hoax or a euphemism for normal asshole
behaviour on the part of regular asshole people. Still, did
find reference in the paper to the funeral of said girl, and an
article online about the bizarre circumstances of her death.

In a world where everyone wants to be a zombie or vampire
or werewolf, I could open myself up to ridicule if I take it
too seriously, but if I've got nothing else to do (and the
paranormal landscape has been unnaturally quiet lately) a
little digging will keep me sharp if nothing else.

With some decent time and effort put in, should be able to
lay this one to rest and return to ACTUAL unexplained
phenomena. Zombies in Toronto. Get real.

Morgoni out.

29.

Kensington was starting to open its secrets to the Redhead. She'd realized that strangers, at least, weren't particularly put off by her appearance. The alley behind Vegan Goodness was all but deserted 24 hours a day, and she'd even found some old magazines, a few cushions, and a solid, non-stinky garbage bag or two to make her hidey-hole beside the dumpster a little more comfortable, if not precisely homey. With the appearance of maggots on the edges of her chest-sutures, and probably more on the knot on her skull, she couldn't be *too* picky about cleanliness or worry about live-person concerns like bed bugs.

At this point, bed bugs might be nice company. She'd given up on the peanuts, and had tried to entice a squirrel over with them to have at least *some* contact with another living thing, but it had been too wary to come close. Later, upon waking, she'd found all the nuts gone. Crafty little buggers. She needed some survival skills like that. It was ridiculous that a rodent could out-thrive her in the middle of a city built by humans. Her people, at least nominally. At least *once* they were.

She'd never been more grateful for Toronto's surplus of free papers. They passed the time, they didn't cut into her very meagre resources, and they made good makeshift wallpaper for her alcove when used in conjunction with some soured milk and a half-flexible paintbrush from the dumpster.

Soon, though, she was going to have to figure out a way to do better. Even hoarding her cash, it wouldn't last long, especially if she managed to find something she could eat. Her experiments so far had been entirely unsuccessful, except for a half-rotten apple that had gone down surprisingly well. The brown bits seemed especially tasty. Where the flesh on it remained white and unbruised, both her stomach and her mouth had seemed to rebel. The texture felt wrong against her teeth, and the first bite had made her stomach churn when it made it down her gorge.

Okay then. More experiments were needed, but she thought she might be on to something.

She'd refilled her water bottle at the library when she'd checked her email. Amazing, that even with its owner dead, her Hotmail account continued to collect dozens of pieces of junk mail every day.

Leaving the chair after her session, she'd been horrified to see she'd left a bit of staining on the seat and a couple of maggots near the keyboard. Hoping no one was paying attention, she used a Kleenex to remove the evidence. She'd have to be *much* more aware of her surroundings unless she wanted more reactions like Monica's and Dave's.

Now, she was exploring Kensington as a potential consumer, looking for anything that might make her life-after-death more bearable. She'd picked up a knitted afghan or shawl with a hood, made of thick, dark wool, that would hide the dress a bit if she felt it was too flashy, and would also be something she could throw around her shoulders if her imperviousness to the cold was likely to attract unwanted attention.

It also was nice to snuggle into when she tucked herself behind the dumpster to sleep, even if it wasn't really necessary for warmth.

All in all, she was doing… okay. Not well, not badly. But definitively, undeniably okay.

On Augusta, a bright, cluttered window caught her eye, full of comics, graphic novels, and toys. This was the kind of window shopping she'd never gone in for much as a live person, but it was something to look at and actually kind of cool.

She didn't recognize many of the characters depicted on the books, especially the round headed, huge-eyed Japanese characters with hair more vivid than hers and in every colour of the rainbow. That was a crazy trend, the blue and green and purple locks topping pointy-chinned heads on small torsos with legs so long and skinny they'd put a spider crab to shame. Spider crabs. *Shiver.* People thought zombies were scary?

On the zombie theme, the Redhead was astonished, although not entirely surprised, to see that a huge amount of the merchandise on display was devoted to depictions of the undead. She knew about the recent zombie craze, even if she hadn't been a fan of the specific shows or films that took advantage of it. Uplifting animal documentaries. Light romantic comedies. The occasional action film, as long as it wasn't *too* violent. That was Sharon's taste.

The Redhead, on the other hand, had better educate herself. Especially—if the stuff in the window was any indication— if most people figured the only good zombie was a hacked-to-pieces one.

She shivered again, this time feeling the skin at her throat crawl a little. At first she thought she was having a quite visceral reaction to the cover of one of the comics depicting a muscular man in a ripped shirt in the process of removing a drooling zombie's head with a fire axe.

Touching her neck, though, it was just a maggot who'd escaped her cleavage for fresh (rotten) pastures. Not worrying this time about the surprising strength of her fingers, she crushed it and tossed away what was left.

But immediately after she'd done it, she felt bad. Maggots were living things too—or rather, they were living even if she was not. They just wanted something to eat, and she couldn't deny that she was a walking bug-buffet, if she continued to rot.

And what if they were actually beneficial, a kind of Redhead-cleanup-crew, ridding her of dead(er) skin, but getting as bad a rep as that garbageman-hero of the natural world, the underrated turkey vulture? Also, who was to say the maggots had any less right to thrive than she did? Another troubling philosophical question, she supposed. Did she have a right to interrupt the circle of life? As a dead Canadian, did she have any rights or protections under the law from anything that might happen to her?

It had to be an unprecedented situation, or for sure she'd have heard about it somewhere. There'd be petitions for recognition of zombie rights, and undead marches… That sparked a memory but this one was too vague to capture. Not a memory of something she'd done, but of something else. Zombie marches? She'd have to look it up, if she thought she could stand being in the library again. It would be mortifying to ruin a chair with her… juices leaking. She might get kicked out, or worse, get a lecture from one of those terrifying library ladies with the stern faces and gold-rimmed specs hanging from chains around their necks.

And people thought zombies were scary? They'd obviously never had to face the humiliation of being blamed (in error no less) for someone else's too-loud laughter in a public library. That memory came to her very clearly and painfully. Just another time when she'd covered for Dorri, and never been thanked.

A title in the window caught her eye. Really? She read it again, checked the price on the sale sticker in its corner. It seemed like the answer to her prayers. For once, fate was intervening to help her out.

She opened her clutch and counted her money. Yes, she had enough. It would pretty much break her, but if it could help her understand what to do next, it was well spent.

The Redhead went into the comic book store.

Rescue Party

30.

Malcolm slid the air out of the mylar bag and taped the flap shut with long-practiced efficiency.

"She had a what?"

"A bouquet. Like she'd been to a wedding and didn't want the memories to end."

Jason Terry, owner of Kensy Comics, handed his employee one of the mugs he was carrying, and took a sip from his own.

"That's freaky," said Malcolm. "Wish I'd been here."

"Seemed nice though. Don't know what the story is there."

Malcolm laughed. "You're talking to the guy whose sister is sharing space with a bone fide Lone Gunwoman."

Jason laughed. "How is Teeny?" He perched on the one stool behind the counter and watched Malcolm bag another comic from the stack.

"Back at school, thank god. Doing great, actually. I think having a roomie who's stranger than science fiction kinda keeps her on track."

"By the way," said Jason, "how did we end up with me making *you* coffee?"

Malcolm shrugged. "Because I suck at it. That demon machine barely tolerates you; me, I have nightmares it's trying to coffeeboard me to death in my sleep. And because then I don't start whining that you sit on your ass while I do all the work around here."

 A passing figure caught his attention—unmistakable with the hunched walk, watchcap, and dreads.

"Speak of the devil."

Jason turned to check the window and saw her disappear past the shop. "Don't say her name, man. Three times and she turns around and comes into the store." He gave an exaggerated shiver. "Spooooky."

"Hey, man. It's Kensington. You wanted normal, you shoulda opened up in Bloor West Village."

"We are normal," said Jason, mock offended. "What you mean is average."

"Utah Phillips. *The Past Didn't Go Anywhere.*"

"You know it." He held out his fist for Malcolm to bump. "Hey, less talk, more bagging. How can I enjoy my coffee if I have to worry about you not working hard enough?"

*

31.

The Redhead saw the cracklady sitting on the curb not far from the grocery store she'd targeted as a good bet for continuing her research into what might cure her hunger. So far, she'd staved off the worst of it with rotten produce from dumpsters, but there really was something of an "ick" factor involved. It wasn't the condition of the fruit, per se, just what she needed to scrabble through to get them.

In fact, she had pretty much come to the conclusion that she was still a Vegan despite zombification, only her tastes seemed to run to the extremely overripe if not downright spoiled versions of what she used to eat. It had occurred to her that if she talked with the produce manager of a smaller supermarket, she might be able to score a reliable supply of unsalable fruit and veggies past their best for the general public. Maybe they wouldn't even charge!

Despite the fact she was entirely alone, the cracklady had her hand out. As the Redhead came up, she heard the woman say, "Change?" to no one.

The Redhead tried to make a little noise as she approached so she wouldn't startled the other woman. All she managed was to stumble a little, almost dropping the plastic bag carrying her new book. "Sugar, sugar, sugar!" she said.

The cracklady turned, gave her an intense look with one eyebrow raised, then grinned. "Hey, I know you."

"Who were you talking to?" the Redhead asked, rubbing her heel.

"Just practicing. Gotta stay sharp." The cracklady put a

finger to the side of her nose again.

The Redhead smiled back, liking this feeling of being a co-conspirator allowed to know someone else's secrets. Then, another thought struck her. "I, uh, I don't have any…" Her resources, especially post-comic shop, were very slight.

"Don't worry, hon," said the cracklady, waving an arm expansively. "I don't beg from my peers."

"Huh," replied the Redhead. It was a *kind* of belonging, she figured.

"You doing okay?" the cracklady said, waving the Redhead to a spot on the curb next to her. "Found something that agrees with you?"

"Sort of," she said, sitting, grateful to get off her feet but a little worried about flashing her undies to the world. She tucked her legs to one side and put her clutch and the bag in her lap. "I seem to be good with… really ripe fruits and vegetables. I thought I might go in and…" She indicated the supermarket.

"How'd it go with your man?" the cracklady asked. "You look him up?"

"Sort of. Didn't go well." That was an understatement, but better that than relieving the drama. She'd never been screamed at before. Well, not like she was something in a horror movie, anyhow.

"Well, screw him," the cracklady said. "Wash yer hands of the bastard and move on."

The troubling presence of Monica at Dave's place and the implications of what she could recall about the weeks leading up to her death were her own drama, the Redhead supposed. Who would have thought she'd be second-guessing everything she knew about Dave as she remembered it?

"I think he might have been sleeping with my best friend," she said, tentatively, and was rewarded by the cracklady turning to her with an over-serious look of horror that, oddly, encouraged her to go on.

Sharon smoothed the bridesmaid's dress, checking the fit in the mirror. It looked like it hung right, even if it felt like a sausage casing. And the colour… "Sallow" didn't begin to describe how it made her skin tone look.

From the next room, she could hear Dave's voice, but he didn't seem to be talking to her. It was him though, not the TV, she decided.

"Look, I can't talk now," she thought she heard him say.

"Dave?" she called out. "Who's that?"

"No one, honey," he shouted in reply. A moment later, he came into the room and joined her at the mirror.

"How do I look?" she asked, fingers crossed that he would either lie to spare her feelings, or tell the truth and confirm her opinion. Anything, but be ornery and start a fight.

Dave smiled. Sharon noticed he was holding his phone. By his leg. As if hoping she didn't notice.

She was babbling, decidedly. But the cracklady was gazing at her with a tender sympathy she wasn't used to, and kind of liked. "Monica… I think she and Dave might have got together behind my back. Sometimes, he'd be on the phone and pretend he wasn't when I came in. Or he'd close the browser quickly when I saw him on the computer. I thought he was just looking at porn."

"Reasonable," said the cracklady, nodding sagely.

"But… you know. I never thought it was true, that you always know when someone's cheating. I didn't, not really. I just knew… I knew from the start Dave and I were wrong for each other. I just kept pretending I didn't."

Sharon heaved a sigh that seemed to verge on an actual sob. "He kind of vanished at this wedding we went to together. Between the service and the photos. And when he came back, I realized Monica had been gone too. Monica, she was… I guess we were best friends ever since high school. It was kind of because of her I was a bridesmaid. We were both bridesmaids, for Dorri, but I wouldn't know Dorri except for Monica…"

They sat in silence for a moment. The cracklady stuck her hand out as couple of pedestrians passed, but they ignored the two.

"Always a bridesmaid, huh," said the cracklady, when the strangers had gone on.

The Redhead snorted. "Once was enough for me. Believe me."

"That the bouquet?"

The Redhead had almost forgotten she was carrying it. For some reason, she didn't want to lose it, which meant keeping it in hand. Who else wouldn't just assume the wilting flowers and dried-out foliage weren't just so much trash? Besides, it was the key to her death—she was sure of it.

"The last thing I remember, Dorri was getting ready to throw it. Monica had this look on her face like she was going to kill anyone who got in her way… and I don't know. It's not like me at all, but I just remember thinking, 'Outta my way, bitch. That thing is *mine.*' And then…?"

"Looks like ya got it in the end."

The Redhead snorted again, more sadly this time. "Not to mention this gorgeous dress."

"The colour is…" started the cracklady, then seemed to think twice about what she'd been planning on saying. "It's really…"

Speechless, thought the Redhead. *I guess I wasn't wrong when I thought it was hideous. At least with this hair…* "I can't believe this is what they buried me in! My over-priced, sixteen fittings to *still* feel like a sack ugly, ugly, clashing, nasty… and of course the dyed-to-match torture devices Dorri picked for footwear. Ugh, this dress!"

"You never ever get a chance to wear those things again," said the cracklady.

"I'd give anything just to get it *off* me."

The cracklady rose, creaking, to her feet, and held out a hand to the Redhead. "Then that's what you gotta do!"

Her enthusiasm caught fire inside the Redhead. *Yes, damn it. They might have buried her in the damn thing, but she could change. Everything could change. Why not?* She moved her hands to the zipper of the dress, but just like with the peanuts, she couldn't assess how hard they were holding on, or even feel the tab.

"Here, hon, let me," said the cracklady and moved beside the Redhead to reach the zipper. But the woman's creased hands were shaking like china in a San Francisco quake. The crack? The Redhead reached back to try to help. A fingernail fell off and hit the pavement. "Was that you or me?" asked the cracklady.

After more struggling and a lot of groans of exertion on one's part (the cracklady) and what might have been the start of a sprained neck muscle on the other's (the Redhead), the zipper moved downwards about an inch. Both women cheered.

Then— "Hang on," said the cracklady. "Do you have anything to change into?"

Silence. *Nope. And no money to waste on that either.* Resignation. The Redhead sighed.

"Okay. Back up again," said the cracklady, and the fumbling began again.

"Oh heck," said the Redhead.

32.

It was mid-afternoon, typically the time of day when the shop traffic was confined to kids skipping school. So Jason was mildly surprised to see the zombie come in.

"Hey," he said. "I was going to ask you—the Zombie Walk.

I thought it was in October or something."

Zombie Walk. That's what it was, what she'd been trying to remember. She'd have to look that up when she got up the nerve to go back into the library. For now, she was getting used to explaining the way she appeared the easiest way she knew how.

"It's more of a… look," she said.

"A lifestyle choice, then."

"Not so much," she admitted, "but that's a good way to think of it."

She wandered closer to the counter and pretended to be browsing anime miniatures in a sale bin near the register.

"Can I help you?" Jason said finally when it was clear she wouldn't ask.

The Redhead fidgeted. "I'd like to return something. If I could. Please."

She put a Kensy Comics bag on the counter and removed the copy of *The Zombie Survival Guide* she'd bought the day before.

Jason could see it had been thumbed through but it was still in decent shape, if you ignored a little bit of stained on the edges of the pages, which of course most of his customers wouldn't. Except the collectors, who noticed *everything.* "Yeah?"

He looked at her for an explanation.

"It wasn't what I thought," she said, embarrassed now.

Interesting… "Okay…" he said, apologetically. Policy was policy though, and he didn't think he could resell it in its current condition anyhow. "We don't take returns on books."

"Oh," she said, disappointed but not really surprised. Of course.

"Sorry about that."

She fidgeted more, and he felt even worse. There was something about this girl… it wasn't a helplessness or anything. She wasn't exactly a damsel in distress, not looking more like the monster the damsel'd be fleeing from. Not that she wasn't cute, just—well, lifestyle choice or not, the zombie thing was a little off-putting.

But there was something interesting about her, nonetheless. They'd actually had a nice chat when she'd been in before, as he'd told Malcolm earlier. When she got excited—they'd been talking about how fairy tales she'd read as a child were creeping into a lot of recent comic series, and he'd been showing her just how much—she'd been animated and really funny. It was like she'd entirely forgotten the persona she'd chosen to convey with her dress sense and that creepy-ass makeup…

"I kinda really need the money," the Redhead said, sounding more than a little apologetic herself. He could tell she was one of those people who really didn't like to be an imposition, and it made him feel more inclined to cut her a break. He could, of course. After all, he *was* the boss.

Still, he said, "I'm really sorry."

"That's okay," she said, nodding. "It was a fun read. Even it if wasn't…"

"…What you thought," he finished for her."

She agreed. "Yeah."

"Look," said Jason abruptly. "I can give you store credit."

"I'm not sure that helps," she said, hoping she didn't sound ungrateful. Her cash was *really* low. Amazing she'd lived on it this far. Well, not exactly *lived* of course…

"Sorry," said Jason, really sounding like he meant it. "That's the best I can do." That would actually still be a hit; he'd have to mark down the book for it to move. Maybe as much as half off.

But it was worth it to see the smile on her face. Too bad Malcolm wasn't here; he'd really like this girl. And he deserved someone sweet and fun and smart in his life: Jason had seen too many girls who were *none* of those things chase his personable employee.

Too bad Malcolm hadn't made it back from lunch. His loss.

The Redhead had made a circle of the shop, but it was clear she'd homed in on one something specific just as soon as he'd mentioned an exchange.

She held up a cute backpack. "How much is this?"

*

33.

**From the case files of V. X. Morgoni,
cryptoparapsychocriminologist**

More proof of the steady decline both in intelligence and
manners in the common human animal, and I do mean
animal. Today, filing a report on the deplorable state of a
particular cafe in the vicinity (which shall go by the name of
Cafe X until I am ready to go public with my findings), I
was interrupted by possibly the rudest group of young
females I have ever had the misfortune to share oxygen
with. I am quite sure all of them respirated solely through
their mouths, if you get my drift.

Ugh. Save me from the kind of people that believe their
own conversations are fascinating enough to inflict on
everyone within a mile radius.

I had hardly begun shooting my report when one of these
arrogant, useless women who had been talking nonsense at
the top of her lungs snuck up behind me and *actually ripped
my video camera out of my hands.*

Stunned at this intrusion and the blatant theft, I was hardly
swift to react. Instead, I found myself pulled into their
idiotic interaction, like they were some kind of black hole of
stupidity invading my unsuspecting solar system and
sucking out all the sense.

As soon as my initial shock abated, I immediately went to
the counter and demanded to see the manager. Meanwhile, I
kept an eye on the foul thief who'd grabbed my camera.
Every time she moved, I was sure she'd drop it, the entitled

bimbo. Eating up my memory, on some vapid congregation of like-nul-minded morons.

The manager took his sweet-ass time coming up to the cash. I'd dealt with this numbskull before during my investigation, and I could tell he was spoiling for a fight. A total lack of professionalism on his part, which is probably a combination of the piss-poor training and his own mental deficiencies. I could see my complaints were barely impinging on his feeble little brain.

Obviously, even in its current covert phase, my investigation into the shoddy conditions at this cafe are registering on one of its greatest malefactors. He seemed to take a childish pleasure in pretending he didn't see "the problem" if the bimbo had "asked if she could borrow my camera." Well, lah-di-dah, useless turd. I didn't say *yes!* I wasn't even given the option before she snatched it out of my hands.

As if I *would* lend any of my equipment to someone I didn't know, especially someone barely evolved enough to stand upright much less treat a piece of electronics with the care and respect it deserves.

Finally, I was able to disengage myself from the useless interaction with the insipid manager, and take matters into my own hands. By this time, a now-familiar figure had joined the group, that odd girl in the pink dress who had threatened me at the bus stop no less. Yes, I said *threatened.* Upon review of the footage I took that night, it was pretty damn clear to me that she had approached me in a manner obviously prepared to do harm. It was only by my own quick response that I derailed her intention and sent her on her way.

Hmmm, maybe this is the new menace—the kind of loon that will not just *dress* as a zombie, but who believes she *is* one up to and including trying to eat human flesh. Or brains.

Suddenly, I am glad I had decided to keep the footage shot by the sneak-thief in case the matter of her crime against me goes to court. Maybe there's something in that footage I can use in a new investigation…

One last note: although I called the criminal bitch a fascist when I reclaimed my property, it was clear she had no idea whatsoever what the word meant. Idiot.

Morgoni out.

34.

It had been a disaster, but that was probably what she *should* have expected. First, she was too nervous even to go into the cafe. It was bad enough that hadn't thought about bringing a good-bye present for Sylvia, but to be late on top of that…

In her own defense, she hadn't quite realized how long it would take to walk. And she needed to make sure she saved as much of her remaining money as possible. The backpack was a nice addition to her current stock, and a way to carry her few possessions (including the bouquet, in the Kensy Comics plastic bag to stop it from shedding) that almost made the expense worth it.

But she'd decided to take the TTC to her old neighbourhood again, just to see if anything was left behind the building in the box near the dumpster, and really couldn't afford to take it back as well. She'd managed, though, to find a couple of bits and pieces of her past including an old school essay (The Themes and Conflicts in Thomas Hardy's 'Tess') and her public speaking trophy. Little enough for a life, but maybe enough to anchor a life-after-death.

Walking back had made her late, though, so she'd hovered in the alley besides the building for a few minutes, trying to work up her courage enough to go in.

It was nice that Sylvia's friend what's-her-name from Burlington had come out and convinced her it would be okay. Well, maybe she didn't actually say as much, and it was clear she didn't remember the Redhead from her Sharon days when they'd all gone out to Montana's together for drinks, Sylvia and her posse of friends, including a considerable overlap from Dorri's circle.

Inside, it was pretty clear that her attendance at Sylvia's going-away party was not just unwelcome but downright disruptive. She'd had her eyes opened there, that was for certain.

Apparently, Dave and Monica were official, something that didn't really surprise her, and shouldn't really concern her since, well, he'd only started dating her openly when Sharon Backovic was dead and buried (actually of course neither, really, or at least only one for certain) but he wasn't to know.

Not only that, but they'd issued a joint statement about having seen Sharon, or a reasonable facsimile, outside his place—and added their own opinions about just how that had come about.

Apparently, Dave was of the opinion that Sharon had somehow appeared to come back to life, because of some rare condition that made it difficult for doctors to tell if she was really dead or just in a deep coma. He put down what he called her "inappropriate behaviour" to post-coma confusion, or post-traumatic stress.

He would, she thought. Dave was always Googling everything medical he heard about and then spouting off as if he was an expert. It was something that really got up her nose every time she'd had the sniffles or was a little tired. There went Dave, telling her exactly what he thought was wrong with her and what she should do to solve it. *If only he'd just taken a break from being Dr. Boyfriend long enough to be sympathetic or, I don't know, make some soup!*

Monica was a lot less charitable. She had spread the very nasty idea that Sharon had faked her own death for attention, believe it or not—and it seemed clear that at least a few of her best friends (besides Sharon of course) had come on board. So now, the Redhead would have to deal with not only the knowledge that somehow Dave and Monica had been let *entirely off the hook* for their duplicity because of the creative forward-dating of the start of their relationship, but they'd taken it upon themselves to smear Sharon's reputation as much as they possibly could.

Not to mention that her former best friend had apparently declared war on the memory of their long time together, *and* stolen her boyfriend to boot.

Now, the Redhead was left with a couple of thorny issues to work out. First, to prove that there was no malice in her return to whatever kind of life this was. She hadn't *wanted* to wake up that day in her own coffin, on the way to six feet under of eternal solitude. It wasn't like this was her plan all along, just to make Dave and Monica unhappy. Seriously, if Dave had just been honest about moving on in the first place, maybe they could have found a way to split up amicably before Dorri's wedding.

Second, and this was an altogether more troubling thought: what if they were right?

The Redhead had kind of gotten used to life post-Sharon, to the idea of being somehow reanimated and irreversibly altered into some kind of zombie or walking-badly-on-high-heels dead.

But what if she was simply a medical oddity, a girl who'd been knocked out, however it had happened, and woke up just in the nick of time to not be buried alive? In that case, she really had to get over what had happened, and move on with things. With her *life*.

It was in that spirit that she'd called Dorri, from a payphone (who knew they still had those, huh?)

When she'd identified herself, she was surprised to discover that Dorri was more put out than shocked that her former friend was on the line. And now, here they were, at the same cafe where Sylvia had basically brushed her off earlier in the day, sitting across from each other. Sharon and Dorri, Dorri and Sharon. Dorri and her errant bridesmaid. Sharon and her crazy dead eyes and taste for bruised kale.

Dorri had just had her nails done, the Redhead saw. Dorri had always just had her nails done. At least that hadn't changed.

Dorri tossed her perfect hair back over one perfect shoulder and sighed dramatically. "Let's—just get this over with. Okay?"

The Redhead found her inner mouse kick in with a

vengeance, like it always did around Dorri. "Thank you so much for coming," she said, babbled really. "Can I get you a coffee? Green tea? Maybe…"

Dorri tapped her nails on the tabletop, and the Redhead braked her mouth. If words could come to a screeching halt, that's what the tap of Dorri's nails did to her.

Dorri tapped a bit more, than looked at the Redhead expectantly.

"Okay," stumbled the Redhead. No coffee…"

"You look like crap," interrupted Dorri.

The observation made the Redhead defensive, but also returned to her just a hint of backbone. "I'm kind of… a zombie," she said.

"No shit," said Dorri. "Or you're the medical marvel of the century, *or* a totally sick fuck who wants to give her friends heart-attacks. Something they aren't going to miraculously recover from."

This was *not* going like the Redhead had hoped.

From her something-something designer bag, Dorri retrieved an oversized, cream-coloured wedding album. It had gold corners on the covers and satin ribbon woven into the motif.

"Do you want to see what you did? How beautiful my wedding photos are? With you and Monica trying to kill each other…"

That seemed a little unfair. "Um," said the Redhead. "I actually *did* die. At the wedding. At the photo shoot I mean." Or something. Dead or at least apparently dead. It seemed a little cruel to put wreaking her photos on someone who was dead. Or something.

Dorri had an answer to that. "Yes, and as long as you stayed dead, it was tragic. Totally. I get that. I mean, hell. Anniversaries were already going to be kind of a downer with you dying at the wedding…"

A memory started to emerge in the Redhead's mind. She *had* been the one to catch the bouquet. She was absolutely sure of that now. She could almost feel it in her hands, and the surge of elation that *she'd done it! She'd really done it!* And then… "Monica pushed me," she said, suddenly just as sure of that as she was of the rest. Was this how she'd died? "I'm pretty sure," she finished, a little lamely. Dorri had to know all this. She was there too, and didn't have the intervening period of death to confuse *her* memories.

Dorri, however, was still talking as if she hadn't even heard. "…but then you come back like this. I mean, *freakshow* much? Showing up at Sylvia's party without so much as a warning…"

"I don't think anyone was exactly scared…" the Redhead tried to explain.

"…and now, not only is my wedding day ruined for all eternity, you're probably going to show up at, I don't know, my first child's birth, eating some doctor's brains."

Even now, it didn't seem like she really wanted either an explanation or an apology from the Redhead as much as she wanted to vent. Well, fair enough, but the brains thing…

"I'm a Vegan," said the Redhead. "At least…"

But Dorri cut her off sharply. "Okay. Fine. Whatever. So say what you're got to say, and then just leave me alone."

A silence descended between them that the Redhead abruptly felt afraid to fill. Being told in such explicit terms that even such a fraught friendship was at an end was upsetting. Even if she'd never really felt that close to Dorri despite all the protestations both had made over the years, it *was* one more person the Redhead's current situation had alienated. Would she find herself more and more on the other side of a gulf, separating her from every other human being who *hadn't* experienced her own funeral?

Although it seemed insufficient to the circumstances, the Redhead managed: "…I'm sorry?"

They stared at each other for a moment, the Redhead questioning, questing for some kind of salve, and Dorri with cold fury.

"You're sorry?" said the latter.

"Really, really sorry?"

"Huh," said Dorri, with dripping disdain.

"Really, really, really sorry?"

"You can't make this right," Dorri spat.

That sounded pretty final. "Oh," said the Redhead.

Dorri tapped her nails. Maybe that was a way to open the lines of communication again.

"I like your nails," said the Redhead.

"Don't change the subject."

The Redhead lowered her head. "Okay."

She heard Dorri huff out a breath, as if all the offense she'd had to take just *sitting* with the Redhead almost added up to a mortal wound. "Here's the deal. I only came because Davin is still the world's biggest geek. I love him, but his taste is execrable. So. It won't make up for ruining the happiest day of my life, but Davin's birthday is Saturday, and you're going to be his surprise."

"I'm…"

"Don't look at me like that, freak. He's all crazy about zombies."

Taking out a notebook (also cream with gold corners and satin ribbon accents), she scribbled down a date and address and tore out the page, using one long nail to guide the tear. "You show up here at 3 pm in your shambling, mumbling best and let Davin and all his little buddies get their pictures taken with you. My hubby's happy, and you start, just *start* to make up for what you did."

The Redhead took the page. "Okay," she said, in a very small voice.

Satisfied, Dorri sat back in her chair. "Now you can tell me you like my nails and get me a coffee."

The Redhead managed a tiny smile, but it felt forced. Or maybe just wounded. "Friends?" she said.

Dorri frowned. "Don't push your luck."

102 - undead redhead

Second Variety

35.

It was late, but Morgoni was still at it. Teeny finished up the dishes and danced through the living room, just to check.

Their third roommate, a nice boy named Jackie who was studying to be a nurse, wasn't around, and his door was open just a crack. Teeny was tempted to sneak a peek and see if Morgoni had driven off yet another poor flatmate. So far, their record had been abysmal, and while it was nice to have more room around the place, it was not a good thing financially.

Oh well, that could wait for tomorrow. Jackie was paid up until the end of the month, whether or not he was capable of sticking it out. Sad, though: he was quiet and it seemed like a perfect situation, since his hours were so long he was hardly home anyhow. Maybe that's all it was—although there was an odd feeling of emptiness about the place that made her suspect otherwise.

Still, she was in too good a mood tonight to let those darker thoughts intrude.

"Going to bed, Morgoni!" she called out, trilling it. She blew the huddled figure at the desk in the corner, illuminated only by the glow from her monitor, a kiss.

"Don't care…" she heard Morgoni mutter back from the darkness.

Just out of perversion, not from any real sense of potentially satiable curiosity, Teeny decided to slip into the big, comfy chair on the other side of the room. It was made almost invisible from the desk by Morgoni's stacks of investigative material and the bookcase she'd erected mostly to hide her work from casual scrutiny. While not a real barrier, it and the white board propped beside it definitely said "Keep Out" of her half of the supposedly communal area. The back of the white board faced into the main part of the room and Morgoni had strung police barrier tape over it, as if her demeanor itself wouldn't stop most people from trying to see what transpired beyond its forbidding boundary.

Teeny realized that most people wouldn't be capable of living in a building housing someone like Morgoni, much less the same apartment. Their parade of flatmates proved that. But she kind of liked the odd energy created by the other woman's intense privacy, not to mention the educational opportunities provided by Morgoni's infrequent but always illuminating gregarious moments.

Pulling a book of Borges poetry from between the seat cushions, Teeny settled in to read while Morgoni continued to work, murmuring to herself under her breath.

It was hard not to giggle, not out of unkindness but because of the disconnect between Teeny's own easy-going nature and her roommate's deadly seriousness. Teeny had to literally bite down on her lips a few times as Morgoni's mutterings reached discernible levels.

"Judging by the apocalyptic if not precisely atavistic…" she heard once. A few minutes later, it was: "If the retrogression proceeds and it's not merely a felonious…"

Social niceties might not be Morgoni's strong suit, but her vocabulary was magnificent.

Teeny watched out of the corner of her eye from the cover of the chair as Morgoni's hand reached for her camera bag, never apparently taking her eyes from her computer screen. A moment later, a string of indistinguishable curses emerged from behind the barrier.

Although tempted to sneak around for a look, Teeny forced herself to stay put. But not listening was impossible, and what harm could it do?

She heard digital voices, faint but audible enough to catch most of the words. First, a young woman, concerned: "Are you okay?"

Then after a moment, a second, this one a little more nervous, pitch a little higher, words a little tighter. "Just… not sure. Do you think it would be okay if I went in? I mean, I know I'm a little late, and…"

Then the sound of Morgoni scanning forward in the footage, followed by the second woman speaking again: "I'm sorry, I just wanted to come to your going-away party. I mean, you invited me on Facebook."

Another voice, this one older or at least more authoritarian: "But you're dead."

What?

The previous voice, who Teeny automatically dubbed "DeadGirl," said, "Not totally."

The voice of authority, dripping with sarcasm. "Okay,

you're undead. We heard from Dave and Monica."

This was a little more interesting than Morgoni's usual ambush-interviews, thought Teeny. Maybe she would… sneak a little look…

But then there was silence on the recording and Teeny froze without doing more than tensing her muscles in preparation to get out of the chair. Then, a new voice, sounding a little more well-meaning and friendly, as if trying to undo the severity of the sarcastic woman: "Did you see the pictures on Facebook?"

Authority: "She doesn't want to know about those."

But DeadGirl did. "Wait, what do you mean?"

Friendly: "Of you in the fountain. When, you know. When Dave pulled Monica out."

And DeadGirl, a little sharper: "Wait—he pulled *Monica* out? Not me? Didn't anyone pull me out?"

"I guess they were too busy taking pictures," said Friendly, and Teeny abruptly felt a tug on her empathy bone. *This had to be some kind of movie, or performance art thing. But why would Morgoni have a copy of it?*

Unable to resist any longer, Teeny slipped out of the big chair leaving Borges perched on the arm. She padded on her toes quietly around to Morgoni's side of the desk where she could see her roommate's ubiquitous video camera cabled into the computer. The monitor showed a group of young women and a couple of men sitting in a cafe around a low table. One, who Teeny immediately pegged as Ms. Authority, sat in the nominal center as if holding court. Closer to whomever was shooting the scene stood a girl in a bright fuchsia gown, a little formal-looking for an afternoon coffee klatch. She had vibrant red hair and pale, pale skin, at least what Teeny could see of it with her head turned mostly away from the lens, focused on the people around the table.

Teeny thought that maybe Morgoni had paused the recording, but then she noticed that the people in the chairs were shifting, uncomfortable, waiting for some kind of reaction or response. Ms. Authority had a stern, castigating expression, staring right at DeadGirl.

Then DeadGirl, sounding somewhere between petulant and hurt, said, "Why didn't anyone tag me in the pictures?"

At that moment, she turned her head and looked right into the camera lens and Teeny saw Morgoni stiffen and hit "pause" on the camera. Curious, she tried to come closer to see what it was about DeadGirl's face that had startled her so.

"See something spoooooky?" Teeny said in her best Vincent Price, and Morgoni jumped about a foot.

"Sorry!" said Teeny, again trying to hide her amusement. Morgoni had already clamped her hand over the computer screen, and, regaining her composure with cat-speed, growled at Teeny.

"Do you mind?"

36.

Water, in her nose, in her mouth. She struggled to her feet, fighting the slipperiness of the interiors of her shoes. She fought the water even as she raised herself up out of it, the fabric of her clothing suddenly stiff and bulky. When she managed to get the spikes of her heels properly under her, the dress, wet but somehow not saturated, sucked itself onto her body like sopped lettuce.

It felt disgusting, actually; although it was hard to imagine this outfit could feel like it fit any worse than before, it had achieved something like megastar status for unwearability.

Sharon shook her fingers, removing an absolutely insignificant amount of water. One hand, miraculously, was still clutched around Dorri's bouquet. Her hair was in her face—but before she could remove it, something hit her like a pissed-off linebacker.

This time when she went down, it was backwards. Backwards, water surged up her nose. Backwards, she felt the back of her head take a sickening *crack* against the edge of the fountain, and her vision lit up like a solar flare.

Still clutching the bouquet, she fought to turn herself over. She could see the red of her hair floating in front of her face, and with it streams of redder than red blood. Her free hand reached to the back of her head where the pain had blossomed with the blood into the whole bloody world.

Through the agony, she heard Dave's voice: "Oh my god! Monica!"

37.

"…your creepy zombie ex-girlfriend," Monica was saying. "It's a little hard to concentrate on us when…"

Dave interrupted. "Hang on…"

They had been walking arm-in-arm in the ravine near Dave's, part of the network of trails running up and down the Don River Valley. The new leaves were that bright green that looks almost chemical, and it had been so pretty: the yellow forsythia just coming into bloom, a few other early blossoming trees showing their pinks and whites.

He motioned to Monica to stay put, and moved off the path toward what had caught his eye. Pulling back a branch heavy with last year's dead vines, he uncovered—a very abashed and meek Sharon.

Monica, in as much exasperation as disbelief, groaned, "Oh, come on!"

"Hi," said the Redhead, rubbing her arm as if searching for some kind of universal "control Z" key to allow her to take back Dave's discovery.

Monica opened her mouth, but was stopped cold by Dave. He put up a hand, never taking his eyes off Sharon, and said in a tone that was a little *too* reasonable, "Monica, could you give us a minute?"

As he should probably have predicted, Monica's mouth dropped open with an expression of aggrieved shock. She stared at him, drop-jawed, but Dave didn't even seem to notice.

Sharon did, and couldn't quite believe that, instead of rushing back to Monica with a heartfelt "Oh, sweetie" or "Oh, baby, I'm sorry," he just kept coming, toward her.

This was not the Dave she remembered. Even when they'd been together, Dave had never looked at her like he was looking at her now. Oddly, he'd been all gentlemanly hearts and flowers for girls he *wasn't* dating, but never for her. Was it something about the way he'd rushed to protect Monica when she'd seen them together outside his townhouse, the way she's thrown herself into his waiting arms, that made her imagine that they had a totally different relationship than what she'd had with Dave herself?

How did she have what felt like a memory of Dave and Monica together, when that could never have happened, at least not in her presence, before she'd (died) gone out of circulation? There was a memory, not quite hers, in which she saw them so clearly it made her ache. No, not clearly; obscured but still so plain for all that she seemed to be watching them through—a window? No, through a pane of glass separating two sections in a coffee shop.

She remembered, as if it had really happened, that Dave held Monica's hand like it was a piece of soft leather, stroking it gently. Monica rested her free hand on her chin, and they both leaned in to the center of the table, ignoring their half-finished drinks.

"I will," Dave was saying. "Oh baby, I am so sorry it's been so hard. I want to tell her; she's just so fragile."

Monica responded with a much toned-down version of the look of imposition Sharon had just seen her use, a whispery folk song to the operatic tour-de-force aria of the more recent performance. "Dave," she said, "I don't care what's fair for her. I want what's fair for *you*. And you're drowning in that relationship. You have to get out, before you go under for the third time."

Sharon watched, with eyes that didn't feel her own and with a slow burn of anger rumbling through her insides that wasn't hers either. *They are so fake,* she heard the thoughts coming from somewhere other than her own mind. *He doesn't deserve her, and she deserves to know.*

And then a shiver, as if she knew what the right thing was to do (*tell her—you can save her so much pain if you just tell her*) but was absolutely, utterly unable to take the path to correct the great wrong in front of her (his?) eyes (*oh Sharon, how can you be with him? He doesn't love you. He's no good!*)

Then, just as an afterthought, she found herself (and this really was her own thought this time), she told herself, *Go under for the third time? Huh—she actually believes that dumb urban legend.*

All this flashed through the Redhead's mind in the seconds it took Dave to wave off his new girlfriend and saunter (yes, saunter) slowly up to his ex with an expression that was nearly goofy-sweet.

"Hey, Sharon," he said. Was that actually a sideways smile on his face? Was he *flirting?*

"Hey, Dave," she replied, figuring she'd almost made it into a question. But he was acting… well, strange hardly began to cover it.

He struck a casual pose the Redhead immediately thought of as "cock-eyed casual." And he grinned, crookedly, the way he only ever had when he watched classic Disney. And when he didn't know she was spying on him watching classic Disney, just to see that smile.

He'd never used it on her before.

But he was mock-serious when he said, "Monica says she's seen you around. Like, following her."

"No!" Sharon was horrified, but less than if he'd been talking to her in his Dave-the-censoring-Professor voice. "Seriously no. I wouldn't."

"So—it's just some kind of coincidence?"

Connected to…? "As in…?" Sharon asked.

He smiled, maybe even winked a little. "You just happen to be wherever she is?"

Now Sharon blushed and looked down at her nasty fuchsia heels. "No, it's just you never notice me."

Dave didn't lose the coyness. "I never?"

"Yeah, you know," she said. "I didn't remember a lot about the day—you know, the day—and then it started to come back to me and…"

Now his voice took on a little of its more usual edge. "You're following *me*? Do you know how creepy that is?"

Startled by the change in tone, Sharon asked, "…it would be better if I was following Monica?"

Dave sighed. If Sharon didn't know better, she'd think he was still a bit amused. But that wasn't Dave; David Jules Swinson made the jokes; he didn't laugh at hers. But his words were more than a little distancing. "Sharon, you're part of the past for us. We've moved on." Then, as she gained a little courage, which must have shown on her face, "What?"

"It's just…" she started tentatively. "You know. I kind of picked up that you might have moved on a little before we split up. I mean, before I drowned in the fountain. I just thought that if we could talk a bit…"

That was enough to bring the rest of the old Dave back. "That's low, Sharon. First you wreck Dorri and Davin's wedding, then you come back to break up me and Monica?"

"I died!" she yelped.

"Not very well! Seriously, Sharon, you know we were going to break up. It was only a matter of time."

But she didn't, not really. I mean, it wasn't a perfect relationship. She wasn't really growing within it, and sometimes she wondered if they'd ever been good together. But he'd never given her the least hint that he might have felt the same way.

"I mean, you had to know," he went on. "Monica was there for me at a very difficult stage in my life. There were so many things about you that just weren't working for me."

"Things about…"

He lowered his voice, but not enough that Monica probably couldn't still overhear them if she was trying. "I needed a girl like Monica. We're just more…"

He trailed off, and Sharon found herself getting, well, a little annoyed. "Cheaters?" she supplied.

"Compatible," he finished. "Although, I have to say I like this new side of you." The coyness returned. "Maybe if we'd met now instead…"

"You like me better as a zombie?" Was that it? The answer to the coy solicitousness? The reason he was… flirting with her?

"I'm not saying it would have worked out, but we could have had some fun, if—you know what I mean."

Was he trying to suggest an after-life *booty call*? Her eyes widened. This time, she was starting to sound even more annoyed, maybe moving into *pissed.* "You *like me better as a zombie?*"

For the first time, Dave dropped his voice so that only Sharon would hear. "Shh—Monica doesn't need to hear this. Seriously, Sharon. The sight of the two of you going at it like a pair of angry Pussycat Dolls…"

"Seriously *gross*! I *died*, Dave."

He grinned. *Crooked like a fox…* "That's even better. You died, and look at you now. Cat fight to the death and it's no harm, no foul."

That was it. Like she was suddenly seeing him for the first time, like she finally could say no to him, the Redhead said, "I gotta go. Have a nice… life, Dave."

She hoped that sounded sarcastic enough.

Monica, tired of waiting, stomped up.

"Are you done?" she spat. Sharon wasn't sure if it was Dave or her she was speaking to.

"I am," she confirmed, "Utterly."

Monica grabbed Dave's arm and started to pull him away. "Stay in touch, Sharon," he called over his shoulder.

"She will *not,*" said Monica. It sounded like she was talking with her teeth gritted.

"Have a heart, Monica," the Redhead heard Dave say. "She *died.*"

The Redhead began moving into the brush as fast as she could in the opposite direction. "Live people," she muttered, seeing it so clearly for the first time, "are *fucked up.*"

38.

What a difference a day makes.

Yesterday, she'd wondered if maybe her Sharon Backovic crusade had run its course, ready to be relegated to the closet with other ideas that had seemed so promising at first until they'd tapped out having done *nothing* to make her either famous or rich.

Today, there was magic in the air. Hope was restored, if it had ever truly been anything but a little tired out and resting.

It started simply enough with an email from a fan in Michigan (*You can see Milwaukee from here!*) telling her to check out a video blog from Toronto, *Morgoni Investigates.* She'd never heard of it or the obvious freak who ran it, and it looked like it had found a small international audience but nothing to text home about. Nothing like the numbers she was planning on running.

So, this Morgoni weirdo claimed to be investigating a zombie, living in Toronto. Or dead in Toronto, or what have you. Even claimed to have footage *and* multiple personal sightings, although that seemed a little too much to believe even for a conspiracy freak. Of course, she hadn't *posted* the footage, just a transcript. *Lame.*

It did sound like Sharon Backovic though. Sharon, the Redhead. The… the *Undead* Redhead. Undead Redhead.

She hopped on Whois and checked availability. Crud— some loser had already picked up the dot com. *And* not bothered to develop it. Asshole speculators. Probably some big company that kept renewing potentially profitable domain names just to screw over the little guys like her.

But dot CA was available, and the more she thought about it, the more she loved the idea. A Canadian domain name would just add credence to her new identity. She could almost see the logo and the splash graphic at the top of the home page. Had to feature the hair, of course. Maybe a close-up on the top half of her head and face, long red bangs pulled over one eye, pale skin, some artfully applied cracks and fissures. What did a zombie's eyes look like? She'd need some custom contacts of course. Bloodshot, for sure. She could get some of the look going with red eyeliner, and hell, if she was going to really commit to the part, she could irritate the whites with a bit of onion before the shoot.

The irises should be startling, glowing acid-ravaged green apple, brighten up her own color a bit like she had before in Photoshop, and maybe have a slightly artificial look or texture to them. None of the pictures she'd found on Sharon's Facebook helped to figure out what her actual eye color was, but hell, it wasn't like the *real* Sharon was going to be coming around anytime soon to complain she'd got it wrong.

This was *brilliant,* if she didn't say it herself. There had been ideas, and ideas, but only one stroke of pure *genius.*

She was going be famous.

She pulled up Morgoni's latest vlog, and watched it for the tenth time, a lawyer cramming for the bar, a surgeon boning up for a difficult procedure—hell, call it what it was: an actor studying for the role of her lifetime.

There was little video of Sharon online, not as much as she'd like for authenticity. None of it was focused solely on Sharon either; she always seemed to be a secondary or even tertiary character in whatever bit of footage had been posted.

Look at all the friends she'd had, and not a single one was true enough to manage her page post-death! Not a single one had posted a pic of the funeral, or a dweeby little anecdote about something that had happened in grade two, or even a four line poem cribbed from a Hallmark card.

Even if she didn't feel so connected to Sharon, she'd want to do this. She'd want to even if she wasn't so sure this would be the greatest, most incredible, amazing, blow it the world outta the water chance of her whole life to really *be* someone.

118 - undead redhead

Not With A Bang

39.

Malcolm Sinclair was trying *really hard* not to smoke. Sadly, this was a battle he lost more often than he won.

"You're going to die with black lungs," his little sister said once when he'd dropped in on her, after he'd excused himself for the second time to slip onto her balcony for a drag, "and that's just kinda yucky."

"And when they cut *you* open," he'd shot back, "they're going to find just vegetation, nothing animal at all. I bet even your tendons are meat-free by now. Even your toe cheese is probably dairy-free."

"Don't knock Veganism," she said, punching him. "And remember, I am a vegetarian, not a Vegan. I *DO* eat dairy, so that last crack was not even apropos of me and my ilk."

"Did you just say *ilk*?"

"Don't knock vocabulary either, brother!" She handed him the fruits of her current labour, the reason for his stopping by. Rather, not the fruits but the double chocolate fudge brownies she'd promised would take his mind of cigarettes if anything could. "My roommate is like a word-a-day calendar, and she's *bad-ass*."

Malcolm'd snorted. "Yeah? I thought she was just nuts."

"As a fox," she agreed. "But as long as I stay out of her way, she's surprisingly tolerant. And she loves my brownies. At least I'm assuming that's what that particular grunt meant when I gave her one…"

The brownies hadn't lasted long, of course, and neither had their impact on his dirty little vice. As he slipped out the back door of Kensy Comics into the back alley, he grinned to himself, thinking that Teeny probably *would* be Vegan if it didn't mean giving up milk chocolate.

He already had his lighter out, cigarette between his lips, when there was a noise from the darkness beyond. He had the back door cracked a couple of inches, just enough to see his own hands, but between the time of night and his indoor-adjusted eyes, he could see nothing in the gloom.

Another noise, this time a scrabbling kind of sound, something shifting in the darkness. Then—BANG! He jumped back toward the shop door, dropping his smoke.

Cat? Raccoon? Confused squirrel?

Another person? Someone sneaking around in the back alley with something other than sunshine and lollipops on his mind?

Another, smaller BANG! And a little voice, female and exasperated. "Jiminy Cricket!"

"Hello?" said Malcolm.

He relaxed a little. A girl, and unless she was hopped up on something nasty, probably more a danger to herself than him.

A crash. And her voice again, as if she hadn't heard him: "Dang it all to heck!"

Amused, he moved out of the small pool of light spreading from the back door. "Are you okay?" he asked the darkness.

He still couldn't see her, but thought the sounds and the voice had been coming from the general direction of the dumpster at the end of the alley, close to the rear exit from Vegan Goodness. "Hello?"

Then, obviously finally hearing him, a panicked response from the dark figure he was just starting to be able to make out as his eyes adjusted. "Don't come any closer!"

The dark shape ducked down behind the dumpster. She didn't *sound* stoned or high, and the quickness of her movement made it unlikely that she was drunk. But still, she didn't sound… right.

"I just want to make sure you're all right. Don't worry, I'm not… I mean I'm just a guy who wants to make sure you're okay. Okay?"

He flicked the lighter, both to let her know where he was and to see if he could catch a glimpse of her. Nothing. Then, a shuffling sound from beside the dumpster, just out of his line of sight, and a bright neon pink shoe that had seen better days poked out. The way the foot had shot out, it looked like she was probably on her knees, or half-crouched anyhow. He guessed she might have slipped back there, trying to hide.

"It's okay," he said, soothingly. He inched closer, holding the lighter high, flicking on the flame for as long as he could stand the heat. Rounding the corner of the dumpster, he got his first look at her, curled up half on a bag of trash, and apparently interrupted by him in the middle of scrabbling through another. Her face was in deep shadow, but it looked as if she was in rough shape, skin devoid of colour, and marred by old scratches.

He'd seen some pretty sad things in this alley, in this neighbourhood, but this sight really captured his pity. "Are you hungry?" he asked gently.

"So hungry!" she agreed, then, as if her boldness had shocked her, drew back even further into the shadows. Wanting a look at her face, he raised the lighter high and flicked it on.

"Oh my fucking god!"

Malcolm stumbled backwards, slipped, caught himself against the wall, slipped again.

Her face was the face of death, of a person long dead, bloodless, eyes unnaturally fixed and staring, a small tear in her cheek near the jawbone gaping, and flaking skin.

She was babbling, emerging from the dark corner tentatively, as ginger about approaching her as he had been easing himself into the shadows a minute earlier. "Sorry, sorry sorry!" she cried. "I told you. I told you to stay back!"

Malcolm shifted himself against the wall and tried to regain his composure. *C'mon, man,* he told himself severely, *you of all people should be over how someone looks.*

"No, I'm sorry," he said, making his tone as gentle as possible. "I didn't mean to react like that. What… uh… your skin?"

"I know," she said, sounding more frustrated than distressed. "I'm gross. I can't keep all the skin on. It just keeps peeling off. Not everywhere, but a little. No surprise, but... oh! Uh—I'm dead. Kind of."

Realizing that she'd brought the garbage bag she'd been searching with her, she stuffed it behind her back. As if that was the most bizarre part of this situation... Malcolm groped for sanity.

"I'm kind of—you know. Zombified," she said, then put her arms out in front of her at shoulder level and stumbled forward. Her face twisted into a rictus of horror. "Arrrrgh... Brains..."

Malcolm shot backwards, slipping again and landing on his seat on the pavement. "Don't..." he began.

She seemed shocked she'd scared him, and slow to realize why. Then, "Oh come on! I'm not going to eat you. It's just... when I was alive, I was Vegan, and I guess I still am. There's this awesome restaurant I used to love and..."

It made a *kind* of sense, he supposed. "...this is their trash?" he asked. "Vegan Goodness?"

"Yeah," she said sadly. "Could I be any more pathetic?"

"So..." he said, thinking maybe he almost had it together again, even if it was totally mad, "you don't feel like eating *people*?"

"No!" She almost jumped as she said it, not so much offended as really, really wanting to reassure him. "I was a Vegan, you know, before I woke up again, and I guess maybe the whole meat thing just isn't going to agree with me. Even if it's what, you know, what I'm supposed to eat. I just can't. God, I am *so* pathetic."

She shivered, and moved back away from him far enough to slump back onto her black plastic bean-bag chair substitute, the garbage bag beside the dumpster.

Malcolm felt a wave of sympathy. "I don't think you're pathetic," he said, and he meant it. Yeah, she looked like hell, but there was a genuine sweetness and humour about her that made him more inclined just to think of her as someone who was struggling, not someone who'd given up.

"You don't?" she asked. It came out pretty quietly, and definitely seemed to demand a bit more reassurance from him.

"No," he said firmly. "It just looks like you're, you know, dealing with a lot."

She snorted, as if to say, *you have NO idea,* then shrugged. "I got killed at a wedding. Over the bouquet. My best friend Monica drowned me in the fountain, and my boyfriend saved *HER* instead of me. And now they're dating, and not only did I find out they started seeing each other before I died, it turns out he actually likes me better now because he's got some creepy zombie-fetish thing happening that I'm actually glad I didn't know about, and everybody hates me—I got de-Friended like fifty times just today, and I don't even have a place to live anymore so half the time I sleep right here. Beside a dumpster. Because I might find some good leftover couscous that someone didn't finish. Yeah, I'd say I'm dealing with a lot."

Malcolm swallowed. "I kinda meant, being a zombie," he quipped.

She responded with a brief laugh. "That's almost the easiest part."

"Seriously."

"Yeah." She smiled now, and even with the way the change in the shape of her mouth made the cut on her jawline gape a bit, it was kind of a nice smile. Suddenly, instead of feeling out of his depth (if not out of this *world* altogether), Malcolm found himself remembering that he'd always had a thing for smart redheads. Now *that* was another kind of odd altogether.

Trying to sound as sincere as he felt, not a mean feat since he was apparently talking to someone convinced she was a sentient dead person, he said, "I'm not going to pretend I get what you're going through, but I know how hard it is to cope when you've lost your self-respect and your support system."

"Yeah," she said, looking away. Then, as if the fact he was being serious had taken a moment to register, she repeated it. "Yeah?"

"I do," he said, and now he was seeing her differently. Dead? That was the most ridiculous thing he'd ever thought, except maybe that a degree in comparative literature would make him instantly employable after university. He indicated the trash bag. "Anything good in there?"

She shook her head sadly. "No. Vegans are usually so hungry, we always clean our plates."

Not sure if she was making a joke or just stating a truth, he nodded in return. Suddenly inspired, he cast a glance at the Vegan Goodness back door and said, "What's your favourite thing on the menu?"

"Couscous," she replied, again full of sorrow.

"You wait here," he said, finally managing to get to his feet. "I'll be right back with a big plate of couscous that *didn't* come out of the garbage."

She blushed, almost as red as her hair. "Oh my God, that is *soooooo* romantic…" Then, starting as if she'd just realized she'd gone way too far, she amended, "I don't mean anything…"

That made Malcolm smile. "That's okay. You find whatever you want romantic. Self-respect. Okay?"

She nodded, and smiled a little shyly as she settled herself more comfortably on her makeshift chair.

Malcolm decided to go the long way around the block to get to the restaurant instead of taking the short cut through the shop; that way, Jason would just think he was taking an extra long break. He wasn't entirely sure just yet what was happening, but the more he thought about it, the further away he walked from the girl sitting there in the shadows by the dumpster, the more he had to laugh at himself. A *zombie?* Right. Just a girl, with some pretty creepy make-up or at least some kind of not-so-nice skin condition. But nice herself, a good spirit. It was well worth the cost of a Vegan dinner to see her smile again.

Back in the alley, the Redhead smiled to herself. She wasn't sure she'd be able to eat the couscous, but it was a very nice thought. Not only that, but he was cute, not to mention a real gentleman.

Of course, that's how Dave seemed at first too, so she'd

better not get ahead of herself. Especially not with, you know, the dead thing. Or the back-from-the-dead thing. One way or another, she was still homeless, friendless (unless you counted the cracklady), and destitute. She'd used just about her last little drip of cash to buy a refillable water bottle (at least hydration seemed to be something worth keeping up with, even if she hadn't cracked the nutrition enigma). This guy deserved something better than a redhead with crazy eyes and peeling skin with no prospects, no resources, and, really, no clue.

But the couscous would be very, very nice. If it wouldn't go down properly tonight, she could always let it sit out in the sun for a day or two and see if that was better. Her mouth watered just thinking about it.

40.

From the case files of V. X. Morgoni, cryptoparapsychocriminologist

Video Blog, Investigation Zombie Watch, Day One: Recording. [transcript]

(LOCATION: converted Victorian house, Nassau Street. 6 apartments. Establishing. Moving inside.)

(To camera.)

MORGONI

I have been following up a new and possibly deadly local threat which has potential global implications. I'm here following a tip from Juan Carla that our "zombie" friend was sighted entering this building earlier today.

(The camera pans to show a plain door with 'SUPERIN-TENDENT' and 'A1' written on it in black stick-on letters. Knocks on door.)

(A large and fierce woman appears at the door, wearing a bathrobe with her hair in rollers. We will soon learn she is MRS. WOCIECZOWSKY [sp?], widow, 54, superintendent, Polish immigrant of 18 years.)

WOCIECZOWSKY

What the ▮▮▮?

MORGONI

Good afternoon, ma'am. Can I have your name for the people?

WOCIECZOWSKY

Why the ▮▮▮ you want name? Is this on television?

MORGONI

Internet. My name is…

WOCIECZOWSKY

What the ▮▮▮ I want on Internet?

MORGONI

It's just a… Can I have your name for the people, please?

WOCIECZOWSKY

Wocieczowsky. Mrs.

MORGONI

Okay… Mrs… Mrs. W. Okay.

WOCIECZOWSKY

What the ▮▮▮ you want me on Internet?

MORGONI

I understand that a certain individual was seen leaving this building earlier today…

WOCIECZOWSKY

You mean falling apart zombie █ who want to rent my room?

MORGONI

…Yes! The zombie…

WOCIECZOWSKY

Some zombie █ with weepy skin want renting my room. I tell you. In Krakow, never.

MORGONI

Uh… right. Never. We want to find the zombie.

WOCIECZOWSKY

I send zombie █ packing. No falling off skin zombie █ in my clean room. I run extra clean house. No bedbug. No brains-eating. No maggot.

MORGONI

Right… I understand this zombie…

WOCIECZOWSKY

What I caring about sob story? Everyone have sob story. I come to this country with nothing but no good man who meet me on no good Internet. So I say, what the █ I want on Internet? Internet giving no good to me! No good.

MORGONI

Mrs… Mrs. W., I just want to know where the zombie went after she left here.

WOCIECZOWSKY

What I care? She is no renting room from me. You, you
look nice clean boy. You want renting my room? Wait—you
are maybe from reality TV show? Wait. You are boy? Girl?
No ███████ telling.

MORGONI

I have a weblog.

WOCIECZOWSKY

Weblob? What this, weblob?

MORGONI

Weblog…

WOCIECZOWSKY

If you no renting room, you get out!

(Mrs. Wocieczowsky grabs a broom from inside the
doorframe and starts poking it toward the camera. Makes
contact. The lens goes wild.)

MORGONI

Cut! Cut! Screw this…

WOCIECZOWSKY

You go! I have clean house! Clean room! No zombie!

(Retreat to exterior of building, lens swinging wildly as she
goes. To camera again.)

MORGONI

Okay. Struck out here with Juan Carla's tip. I'll pick up the
story at home.

(Lens swings downwards. Frame filled with view of grass
and sidewalk, shin. Hand pulls up pantleg to reveal

developing blackness.)

MORGONI

Ow. That is totally going to leave a bruise.

41.

The couscous was a bust, but Malcolm was so nice he actually heard her out on her idea of leaving it to "ripen" a bit before trying again.

Malcolm, in short, was terrific. For the first time since she'd woken up in the cemetery, the Redhead felt, if not herself, than at least on solid ground. Rather than *in* solid ground, which would have been pretty horrible.

She honestly couldn't tell if he believed her, that she'd come through the kind of trauma that usually makes for a pretty damn scary Dateline special, or if he thought she was just a loon, but he was willing to listen and even entertain her notions of what she might need to survive in her new (life) incarnation.

His picture of her as a kind of earthy phoenix, rising from her own ashes-to-ashes, was far more appealing than her own stubborn feeling that it was all some big cosmic joke with her as its butt. Maybe she could borrow a little of his seemingly indefatigable faith that she'd be okay and figure it all out. Maybe pigs could fly like pigeons someday too, but she was willing to go a little further with him.

He was actually so great that she already felt a little afraid of disappointing him, as if showing any weakness or lack of resolve might in fact make him disapprove of her, and lose her his friendship. For the first time in her life (or at least in memory), Sharon Backovic was not the most optimistic and positive person in the room.

Malcolm had even been amazing in the area of finding her something to at last sate her hunger. Maybe it was the shock that had changed her food preferences. Maybe it was something else, but at the moment at least, she was just going to go with it. With Malcolm's help, she'd come to a nice arrangement with the produce manager from that grocery store after all, and quite easily. He'd save the best of the rotten fruit and veg for her from the garbage ("best" being in this case, of course, a definitely relative term) and she'd help him with his stats homework, something she discovered she remembered just fine from her first year of university.

Overripe organic matter had taken care of her dietary requirements. But if she really *was* alive, and merely traumatized, didn't that change everything? How to explain the eyes, the wounds that didn't bleed, and the penchant for spoilage?

For a day or two while his roommate was out of town with family, Malcolm said she'd be able to sleep on his sofa instead of the ground behind the dumpster. Maybe even wash the dress, or herself, although in the latter case, she was afraid she'd rub more of herself off than she could afford, and in the former, well, not only did she still not have anything to change into, but she'd have to ask Malcolm's help getting out of it, and that was a little *too* familiar. She'd managed a little bit of grooming in his bathroom when she'd first arrived, but even that felt like imposing.

As Malcolm set up the couch with some rubberized camping sheets, the Redhead sat at his desk surfing the 'net.

The afternoon's abortive apartment hunt notwithstanding, she had a pretty good feeling about finding a place to live and generating some kind of small income that would allow her to keep herself together. The last thing she wanted was to impose too much on Malcolm's kindness. It was strange; it felt like he'd been a friend for years even though they'd only just met.

That's why she felt so bad about what she was doing currently.

Malcolm finished with the makeshift bed and paused at the door to the kitchen. "Do you… want anything? Uh, what do you feel like?"

They'd brought some leaking oranges and squashed lettuce back from the grocery shop earlier, but yes, she was starting to feel peckish again. "Is there any more of that rotten kale? I'm sorry—that's gross. I can come and get it. You don't have to…"

He shook a finger at her, mock-severe. "No, whatever you need. Remember, self-respect and self-acceptance. And I am your willing servant while you get through those ads."

The Redhead blushed furiously, diverting her eyes from him. If he knew… "Thank you," she said, wondering if he could hear the guilt in her voice.

As he was leaving the room, he made it worse. "You having any luck finding good rental prospects?"

She gave a non-committal "Mm hm…" and tried to put herself between the screen and the door behind her.

Who would have guessed it? zHarmony, a real site for

zombie dating! Okay, maybe it was a little soon—but heck, Dave hadn't even waited until she was in the ground before starting up with another woman. And it was fun, and even a little after-life affirming to fill out her profile.

> HEIGHT: She typed *5'3"*.
> HAIR: *Red*
> EYES:

She smiled. *Still have 'em.*

> BODY TYPE:

Couldn't exactly type *flaking* or *decreasing daily due to bits falling off.* She went with *slim.*

> PROFILE PIC: Upload or take new

She found the option to use Malcolm's webcam, dragged her fingers through her hair figuring she was probably doing more harm than good, and snapped a shot. *Could be worse,* she thought. *At least there's no maggots.*

Then, just as she'd almost forgotten he was in the apartment with her, Malcolm's voice came right at her side.

"What are you doing?"

"Oh!" She jumped.

It was the most pissed off she'd heard him, still not pissed off by Dorri standards, but her cheeks reddened guiltily. "A dating site?" he said.

"I'm so sorry!"

He peered over her shoulder. "You're kidding—zHarmony?

Really? And what's this?"

He took the mouse from under her fingers and switched to one of the other open tabs. "Zombie Love Dot Com? Necromatch?"

"I found it totally by accident!" she protested, but she sounded lame even to herself.

"I thought you were supposed to be looking for a place to live," he admonished, and she deflated a little. He was right.

Instead of continuing on that line, Malcolm handed her a slightly rotten apple. It looked delicious. She took it, and there was an uncomfortable moment of silence.

Finally, she said, "It's just… seeing Dave, and you know, Dorri and Davin, and they've been married for—I mean, they've been married as long as I've been dead!"

"Sharon…" said Malcolm. Just hearing her own actual name from her own actual former life was enough to make her burst into slightly damp tears. "I'm so sorry," she began. "I just couldn't help myself."

He bent down beside her chair, and put a hand on her arm. It was a warm touch, almost hot, but the Redhead had come to understand that it was the differential between her skin temperature and that of others, the fact that she was *icy* that made him seem so hot.

"It's okay," he said at last. "I get it. You're lonely."

"I also feel so…"

This was hard, and she almost wished that he didn't prompt

her to go on. "What?"

She sniffed. So embarrassing, to get caught surfing online dating sites and then to lose her composure as well. "You know. Ugly. I mean, I never got told I was pretty much when I was alive, and now I'm peeling like everywhere."

He laughed, and it was a kind laugh, gently mocking. "C'mon, Sharon. You think I would have stopped to help you out if I didn't think you were a completely, stunningly beautiful person?"

That *really* caught her off guard. It took her a moment to recover enough to say, "…No?"

Now he looked at her, right in the crazy eyes. How did he do that without wanting to run away? "I'm not the kind of guy that gets fooled by all that surface crap anyhow. You're going to find a great apartment, and everything's going to change for you."

"You really think so?" she asked. "'Cause I just trimmed the dead skin back a bit, you know, cause I realized the maggots won't stick around if I'm just dead but not actively rotting. That was a good thing to figure out."

"You know it," he affirmed. Then, "You used my nail scissors?"

She looked guilty. "Yes, but I washed them *very well* afterwards."

He considered this and accepted it, shrugging. "You do what you gotta do."

She smiled now, but still felt like a burden. "Malcolm, you're a good friend."

He finally moved his hand from her arm, and there was a little twinge in her, a little surge of sorrow that he'd taken it away. Maybe it was just the warmth? Or was it something more?

"Look," he said, standing, "I threw out some overripe avocados yesterday. You think you'd like one?"

"Yes, please!" she trumpeted, this time in genuine pleasure and relief.

He went, and she could almost feel him looking back over his shoulder as if to remind her *Come on, Sharon, you're supposed to be apartment-hunting.*

She was just about to flip to the ViewIt.ca tab when an ad on Necromatch.com caught her eye.

"You gotta be kidding. Zombie speed dating?" It was wild, unexpected, and incredibly enticing. "Oh my god, at the Royal York! Too cool!"

138 - undead redhead

When Worlds Collide

42.

She put in a call to the AV boys first. They *loved* her—well, at least they loved her boobs, and with boys, that was the same thing most of the time.

Geary, Jerry, and Joe had been following her every move for almost three years, since her first appearance on Jeter Khan's *Voodoo Taboo Tattoo* webseries—a piece of shit, undeniably, but it got the ratings. And it made her a star, at least among a certain subset of the net's better quality trolls and perverts.

The AV boys were a definite step up from the ones who spammed her with requests for underwear and more intimate articles, and they had mad connections. And, bless their little fanboy hearts, they knew a great concept when they heard it.

Ever since the bottom fell out of the online ad market for anything but porn, the boys had been struggling to diversify their passive income streams back to pre-crash levels. An idea like the Undead Redhead thing was pure gold, and it didn't take them any time at all to see the possibilities.

Not that they had any problems with porn, mind you, but they had enough integrity to want at least *something* other than skin sites on their resumes.

"We can get you onto Pargeter tonight," Geary said over Skype, as he typed furiously just out of frame. "Probably not Sheila Grief until tomorrow am, but she's got saturation in Japan so the time differential actually works in our favour."

Behind him, Jerry was sketching out a plan of attack on the whiteboard.

"Awesome," she said. "Don't forget about Dar'eena in Wisconsin. She's always good for the alt market on the west coast."

"Got it," said Jerry, never turning away from his calculations.

"Joe's already on the graphics," Geary told her, still typing. She figured he was probably online with at least a dozen leads, probably more. No one could multi-task like Geary.

"Just work the networks too," she said, leaning in to show him a little more skin, but as if it was totally accidental. They might be pervs, but they liked her to be subtle about satisfying their voyeuristic intentions. It might not seem like much, but she considered that about as gentlemanly as she could expect. Probably as much as she wanted, to be honest.

"Networks take time," Geary reminded her, "and we haven't had much luck there. Crossover outlets are our best best, maybe an affiliate with a strong web presence. That reminds me…"

And he was off and typing again, even faster than before.

She smiled. It was happening. Now it was just a matter of

time, and geek-supplied elbow grease.

43.

Morgoni would have recognized her by her voice as the "Friendly" person on her recording, but to the Redhead, she was just Deanna. They'd probably known each other casually for three or four years, through Dorri again, but Deanna was more a part of Sylvia's clique than Dorri's.

It wasn't like they'd actually spent any time together, just the two of them, but Sylvia and Deanna were seldom apart, so when Sylvia had a party (and you really just *had* to go to Sylvia's parties, or risk being blacklisted altogether), Sharon usually ran into her.

It was probably a personality thing that meant that Sharon more often than not showed up early to functions—"early" of course meaning "on time" according to the invitation and an hour before just about anyone else. Since Deanna was always around to help Sylvia set up (*Deanna, would you mind? Just cut all the vegetables and make the cheese plate, and could you just, I don't know, throw up some decorations?*), and Sharon arrived before things were in swing (not full, not half, more like a stationary swing in an empty playground), Sharon usually pitched in as well.

Their friendship had never gone beyond the purely practical stage of deciding who would chop the zucchini and who the carrots, but each felt warmly toward the other. That's why it was so nice for the Redhead to be contacted by Deanna a few days after Sylvia's going-away party.

The Redhead had been following Sylvia's departure from a safe distance (via Facebook updates) and wasn't surprised that it was only after she'd left town altogether that Deanna felt comfortable reaching out. Maybe it wasn't exactly an abusive relationship, but the Redhead was hoping that, in the absence of Sylvia's often overbearing personality, she and Deanna could actually be friends.

Now, under the hood of a beauty salon dryer, the Redhead reflected on how her path had changed so much so quickly, and through the unlikely mechanism of her own death, or supposed death. She'd met Malcolm, who was a total doll, she'd not actually stood *up* to Dorri for once but had at the very least faced her and not cried once, and she maybe even had the chance to find friendships and even date a bit.

It was all pretty heady and wonderful, even if she was more confused than ever about what exactly she was. Was she alive or dead? A miracle or an abomination?

What happened if she got sick—if she even could? What if she was trapped in her current state, never aging or changing in any way (except for the obvious getting dirty and losing skin)?

Was there anyone she could turn to for advice about her condition, or was she a one-off, doomed to learn everything by trial and error? It wasn't long since she'd honestly believed there was nothing in the world you couldn't learn from a Google search. Was this whole situation just a punishment for that particular hubris?

But neither God, nor science, could help her. There was nothing rational about her state, or for that matter about the fact she'd just had the best haircut of her life, thanks to Deanna's friendship with a stylist in the Beaches. Next, she'd been promised a makeover (*to cover up all those nasty flaws in your otherwise GORGEOUS complexion— God, I'd kill for skin like yours!*) and even a little stitching-up around the jawline.

Kim, the hairdresser, had apparently not even flinched when told about the Redhead's status as possible zombie. She'd made a couple of cracks about how even the Undead deserved a good hair day, and that her extensive training with scissors meant she could defend herself, and that was it. Deanna had had a little more trouble adjusting, in fact. An essentially practical person, Deanna put Kim's greater ability to roll with the circumstances down to her extensive work on Hollywood film sets where she'd in all likelihood seen weirder.

Out in the waiting area, Malcolm sat leafing through a magazine without interest. Deanna hadn't said much—she seemed kind of shy, in fact—and he figured it was up to him to break the ice.

"So… Deanna, right?" he began. Just in case she didn't want to talk, he kept the magazine in one hand. "It was really nice of you to do this for Sharon."

Deanna grinned faintly. She seemed a little nervous, whether because she'd been left alone with a strange man or maybe because she couldn't quite believe she'd set up a beauty appointment for a zombie, he couldn't guess. "Oh you know," she said. "I felt really bad about Sylvia's going-away party. Did Sharon tell you about that? Sylvia all but kicked her out. I didn't think we should turn our backs on someone just because—you know."

"Yeah," he chuckled softly. "It's complicated, right?"

She smiled and rolled her eyes. "You could say that… So, how did you guys meet?"

Malcolm had a vision of the Redhead crouched behind the dumpster in the alley behind the comic book store, up to her elbows in trash, longingly looking for couscous… "I bought her a meal," he said. "She was kind of in a bad place."

Deanna nodded, but Malcolm could tell she wanted to hear more. "She's crashing on my couch for now, you know, just until she can get her own place. My sister Teeny might have a room free; we just have to go and check it out. But for now…"

Now Deanna looked concerned. "On the… how does… Doesn't it…"

It took him a few seconds, then he realized she was asking about the practical matters of dealing with a zombie as a houseguest.

"Oh, plastic bags," he said, "and a tarp. Most of the maggot situation is under control. It's not nearly as bad as you might think. But that's probably because she was embalmed…"

He stopped as Deanna started to turn a shade of green. "Sorry," he said. "Unintended gross-out."

"Is she really…" Deanna began, and Malcolm knew it was the start of what he'd come to think of as *the Big Question*.

"Is she nuts?" he said. "I have no idea. Whatever she's been through, it was pretty traumatic. Do you believe all that about waking up in a coffin?"

"I kind of have to," Deanna replied. "I mean, it's what she said happened, and I know about what happened at Dorri's wedding. It wasn't like we *thought* she was dead. She *was*. As far as I know."

"That's it, though, right?" he said. "As far as we know. Look, Deanna, she's a good person, and she's been through something big. I don't know what it is. But I don't think she's really dead, or undead for that matter. People don't get to come back from the great beyond, into their own bodies, just in time for their own funerals. I mean, I'm Guyanese, so I grew up with a lot of superstitions, and even we're not that nuts."

Deanna considered this. "So you think she's just—I don't know, all PTSD or something?"

"I think we need to let her work through this in her own way," he said gently. "When she's ready to deal with the truth, I'll be there for her."

Deanna's eyes shot sharply to one side behind him, and he turned to see the Redhead standing in the doorway, primped and fluffed and made-up to the nines. How much had she overheard? It was impossible to tell from the look on her face. *Whatever happened happened,* Malcolm told himself. *Maybe if she hears it this way first, she'll start to consider it seriously.*

Kim emerged from the back room, arms loaded, cradling several bottles of product. "Isn't she *fabulous*?" she gushed.

The Redhead seemed to be afraid of the reaction she would get. "Is it okay?" she asked. Gingerly, she turned, showing off the new style and newly made-up face. It looked like Kim had sponged off the dress as well, and it was looking almost fresh again.

"You look great," said Malcolm, and meant it.

"Awesome!" said Deanna, and got up to bounce the curl at

the bottom of the Redhead's new cut. "Fun."

"Really?" asked the Redhead.

Malcolm smiled and came over to take her hand. It was as cold as usual—her circulation must be really bad to make her feel so icy all the time. He didn't want to remark on it though: just another thing to add to her delusions.

"Thanks, Kim," he said. "You stitched up her chin too, huh?"

"A little bit of superglue and a couple of quick darts. She didn't feel a thing."

He looked to the Redhead for confirmation and she nodded. Another sign she could take to prove she was dead, but he knew that the mind was powerful enough to cause even extremes of pain tolerance if the person believed enough. "Looks terrific," was all he said. It did, too. You could hardly see the stitches.

"My pleasure. You don't usually get a makeover this extreme to really challenge you. I do think you're going to need to buy my conditioner, as well as the foundation I used. See how nice it is? But that's only $30 for…"

"That's enough, Kim," said Deanna quickly. "I still have a whole bottle of the stuff you made me buy last time. We're trying to *help* Sharon, not bankrupt her."

Malcolm paid for the cut and touch-ups, and they left the salon. The Redhead grabbed Deanna's arm as they started toward the streetcar stop. "Oh my God! I can't believe you said that to her."

Deanna was actually vibrating; she thought the Redhead

could probably feel it through her hands. "I know! I never did that before. Felt awesome, though."

"Next time, you have to do that to Sylvia… I hate the way she takes advantage of you. When's she back from her trip?"

"Three weeks. And I am *not* helping her throw her own coming-home party."

Malcolm dug in his pocket for tokens, smiling to himself. Dead or delusional, it was pretty clear that post-traumatic Sharon Backovic was having an undoubtably positive effect on the world around her.

His cell chimed. "Excuse me," he told Deanna and the Redhead, and checked his text. It was from his sister—apparently she *had* been correct in thinking her roommate had again driven away the person who'd taken their third bedroom and he could bring his new friend over any time to check it out. He'd run it by Sharon, but the timing couldn't be better.

The Redhead herself was feeling inordinately pleased with her improved appearance. No sensitive girl wants to be thought of as completely vain, but it was undoubtably good to feel clean and spruced up and just a little more, well, human.

Something niggled at her, and she scanned the area, wondering what had caught her attention and diverted her from what was a very pleasant, as well as uncharacteristic, narcissistic haze.

Something about… maybe it was the boy, across the street in the doorway of the sub shop. He looked familiar. His dark head was tousled like a baby chimney sweep's and just as dusky. The bones of his face, at least what she could see (he had his nose buried in a comic book), were fine and shapely. He couldn't be more than sixteen or seventeen, and maybe younger.

She thought he might be Jamaican, or Cuban—there'd been a couple of trips with her parents back in the pre-divorce days. But she was no expert, just liked the darkness of his skin against the even greater darkness of his hair, and the lighter green of his bulky jacket. And the comic book: she was too far away to see what it was, but…

She had it—she *had* seen him before. She turned to tell Malcolm and Deanna. It was…

The movement of her head jarred something loose around her face, and the Redhead squealed. "I think one of my stitches just popped out!" Then, calm again, "Oh no, it's just a bobby pin."

For the moment, the boy was forgotten.

44.

He'd been watching her ever since he'd picked up her trail again after that first shocking moment in the graveyard. Getting into the back of the hearse to undo the thumbscrews had been nerve-wracking enough, and that was before he'd even known, not for sure. At first, seeing her step unsteadily out of the back of the vehicle, he'd been too stunned even to move, and had thought she'd seen him in the trees, immobilized by his own fear and wonder.

Then, as the wonder of it outweighed his shock, he'd

followed, first into the heart of her old neighbourhood and then deep into Kensington Market, and finally out into the Beaches.

What was it that brought her back into his sights just when he thought he'd lost her for good? It happened the first time seemingly just by good luck; he'd lost her on the busy street, and then found she'd not only paused long enough at a shop window for him to catch up but had actually turned back toward the point where he'd lost her. It was as if she knew he was there, tracking her, and wanted to make certain that he didn't lose the trail.

She couldn't know he was there, though. He thought he'd been noticed just now, but then she'd turned away. She couldn't know he was watching and waiting, planning their first meeting, their first words.

He'd run the scene so many times the specifics had lost all meaning. The fantasy had become a generality: he'd say something and she'd respond, and soon her eyes would open in wonder when she realized just who he was and the role he'd played in making her what she was. And then, her gratitude, her happiness…

That's where his imagination usually failed him. After all, what kind of reward could he seek from someone whose honest love was all he wanted? She must not be coerced or manipulated; what she felt would have to come from her heart, not from any sense of obligation.

But there were too many coincidences, too many lucky synchronicities, to imagine that he'd got it all wrong. She was here, and even when he thought he'd lost her, she came back. Even if she didn't know why she'd returned, he did, and that joined them forever.

Oh, Sharon.

45.

Morgoni was hunched over her computer, surrounded by all her high-tech gadgets. The new collage was expanding on the wall behind her every day—articles printed from online editions of the paper, screen-grabs from the videos, her own notes on colour-coded post-its tying all of it together.

A faint chime sounded from her computer tower: a message from one of the Irregulars. She pulled up chat and found a new lead from Dibber. Good, good…

And the air-headed little tramp who shared her space trilled out, "Morgoni! Do you want tea?"

Morgoni fought to ignore her. She was perfectly capable of getting her own tea, if she wanted it, which she didn't. "I need more empirical evidence. Confirmed sightings. This is Roswell all over again…"

"Teaaaa?" sang Teeny. "I'm making some Ooooooooolong."

There was a clatter as she moved into the kitchen and started fussing with pots and pans.

Morgoni raised her voice, irritated. "No. No tea. Goddamn low light photography. I need a better filter to bring out the details."

In the kitchen, Teeny smiled to herself. She heard the most interesting things when Morgoni didn't remember to *lower* her voice after ranting at the roomie. "Okay, I'm putting on the kettle."

A firm knock at the door, which could only mean one thing. Fortunately, the chances of Morgoni disengaging herself from her work long enough to answer it were—no, they just *weren't*.

"I'll get it!" she sang out, just to make absolutely sure.

Dancing to the door, she turned the deadbolt, then the second (no fears about security with Morgoni around) and opened it to Malcolm and a pale redheaded girl with bouncy hair and an eye-shattering dress.

"Brother Mistake!"

"Sister Accident!"

They hugged, both giggling softly, but Morgoni heard enough to grunt her disgust.

"Shh! Morgoni's on the trail of Bigfoot," stage-whispered Teeny.

From behind the partition: "Bigfoot. Ridiculous."

"Can Sharon see the room?" asked Malcolm. "You didn't find someone else yet did you? And Morgoni's okay with it?"

"Morgoni likes paying a third of the rent more than half just as much as I do," Teeny promised. "You're Sharon?"

The pale girl held out a hand. Malcolm and his redheads! "Hi, yes, Sharon. I'm a... well, I'm..."

Teeny saved her further awkwardness. "I'm Teeny, Malcolm's beloved little sister. He thinks we were both accidents—I don't want to break it to him that they actually *WANTED* me."

"Sorry they couldn't hit perfection the second time around," he said.

Teeny gave him a glancing kick to the calf. "You don't always get to choose how things come out, right? I like your stitches. Very post-apocalyptic chic."

Sharon smiled, maybe a little shy. Teeny figured with that skin condition she probably didn't get many compliments.

That amount of socializing in the doorway was apparently enough for Morgoni. A harsh "*Shhhh!*" came from behind the whiteboard.

Teeny motioned them further into the apartment as Malcolm, ignoring her repeated jabs, called out, "Don't you worry, Ms. Morgoni—just fixin' to help you out with a little extra rent."

Sharon, unnerved by the sounds emerging from the living room's dark corner, elected to cross the room rather quickly, almost beating Teeny to the hall beyond. Teeny indicated the door to the spare room, then grabbed Malcolm's arm to hold him back while Sharon went in.

"Are you sure this is a good idea? I mean, Morgoni's been harping on the zombie thing for weeks."

He snorted quietly. "Morgoni couldn't find a superhero at a comic book convention. It'll be fine."

"Okay…" said Teeny, still wary.

"Look, she's got some crazy dating thing tonight—don't

ask. If she likes the room, we'll look for some stuff to furnish it tomorrow, and tonight she can just crash at my place like she has been. It'll be great, Teens. She's… she's a great girl."

Teeny gave him a significant look that he pretended not to understand, and they followed Sharon out of the hallway.

At her desk, Morgoni sat back, swivelling her chair to take in the expanse of paper she'd accumulated on this most intriguing and urgent mission. At the top was the headline from her site, in letters of 400pt Courier: *ZOMBIE IN THE CITY*. Below, the best screen-capture she had of the so-called undead from that video taken by the fascist from the cafe.

Solemnly she swore, "You can't run, and you can't hide. Morgoni is coming to get you."

Then she realized that, despite her protestations, yeah, some tea would been nice.

Twelve Monkeys

46.

Sumptuous.

The Royal York was freakin' *sumptuous*. The Redhead had never had occasion to use that word before for anything, and now she was immersed in it. Sumptuousness? Sumptuality?

Odd, how the more she turned the word over in her mind, the more it sounded like something to do with plumbing than this wondrous, lavish, gold-and-glass filled fantasy-land.

She felt beautiful, as much as she ever had in her life, and ten times more than she'd have thought possible in this terrible fuchsia dress. Deanna had spiffed up the shoes to match what Kim had done with the dress, and with the freshly styled hair and professionally applied makeup, well, she was as much of a princess as a girl called Sharon Backovic from Toronto could be.

Not only that, but she had a place to live, if not the money to pay for it, and things were, to coin a phrase, looking up.

At check-in, she had the first feelings of unease. Yes, there were other zombies there (the site had specified female zombies looking for live men) but she had the distinct and disturbing feeling that the other women were… well, just dressing up.

Where her efforts had gone into making her look as live as possible, the other women had apparently spent all their time upping the *dead* factor. There was a zombie cheerleader, a couple of zombie nurses, and a zombie businesswoman, complete with a briefcase from which half an arm protruded. Most were showing more blood than skin, although skin came a close second. She'd gone to so much trouble to clean herself up, and now it felt like a wasted effort.

It felt, a little anyhow, like she was being mocked.

Worse, she had to seriously reconsider her own prior assumptions about what this night was going to be like. What had she honestly expected? A room full of other undead people who'd at some point stumbled out of their coffins (or gotten out gracefully, depending on whether or not they were dealing with awkward fuchsia high heels), ready to mix with other undead hopefuls looking for love?

What she'd heard Malcolm say at the salon continued to resonate in her thoughts. She'd been down this road before, trying to believe it was all a horrible mistake and that she really was alive. It was harder and harder to get her head around. How could she *not* be undead? There were the eyes, the coolness of her skin, the extreme dietary changes… but then, on the other hand, she could think and reason just as well as before, she needed sleep and…

And *embalming*! That word had sent a shockwave through her. Would that explain the lack, or at least slowness, of decomposition? If she could prove she'd been embalmed, wouldn't that also prove that she was a zombie and not just some girl who'd snapped after being accidentally pronounced dead?

It was a stunning place, though, the Ballroom at the Royal York. The lights were low, and small lanterns sparkled on the tables. Deanna and Malcolm had walked her to the door, and promised to wait in the main floor bar until she was done, although she though she caught both looking a bit askance at the prices on the menu posted outside.

But girls were free at the event, which was a lucky break since of course Sharon was literally down to her last few bucks. It hadn't occurred to her to wonder why until she saw the men.

Ooo, boy. If the women were attempting to be a freak show, it looked as if the men didn't even need to try. Just from where she stood by the registration table, she could see three or four who wouldn't look out of place in a police lineup, not to mention the big guy in the corner who seemed to be sucking his own fingers. She found herself actually hoping it was just compulsive behaviour. Anything else would be… okay, let's not think about that.

"Okay, hon, you'll be at number sixteen. Have you done this before?"

The Redhead gave her attention back to the woman at the registration desk who had made a cursory effort at reflecting the night's theme with a pair of ill-fitting vampire teeth and a trickle of fake blood at the corner of her mouth. Odd, that she could tell the blood was fake just by looking at it—or really, maybe it wasn't odd at all and just a natural assumption with no real proof from her senses or otherwise. Anecdotally, it was much more likely that everyone in the room was dressed up for the occasion and no one (with the possible exception of herself) was actually what they appeared to be.

Looking at the women, she was pretty sure that was the case. Most of the men, however, were probably just being themselves. Which was mildly terrifying.

"No, first time," she said to the woman at the desk, still unable to stop scanning the crowd. Was there a special someone here for her, someone who'd be accepting of her odd and altered state? Maybe this was a bad idea…

She felt a hand touch hers gently, and returned her gaze to the vampire-woman. "Don't worry, sweetie," she said kindly. "It's a bit nerve-wracking for everyone. The boys don't show it, or they try to brazen it out with bravado, but everyone here is just as nervous as you."

She smiled, and the Redhead nodded. "I guess I'm just worried about getting my feet wet… I just—broke up recently. With my boyfriend."

The woman finished filling out the Redhead's form and handed her a name tag and a stiff cream-coloured card. "Here's your scoresheet, and a pen. Just mark yes or no after you finish each date, and if he says the same, we'll hook you up for another connection."

"Thanks," said Sharon, and a tall man in a mourning coat at one end of the room started ringing a hand bell.

"Zombies and gentlemen," he said, in that kind of amused tone hosts use to let you know they're trying to warm up a crowd, "please take your places. We're ready to begin this evening's *Date with Death*."

Cute, the Redhead thought, and wandered until she found

table sixteen and took her seat.

47.

**Transcript of MOCKLIN McLAUGHLIN SHOW
ep 114 s 3**

[COLD OPEN]

MOCKLIN

Thank you! Thank you! You, I don't give a damn, but the guy beside you, thank you too!

Okay, y'all. You hear what I did there? I went "y'all," like I was from the South. That's the south of America, I mean. South of Canada, I'd just be saying, "Why? Why, God, why?" I mean, you ever been to Sarnia? Hang on, anyone from Sarnia here tonight? Good—I'm safe. It's a *hellhole.*

All right, and yes, y'all, we've got a great show for you tonight. My guest is live by Skype—also the name of my extremely unsuccessful but oh-so-ahead-of-its-time punk band from the 90s—live from an undisclosed location, we have the lovely Undead Redhead, recent Internet sensation and advocate for zombie rights. Did I really read that? And I thought we jumped the shark with our "Hannibal Lecter Cooking" segment.

Also, Canadian rocker legends Nickelback—kidding! Sit back down, you. See, I knew that guy was going to be trouble. We'll have a look at Lithuanian Fest, whatever the hell that is—seems like anyone with a flag can get their own festival these days, huh? Next thing'll be Rural Mailman Fest, right, you know, with the little flags on the… do they even do that any more? Anyhow, if there's booze and food, it works for me and Mayor Ford. *I wanna rum, and Coke, but don't try givin' me another of those stupid popcans. You know what I'm talking about…*

Who'da thought Toronto would have a mayor that makes Marion Barry look like a candidate for United Nations Secretary General? *Shiiiiiiiiiver!* What? Too soon?

But first, let's see if we've got the Undead Redhead on the line. Hey honey, can you hear me? Ears haven't fallen off yet, have they?

UNDEAD REDHEAD

[laughs] No, they're still fine, Mocklin. Actually, I think my senses are a little sharper than they used to be. Something like they're compensating for, well, the fact that I'm *living impaired.*

MOCKLIN

Living impaired. That's good. I'm sure our viewers have one very big question—what's it like to…

UNDEAD REDHEAD

…Be a zombie?

MOCKLIN

Hell no! We've all see that movie. What's it like to be an overnight Internet sensation? …Look at that folks, that's the most terrifying smile I've ever seen, and we had Jack Nicholson on the show once… that's a lie, but we did have Gary Busey…

UNDEAD REDHEAD

Uh, Mocklin?

MOCKLIN

Sorry, doll, you know what I'm like. Even when it's all

about you, it's all about me. But tell us, and I'll zip. What's it like to score almost a million followers in a little over three days?

UNDEAD REDHEAD
Well, I'd like to be one of those celebs who tells you it's gratifying, or the culmination of my life's efforts or something vain and shallow like that…

MOCKLIN
Don't be afraid to be vain and shallow, sweetheart. It works better than Dawn dish detergent for stubborn stains.

UNDEAD REDHEAD
I just want to be honest with you, Mocklin. You want to know how it feels? It feels incredible. And it's not just about me, it's about the cause.

MOCKLIN
Zombie rights.

UNDEAD REDHEAD
We're not just about brains anymore. Now, we want your hearts as well.

MOCKLIN
And on that note…

48.

Number One was a bit hard of hearing, and the Redhead eventually gave up trying to make him understand what she'd really said, and went with what he thought he heard:

"Yes, I got my fishing degree at U of T. They have a great

cod studies program.”

“What?”

Number Two had most of his own hair, but it had apparently been washed last sometime around the Middle Ages. Still, he didn’t seem to be a bad guy, just unnerving with the way his wandering eye kept looking up at the ceiling while the other seemed fixed on her ear.

Number Three was a buff and businesslike specimen who started talking even before he sat down, and had apparently managed to assess every facet of her earning potential even before that.

“I gotta say,” was his opening salvo, “you really have a decent package going here. Not just that, but there’s something different about you. That’s not necessarily a deal breaker; just hear me out. Me, I’ve dated models, actresses, big corporate CEOs… You know what I’m saying. I get the pick of the ladies.”

The Redhead could only nod, trying to keep up.

“You can probably tell just by looking at me. Hell, it’s pretty obvious, right? Total babe magnet. The car helps of course, then when they find out what I do…”

He really didn’t seem to want her input, but the Redhead managed a quick, “Oh? What do you do?”

He sat back, waving his hand like that too should be obvious. “Little of this, little of that—high risk, high finance. You wouldn’t get it, but that’s the way me likey.”

“Oh… right,” she said. If her eyes weren’t the size of platters, she’d eat her very pink shoes.

"Once, I dated this supermodel. I mean, she was pretty good-looking, but when you're with one of them, man, no matter how gorgeous they look from a distance you always find something wrong, you know?"

The Redhead cast around, looking for rescue. The dating sessions were strictly timed to five minutes, but not even Mr. Greasy-Hair-Wobble-Eye had made the time pass quite this slowly. And by the looks of the other tables, worse was still to come.

She managed to tune out Mr. Competition until the host rang the bell, and he sidled off, still talking. She could still hear him as the next date sat down.

Number Four didn't look much more than twelve, and his shirt had red stains on it that, after only about a minute in, the Redhead guessed would probably be Hot Pocket sauce.

She fixated on an extra-large pimple on his chin as he sat forward in his chair, hunching his bony shoulders as if his non-existent muscles were somehow stopping him from putting his arms down against his body, and said, "I have to date a good-looking lady, you know, someone my mom would approve of. Do you like sports, by the way?"

"I, uh…" she managed.

"'Cause I'm a sick Halo player. And I, you know, put a little money on the b-ball. That's sick too."

The bell couldn't come soon enough.

Number Five was a man who could have been made of vanilla pudding for all the impression he made on her— when she looked down to her scorecard after their time together, she already couldn't remember him. And when she looked around the room to see where he had gone, she couldn't even remember what he was wearing or what colour his hair was.

Number Six was as sharply-dressed as Mr. Competition but had a totally different vibe. He too seemed intent on making her aware he'd summed up her assets, only this time it wasn't about her status or income. He made absolutely no attempt to hide the fact when his eyes skimmed her cleavage, then did it a second and third time, swinging in a little closer and slower on each pass. She was almost too astonished to be shocked.

"We could just duck out, if you know what I mean. My car's around the corner, but if you can't wait that long…"

"I'm sorry?" said the Redhead.

"I know a couple of alleys. And a storage room they don't use downstairs. You okay with open relationships?"

"Bell?"

Number Seven looked like a movie star, from the fifties. It took him less than thirty seconds to trot out the pamphlets from his church, and less than thirty more for security to arrive to escort him out.

Numbers Eight and Nine were twin brothers from Mississauga whose entire conversation revolved around how unfair it was that they couldn't make the rounds together. Now *there* was a scary thought!

Number Ten looked promising, and was actually quite sweet and interested for the first couple of minutes. He asked her about her favourite books and movies, and told her he didn't need to know about any past relationships, because "we'll start fresh, because that's the only fair thing for both of us."

Immediately after that, he mentioned the woman who'd recently broken his heart, and just after *that* he burst into tears, thanking her for being such a good listener. As the bell rang and he walked away, he was still telling her, "If you could just hold me for a minute, I'll stop crying."

Number Eleven arrived with a speed dating staffer, on the screen of a MacBook Pro.

"I know it's a little unusual," she said as she set the laptop down across from the Redhead, "but isn't it *fun?*"

Quickly, the Redhead dubbed him, "Mr. Greencard..."

After abbreviated introductions, he launched directly into his sales pitch, finishing with, "So you see, there's really no reason to mention marriage—but if I was to be able to stay in your country of course..."

"Marriage" had already passed his lips nine times. She'd been counting.

"Where did you say you're from?" the Redhead asked, just to divert the conversation from potential nuptials.

"Love is very important to me," he said, and she had to admit it sounded soulful when he said it. "Eventually, it would not have to be merely a relationship of convenience."

"That's... very romantic."

He gave a small smile. The screen froze for a moment, then started streaming again. "In my country, girls are often very traditional. Few of them have your…"

Suddenly, the Redhead wondered if she was going to be calling someone *racist* for the first time in her life.

"Hair colour?" she suggested, to steer him away from the danger zone.

"Your skin tone is…"

Nope, he wasn't helping at all. "Hey—" she warned.

"Not to be politically incorrect, of course. It's not the paleness, it's the veins, the slight discoloration…"

He leaned forward into the camera, and just as she thought he might lick his lips…

"Oh, there's the bell!"

She slammed the laptop shut.

And still, she was confused, as confused about the reactions she was getting as she was about her own place in the scheme of things. Who was play-acting here, and who was deadly serious? Who was fully aware that most of the women in the room had put on white foundation and fake scars for the occasion, and which thought at least some of it was real?

If it hadn't been bad enough trying to figure out for herself what her own particular status was (dead, undead, or merely unlucky), the series of men filling the opposite seat had made her realize that perhaps she didn't want to circulate, *anywhere*. It was just too weird in the normal world, even without the added complications of zombie-hood, real or imagined.

As the final date of the evening, Number Twelve, sat down, the Redhead made a mental promise to herself. No matter what, she would accept the fact that her situation necessitated that she be alone. No matter how lonely she got, she couldn't bear to think of falling into closer quarters with someone who might, after all, only be interested in her because of what she appeared to be.

If it had seemed hard to date before death, postmortem love seemed almost an impossibility.

With that in mind, the Redhead also determined not to prejudge the final date, no matter what he looked like.

This was, it was soon apparent, probably not the best time to have decided such a course.

"Tell me, everything. Did you turn when you were conscious? Dig your way out of your own grave? How much of the damage is decay and how much happened on the hunt?"

The Redhead tried to smile in a friendly fashion, but somehow the date she'd dubbed *Mr. Fetish* (while castigating herself soundly for already falling into shallow patterns of judgement) made it hard. It was probably the number of piercings, or more likely the places he'd put them. She'd always liked a nose ring or multiple ear-piercings—on others of course—but she counted thirteen pieces of steel just on his eyebrows before he'd finished his first string of questions.

This, she decided, was a man who was either perfectly happy to believe that she really was a zombie, or a damned good actor.

"Uh," she began, trying to figure out which of his questions needed answering first. "Actually I eat mostly fruits and vegetables… rotting of course…"

She wasn't sure if he'd actually heard her, or if he had so much to ask he couldn't waste the time it took for her to respond. "Are those real maggots? I just want to stroke that loose skin around your throat…"

Horrified, she reached up to her jaw where, indeed, a couple of those pesky buggers had reattached themselves. So much for the beauty treatment!

"Uh, bell?" she said, frantically, although barely a minute had elapsed. "Bell?"

Outside in the lobby, she found Malcolm waiting with Deanna. It was clear they'd had a much better time than she had—at least, they were smiling. That was good; Malcolm deserved to have a nice night with a nice girl. And just as likely, a horror-show like her deserved exactly what she'd got.

The other women had been nice, though. She'd got some tips on how to make herself look more horrifying (apparently, most of them thought she was underselling the look) and had even exchanged email addresses with two.

Mr. Get-It-On emerged with a couple of zombie-women fleeing in front of him, but he kept going as if they were, literally, leading him on.

"Someone's about to have the cops called on him," she said.

Malcolm seemed a little reticent to ask, but—as the hotel security indeed did arrive to help Mr. Get-It-On to the door —he finally said, "So—how was it?"

She had to be honest. At least, it had been free. And they'd given her a glass of pretty nice wine, which went down fine. Probably something to do with the grapes being thoroughly fermented. "I haven't felt so dirty since I lived behind the dumpster."

He laughed sympathetically, and Deanna made an *Awwww* face.

"That bad, huh?" said Malcolm.

"Met some nice women; not so much with the men. I'm starting to think it's not so bad to be dead—or lonely."

"Hey, watch it!" he replied, giving her a light punch on the arm.

Get a load of her big mouth, huh? Trying to alienate the best friend she'd made this side of the grave. "I didn't mean you! Friends?"

"Friends." He gave her an awkward hug, and Deanna joined in.

Out of the corner of her eye, as she was trying to decide how long to hold it, the Redhead saw one of the nicest women from the event, a blonde who'd dressed as a soccer player with strings of blood drooling from each side of her mouth. "I'll email you!" the other woman called, and the Redhead waved back, effectively disengaging from Malcolm and Deanna. *There. Not awkward at all.*

Over by the archway leading into the bar, the Redhead thought she saw another familiar figure—a small boy with black hair and ebony skin. She was too far away to tell for sure… but what would he be doing near her, again? There was something rotten in the state of Sharon, and it wasn't just what the maggots were after.

49.

The memory of it still kept him up at night, no matter how much time passed. It didn't help, probably, that even without spending so much time following her around, he had positive proof of his actions so much closer—in the corner of his own room, in fact.

Sharon II was nocturnal more often than not, and her soft whickering and scrabbling sounds could wake him from the deepest slumber. That was good, usually, because deep sleep seemed to come with the most disturbing dreams.

They weren't nightmares, not exactly. But they took him back to the night it had all begun, and he wasn't sure how to think of that night. Part of him was proud, but the far more Catholic part of him was ashamed of his pride. A tiny, deniable part of him was horrified. It's not like he hadn't killed chickens before, but that was back home, not in cold, windy Toronto where the colours were dull and the people unfriendly.

Back home, if he'd done it, he would have told his grand-père immediately. He'd have walked up to the imperious old man, standing tall on the porch facing the sunset and said, "Papa Georges, I did it, just like you."

Here, though, Papa Georges was a diminished echo of his former self. He sat in a rocking chair in a small room from which you could barely see the sky, much less the sunset. When he was addressed, it could take a lifetime of silence before he responded, and then usually with "Are you speaking with me?"

It was sad. A boy should not have to see his grand-père decline so soon, not before he could show the old man he was ready to be strong for him and protect him in his twilight years.

He'd never thought of Papa Georges as old before they'd come to Canada, just as a mystic force of wild energy, barely kept harnessed by a powerful will that could move mountains if he just made the right gestures.

Killing the chicken had been easy; finding the right one had taken a bit of time, but hadn't been too hard. Oddly, it was finding a place to do it that was the most difficult part of the whole ritual. He'd finally settled on a back corner of High Park in the middle of the night, and even then, he'd almost been interrupted by a group of stoned teenagers with a guitar and a djembe.

 He could remember, though, the nights back home around a fire where good food cooked—the kind with the intense flavours he couldn't find in this washed-out country. Grand-père and Auntie Cecilia (Grand-aunt, but don't ever call her *that*) taking turns weaving tales of magic, and mysterious discoveries, and over and over the wonder of the natural world and how powerful could be the harnessing of its secrets.

Auntie Cecilia was the more evocative of the two, hunching forward in her magnificent layers of shawl and hair: "Yes, boy, the air would come alive. The very air, as if you could wrap your fist around it and then it would be up to you—to close your fingers and choke the life back out of it, or let it free to dance."

And Papa George would pull on his pipe and exhale, the smoke twisting up and around his grey head, making a halo, a living model of the dancing air in Auntie Cecilia's tale.

Just wait, until they heard what he'd done. Now he'd have a story to tell around the fire too.

50.

Teeny made guac, which was usually guaranteed to put Morgoni in a more receptive mood, although the other woman would *never* have admitted to it. There was nothing like a good guac, was there, with just the right amount of lime and a hint of garlic. She even ground her own coriander seeds in the mortar to augment the fresh cilantro.

Morgoni didn't like tomatoes in the guacamole unless it had a chance to sit overnight to meld the flavours, so Teeny skipped those even though she had a couple of beauts from the market, red and ripe and smelling of summer. She figured it was a wasted effort to make her own tortillas like she had once just to watch Morgoni shove a handful in her mouth apparently without even tasting them. The guac, though, that always got a reaction.

She stomped a little as she carried the plate into the living room, to hopefully break Morgoni's concentration just enough so that she wouldn't entire surprise her roommate. *That* was not a good idea, as she'd discovered in the past to her (*ow!*) shin's discomfort. Who'd figure that someone who spent her whole life peering into a computer screen or a viewfinder would have such mad reflexes?

"Hey, Morgoni," she trilled as she got close to the nominal partition in the room. "Knock knock."

Morgoni's head popped out to the side of the caution-taped whiteboard. "What?"

"Thought you'd like something to munch on. You've been working so hard."

Morgoni grunted, but by then she'd recognized the guac platter. "Thanks," she said, making one motion of emerging just far enough to grab the plate and vanish again. Teeny couldn't help being reminded of a moray eel, darting face first out of its hole just long enough to pick a meal out of the water. Oh well, as long as it made her more open to consider another new roommate.

Teeny skipped back to the kitchen for her own share of the guacamole, smiling to herself. As if Morgoni had even noticed the last one was gone!

51.

What's in a name, anyhow? Shakespeare asked it, although it took Sharon a while to grasp the concept. Or at least, a little longer than she was proud of to adjust herself to his language so she could start to enjoy his characters and his ideas.

Shakespeare ended up being one of Sharon's favourite things in high school for all that, and that scene on the balcony with Romeo and Juliet had always resonated with her, but not for the usual reasons.

She didn't understand why most people focused on the romance of the encounter. I mean, you'd have to live under a rock in the back of a dark cave in the middle of nowhere not to realize this particular love affair had a distressingly short shelf life.

No, for her, the important thing was not that you couldn't be with the person you were infatuated with (and what was that relationship about if not the worst kind of misguided puppy love?) but that even after love was gone, you still might not fit into the family of your birth any more than a total stranger.

What was a Montague, or a Capulet, or a Backovic for that matter? It was a name, nothing more. And if you felt enough like a Backovic to believe saying you were one somehow solidified your place on the planet, that was great. But that wasn't Sharon.

Hearing her own name had always been a little discombobulating, in fact, and not just the "Backovic" part either. "Sharon" didn't really sound like her either. The Redhead could turn over the name on her dry, bloodless lips and feel disconnected from whatever it might represent, but the truth was that even the pre-mortem Sharon Backovic didn't feel entirely comfortable with it.

Sharon, like Sharon Stone. Share-on, like an admonition to *pay it forward.* Don't keep that for yourself! *Share on!*

The history of the name Backovic itself was something she could hardly wrap her head around. It was Montenegrin, which was a hell of a word in itself. Her grandfather had emigrated from what was then part of the Kingdom of Yugoslavia, which in subsequent years was annexed by Italy during the Second World War, liberated to become part of the Socialist Republic of Yugoslavia, folded into Serbia after the fall of Communism, and finally became the independent country of Montenegro in 2006.

Maybe a little identity-confusion was only natural under the circumstances.

She'd never been able to get a solid answer out of her parents about where the "Sharon" had come from either; her dad maintained it was her mother's idea, and she said he'd tricked her into it because he'd had a crush on Cagney and Lacey's Sharon Gless and if she'd known at the time, Sharon would have been Carolina.

If her own identity was fluid in the eyes of those who'd given it to her, how could she be firm in it?

Was it really that much of a stretch to go from being unsure about who you were to not actually knowing *if* you were? Because what did not knowing if you were dead or alive really boil down to, if not a difficulty in deciding if your existence was a firm, actual thing or just a figment of chemical reactions and firing neurons? What was life, if someone in a lab in America could put a patent on it?

The more the Redhead felt she had recovered of the pre-funeral Sharon's thoughts and memories, the more she realized that her existence in the days following her reawakening had really had a kind of peace she'd seldom known. For once, she felt like she was dealing with her own place in the world head-on, unimpeded by anyone else's priorities or preconceptions. A crazy thought, when she was now so obviously odd that the chance of being prejudged based on her appearance had actually increased exponentially.

But that's the way it felt: Malcolm obviously had reacted at first with pity then with horror, but had quickly come to treat her like more like the woman she knew she was than Dave ever had. Malcolm was… but that was a dangerous thought.

He was cute, though, and nice, and *reliable.* Who would have thought that reliability would be the characteristic she craved most in a man, but after learning just how duplicitous Dave had been, even before her so-called death —well, a little security was nice.

It wasn't like she'd really trusted Dave before, not if she was honest. She'd been telling herself she *had* to trust him, not that she *did* trust him, throughout their relationship. It wasn't that she'd caught him looking at other women, or that he'd said anything to make her doubt his commitment to their twosome. But she'd always felt there was something missing, something between them that made it impossible to feel always and entirely safe with him.

Part of it was the way he'd introduced her to his family, or rather, the way he'd put *off* introducing her until way too long into their relationship. She'd been up front with him about hers, that if she *DID* for some reason run across a moment when one or other of her parents were in town, or either of her brothers, that it was his choice if he wanted to meet them but he was under no obligation. She'd been clear about how the time she spent with members of her family always made her a little crazy, how they treated her like a semi-moronic child or hopeless charity case, impractical and failing in every avenue of life. And she'd warned him that not only would they probably not like him, there was almost no chance he'd like them. Better for all involved if he just avoided the inevitable censure.

It wasn't like they'd go out of their way to treat him badly; they just wouldn't go out of their way to treat him as much of anything at all. Sharon had got used the idea that her father would treat every guy she dated with suspicion (*Are you a ball fan, boy? Yes? Hmmm… No? Double hmmm…*) and her mother would be excessively sweetness-and-light to his face while telling Sharon behind his back, *well, dear, he's a little odd.*

Even ultra-normal Dave was unlikely to meet with approval —although there was always a chance that Sharon's mother would do the ultimate about-face and, instead of bewailing the fact that Sharon was obviously too poor a catch to date a *really fine boy,* would probably tell Dave he was too good for her.

She'd never felt like any of her boyfriends had been really accepted by her brothers either. It would have been nice if that had come out of some sense they were trying to protect her, misguided though that idea might be, instead of out of a profound sense of male competition that they extended to everyone from the mailman to the barista at Starbucks.

She'd never understood their ability to turn even the most mundane tasks into a fight to the death, from turkey-carving to servicing their cars. *Everything* became a show of macho bravado, and Sharon had had enough of them both by the time she was in grade school.

It wasn't that she didn't love them, not precisely. It was just that her love didn't seem to make much of a difference to them one way or another, and they took it for granted just the way they assumed that bringing their laundry home (from Dubai and South Africa respectively) meant that their mother would instantly assume responsibility for getting everything freshly washed and pressed and, if necessary, dry cleaned.

Sharon had never understood their level of entitlement, and she didn't usually make an effort to see them on the rare occasions when they'd set foot back in Canada. A quick lunch or coffee was about all she could take before starting to feel so small a high-powered electron microscope would be hard-pressed to find her.

She wondered what they'd make of Malcolm, and then blushed inside at the thought that he'd actually have dated her back in the before-time. Malcolm was calm and confident, just a little exotic with what he'd told her was a richly mixed Guyanese heritage full of far-off sunny places and big, laughing families full of love.

He was also fully, completely, and undoubtably *alive*, and that's what made him dangerous, and maybe even off-limits. Until she knew one way or another what she really was, dead or alive, real or artificially reanimated, how could she even fantasize he would feel something for her?

Your Attention Please

52.

First, there's the dog. Cutest, fluffiest little scamp you've ever seen. The camera lens holds on his clever little face with the button eyes and the vibrating pink tongue. Giggles behind the camera. The dog knows he's cute, and so does the woman behind it.

Then the swing to capture more of the park, and the wedding party. The doomed, tragic wedding party.

She wonders what happened to the white-clad bride, the one who held her new husband so tightly as if her heart would break. *Crying for the death of her friend? Of course not. At that moment, Sharon wasn't even gone. She was in the fountain, drowning, head split, hand locked in memoriam around the fateful bouquet.*

No, she was crying for her spoilt wedding, all but stamping her designer shoes in fury as she played the tape forward: here's how I'm going to remember my wedding, not as the happiest day of my life, but as the day when Sharon and that other bridesmaid pushed each other into the fountain.

What was the other bridesmaid's name? It didn't appear in the press accounts, and really, it hardly mattered. She could rename her anything, call her "Ivy" or "Jezebel" or something ostentatiously foreboding of her jealous rage. *Steal my bouquet, will you? That damn thing was MINE.*

She grabbed the phone as it rang. "Undead Redhead," she purred.

"This is Marion Brixerman from KBYK." An NBC affiliate. *The goddamn show.*

"Oh, hi, Marion. Thanks so much for getting back to me."

"We'd like to put you on the air tonight if you can make it to our studio by 5. You know where we are?"

"Of course!" She didn't, but she could Google with the best of them. And if there was any doubt, a quick call to Geary would get her every single delicious fact she needed to make a success of it, down to Marion Brixerman's bra size if she wanted it. Oh—damn it, could he get her a car for tonight? A limo? *That* would be super sweet.

"Ask for me at the door, and someone will bring you up. We've got about ninety seconds, but we'll make it work for you."

She hung up, already dialing Geary on Skype. *Network, bee-atches!*

53.

"This has been on the Internet for how long?" asked the Redhead.

They'd watched it four times, and she hadn't been able to even close her mouth during the first three. The dog, the bouquet toss, Monica coming at her like a—well, like a total *bitch* after she'd caught the thing fair and square. And it wasn't even like she'd really cared that much. I mean, no matter how good or bad things were with Dave, marriage had not really been on her mind. It wasn't so much that she had low expectations for the longevity of the relationship or even that she knew they wouldn't be together forever. It was just that thinking about future with him never failed to make her just a little uneasy.

In retrospect, being with Dave was a little like being in a job that didn't exactly thrill you, but didn't seem bad enough to leave. You were making enough money not to worry about where your next meal or your rent was coming from, but it wasn't exactly something you got up every day celebrating.

Once, about a year into their time together, near their anniversary in fact, she'd found herself going over how she felt, and what she thought might happen in the future if they stayed together. Immediately, she was faced with the rather bleak thought that Dave had little or no interest in her further development in any particular profession or vocation, and was just happy that she was making a good living and didn't complain a lot.

When she'd talked briefly about going back to school to train as a teacher, he'd held her hands, looked deeply into her eyes, and said, "You don't want to do that, sweetie. Think about all the money you'll spend, and then there's no guarantee you'll even make as much when you're done as you do now. It's just a waste of time."

She'd agreed, but there was something *big* missing from her life, now and then, that she absolutely needed to figure out. Dave had all sorts of dreams and goals and plans, and never stopped talking about how he was working on this with

Joey, or sussing out this opportunity with Justin, or just about to close this deal with the Franklins, you know, those Franklins. She'd always been excited for him, even when she had hardly enough information on each of these ventures to really know who the players were, much less what the game was.

So she'd sat down with herself just before their first anniversary and asked herself, kindly but firmly, "Are you willing to be Dave's girlfriend, and not worry about your own achievements? Can you accept that he will never be as interested in you as he is in himself, and that he *needs* you to be more interested in him than you are in yourself?"

At that time, she had decided the answer was *yes*. She loved him, she told herself. And he loved her—hadn't he told her a million times how perfect they were for each other? Hadn't he told her a million times how she was the love of his life? Just because she didn't feel like his equal all the time was no reason to throw away a passion, a *devotion* that strong.

She wondered how long he'd been seeing Monica, and if there'd been anyone else.

When he'd first pursued her, she was still kind of seeing Martin, although they had definitely drifted apart. Had he gone after Monica, or she him, in the same way? "*He doesn't love you—you can see that from a mile away. He hardly looks at you. If I was in the same room with you, I'd never take my eyes off you.*"

Sometimes, their entire relationship seemed like it owed more to the kind of methodology with which her brothers approached life: if something existed at all, it was a stake in a game to be won.

Well, enough of that. The Redhead was no one's prize. She was herself, and screw the *Backovic*, the *Share-On*, the inconsistent family and the rat-snake boyfriend. Time to start defining herself by something other than how she fit into the lives of others.

"How many people have seen this?" she asked, and Malcolm exited full screen mode to show her the stats.

"Six *million* people?" she gaped. "Six million people have watched me die on YouTube?"

"This channel," he said. "I think there are a few reposts, and some mashups as well. Someone did a 'Wedding Fail/Miley Cyrus' mashup that was pretty hilarious."

She gave him a dirty look, but his distress at having made light of it made her laugh. She punched him in the shoulder. "I can't believe six million *plus* people have watched me die on YouTube. What the heck? Three hundred and eighteen dislikes? Who says they hate a video like this?"

He chuckled. "It's the 'net. If you put up a video of Mother Teresa, you'd get dislikes."

"Yeah, I guess."

It was after nine, and the Redhead was feeling tired but edgy. She didn't know how much longer she would have been able to live comfortably on Malcolm's couch. Yes, it was much better than roughing it in an alley, or snoozing on a park bench, but she missed her privacy. Having the ability to close a door and shut out the rest of the world had never seemed like such a luxury.

"Oh!" he said suddenly as if he'd just read her thoughts. "I have some news for you on the apartment front. Teeny loved you, and it's all but a done deal. It's not the Ritz, but it's nearby, and she's never home except between classes—the only caveat…"

"Yes!" she broke in, jumping up to hug him. "Yes, yes, yes, yes, yes! I'd love to live with your sister. Oh Malcolm, you are the bestest best bester of all the best bests in the whole world!"

He accepted the hug, then pulled back a little. "There is one thing you have to know—Teeny's other roommate. She's a little… odd."

"Malcolm," the Redhead said seriously. "I'm a zombie. You don't get much odder than that."

"You haven't met Morgoni," he replied.

54.

Mocklin McLaughlin knew good ratings, and he knew *great* ratings. His three minute bit with the Undead Redhead had already racked up more hits online than any ten of his other interviews combined.

Garvy Barker, his producer of the last six years (from the lean years of cable access right through the first official launch of the Mocklin McLaughlin show on a *real* cable channel) leaned back on Mocklin's dressing room couch. They had all their truly important staff meetings in here, just the two of them, so they could show a carefully preconceived united front when they were in public, or, every now and then, a public disagreement just as carefully calculated to solidify either Mocklin's position as the genius without whom the show would crash and oh-so-brightly burn, or Garvy's as the *only producer who could reign that madman in.*

It was the kind of theatre they both loved so much, the thing that had brought them together initially and still made doing drama worthwhile, both on air and off.

When Garvy had brought the Undead Redhead story to Mocklin, he saw the potential, but he'd never imagine the girl would have just so much of that undefinable X-factor that rocked the airwaves. She was a star in the making, a real future high-flying potential crash-and-burner. You only could love a celeb if they seemed like they could fall from the heavens just as easily as ascend further, and this girl was the real deal.

"Sure, I can get her back," Garvy was saying, "but what do you want to do? Another three? You're pretty good live-to-Skype, but unless we figure out a way to make it a runner, I don't see it flying as an occasional segment."

"I'm thinking bigger," said Mocklin, still parsing it out himself. He could use her, he knew, but he had to be magnificently careful too that he was not lost in the shuffle. He hadn't been put on this earth to help other people establish their careers, unless he got the credit for their success. If he was to promote this Undead Redhead, it needed to make him the hero of the hour.

"How about bringing her in studio then? Do we have a location for her?"

Mocklin shrugged. "She says she's from Toronto, but there's something in her accent and her attitude…"

"You're just saying that because people can still sometimes hear the Ottawa Valley in your voice," Garvy teased, and Mocklin only let it pass because he knew it wasn't true.

"Not just an in-studio either," he said, still thinking. "A rally. A big fucking all-zombie mass attack festival of stinking undead insanity. A… a…what's that thing they do in the fall? In October?"

"Hallowe'en?" Garvy suggested.

"No, not normal people. The… the zombies. The crazy fans. The big march thing they do."

"Zombie Walk?"

"Yeah, that thing." They'd covered it two years ago, and by all accounts (Mocklin *did* like to keep up on events he'd reported on in the past, just so he could take credit if they'd suddenly careened into the stratosphere in popularity) it had really taken off. You had to hand it to an event that somehow exploded exponentially even though it was predicated on the notion of letting people dress up as cannibalistic monsters with an insatiable appetite for human brains. *And* they made it sound somehow life-affirming. That was marketing genius.

"What about it?" asked Garvy, unusually slow on the uptake.

"What do you mean, what about it? Get 'em out! All of them. How many zombies did they have marching last year? And how much more popular is it going to be this year? You can't tell me for a moment those freaks aren't dying for another chance to get out their ripped flannel shirts and chain saws and latex scar kits and go all *Grrr, Argh* on Toronto's sweet behind."

"I only understood about three quarters of what you just said, and yet I agree entirely," said Garvy, already seeing the possibilities. "Fuck MuchMusic. We'll block ten intersections downtown and hold up traffic for a day!"

He could see Mocklin pursing his lips like he did only when an idea was so stimulating he began to salivate. "We've never had a reason to pull out the police barriers before."

"Hell," said Garvy, getting into it himself, "we'll have to hire half of Toronto's police force for security."

"I am so turned on right now," said Mocklin, and Garvy held up his hands in mock surrender—or as he'd quipped a few times, "Mocklin Surrender."

"Leave me out of the turned on part, but give me three days, and I'll deliver you a zombie rally that'll make the G20 look like Lilith Fair."

"Ooh, snap," said Mocklin. "Hey, is there any more of that smoked salmon? I could *KILL* some smoked salmon."

55.

From the case files of V. X. Morgoni, cryptoparapsychocriminologist

Total network breakdown. The Baldwin Street Irregulars have failed me in the most spectacular fashion.

How on earth could Juan Carla and her reprobate cronies have imagined for a moment that I *wouldn't* want to know about some crazy videoblogger claiming not only to be a zombie, but a *Toronto* zombie? This is our bread-and-butter (or their comic stash, if you want to be precise), not something to be *assumed* or *figured*. It has to be *known* and *understood*. Yes, they're children but goddamn it, couldn't they have realized that this was something *kind of important* for me to know?

Not only that, but it is my absolute top and most pressing current investigation, and Fawn at least knows all about it, unless she somehow has managed not to hear *a damn thing I say* while she's filming my vlogs.

So yes. Some redheaded media whore is exploding all over the Internet and even hitting some of the minor American affiliates to talk about, get this, *zombie rights,* claiming to be some Toronto girl killed in a weird-ass wedding bouquet toss accident that apparently both Juan Carla and Fawn have watched *dozens* of times without ever thinking that this could conceivably spark my interest.

Even a cursory viewing has shown me that this so-called "Undead Redhead" bears a striking but not certain resemblance to the girl on my videotape. *Is this the same person who I have now seen twice in person, and is there something real to this investigation that goes beyond mere play-acting?*

And now, yes, back to the Irregulars.

What the hell have they been doing the whole time I've been mentoring their little idiot asses anyhow? Yes, they do a good job of covert surveillance (with the exception of letting me down *SIGNIFICANTLY* over the Morlock business). Yes, they can find anything on the Internet give a Wifi connections and thirty seconds. Yes, they are dirt cheap. Yes, you get what you pay for. But *REALLY,* to miss out on informing me that someone claiming to be a zombie is living in Toronto actually might *be* one, and all while I'm breaking my back investigating the fact, don't they think I *MIGHT JUST HAVE SOME TINY INTEREST IN IN KNOWING MORE ABOUT IT?* This is unfor-freaking-giveable.

Barring some particularly juicy and useful intel, I'll have no option but to limit this cycle's payment to 80s comics of the strictly second tier variety. With any luck, they'll actually *notice* this time I'm giving them substandard titles instead of going all goo-goo over comics no decent store owner would pay a penny for. A *POUND*. Starting with *Dazzler.*

56.

Outside Malcolm's apartment, the Redhead hesitated. He'd treated her to Thai, because the soup always seemed to work okay for her no matter that it was fresh and not rotten. She thought it might be something about fish-based broths.

Whatever the reason, she felt reasonably warm and sated tummy-wise, but very, very uneasy in the mind.

"What is it?" he said, when she didn't make a move to follow him up the stairs after he'd unlocked the front door.

"Malcolm," she began, the questions forming as she spoke. "If I'm a zombie, what exactly does that mean?"

His mouth made an open smile that was almost more an intake of breath than a facial expression. "Well," he said, "why don't I show you? At least—what the common wisdom on the subject is."

They circled the block to Kensy Comics, and Malcolm put another key from his chain into the lock.

"Hey!" she said. "I've been in here. Why do you have the key?"

He laughed, staring a bit at her. "Out back? When we met? I work here. The alley you were in, it runs along the back of the store."

She'd never realized; Vegan Goodness was around the corner, although it backed onto the same laneway.

"But… there was another guy, an older guy. He was nice…"

"Jason," Malcolm confirmed. "He's my boss. I've been working for him since I left high school; started as a customer when we came from Guyana when I was twelve."

"That's…"

"Yeah?" He paused, without opening the door, as if he expected her to ridicule his choice of job.

"So, so cool!" she finished breathlessly. "You're a comic book guy!"

"Yeah, but not like the Comic Book Guy comic book guy I hope."

She giggled. "No, never. Like the super cool, knows what everyone collects and can tell you what episode so-and-so first appeared in and when they met whats-her-face…"

"You seriously know your comics," he teased. He opened the door and disarmed the security system. "Zombies? We're here for a reason, girl."

She made a *pshaw* noise. "Girl? Okay, homey."

The Redhead followed him in and waited as he locked the door behind them and put on a light. Coming into Kensy was somehow intensely, warmly comfortable, like she had a neighbourhood hangout suddenly for the first time. *Kensy Comics? Yeah, I hang out there all the time with Malcolm. It's cool.*

"C'mere," said Malcolm, making a quick circuit and collecting a few books and mags from various shelves before laying them on the counter. He made her perch on Jason's stool, and spread them out in front of her.

"Basically, zombies got big when George A. Romero made Night of the Living Dead in 1968. They've been around in popular fiction and in legend for a lot longer, but that's what really made it take off. Really fucked up a whole generation of filmmakers, this idea of mindless, hungry, relentless killing machines that just kept coming and coming…"

The Redhead made a grunt, part disgust and part discomfort. Was this how he saw her?

"Then there was a whole series of remakes, and sequels, and different takes on it. Sometimes there was a plague that made people into zombies. Sometimes it was a meteorite from space with some kind of infection that mutated them. Or some creepy government experiment going horribly wrong. It crosses over from sci fi to horror pretty effortlessly, even fantasy sometimes. Did you see those Pirates of the Caribbean movies?"

"I think so…" she said, but she was drawn into the pictures in the books he'd arranged in front of her. Gape-mouthed rotting corpses, slathering from their jagged-toothed mouths, clothes torn to ribbons, flesh the same.

"28 Days Later made it kind of classy—zombie films, I mean, and guys like Zack Snyder remade the original Romero flicks… Some takes made it funny, like the Evil Dead series. Even Stephen King played with it in books like Pet Sematary."

"This…" She touched a full colour illustration of a zombie woman with huge breasts barely covered by a skimpy and torn nurse's uniform, eyes rolled back into her head, hands stretched out with the wrists limp, fingernails torn and bloody. "This is what I'm supposed to be?"

"Sharon," he said gently, and closed the graphic novel she was staring at. "Sharon, look at me."

She did, and his eyes, so kind and concerned, almost made her die again right there. "What?"

"Do you really think you're one of these things? A reanimated corpse, decaying and… and hungry with no capacity for reasoning, for empathy? Do you really think you're dead, that you died?"

"…Yes?" she said.

He accepted that, but also the way she'd made it almost a question. "Okay."

"Well—maybe?" she said. "I'm so confused, Malcolm. What else can I be? I died. Six million people saw it. Three hundred and some odd even saw it and hated it. Do you think they hated the fact that I died, or just the video? Did they hate *me?* But it happened. I woke up in a *coffin,* just before my own funeral. If I hadn't, I would have been buried…"

"…Alive?" he said.

"Buried *something*. Alive, undead, but conscious. And capable of starving to… to death, or to unlife. Or to eternal really, really hungriness. I don't know! I don't know anything! But I woke up in a coffin, after a doctor said I was dead, and nothing has been the same since."

He left a significant pause for her to collect herself before putting a hand gently on her arm and saying, "Sharon, I want you to consider what I'm about to say. I'm not saying I'm right, but just hear me out."

She bit her lip, and nodded.

"What if," he said, "what if you were just unconscious, in a deep coma? These things happen; they're documented. It's not common but, you have to know. There's no firm test for cessation of life. Brain activity can drop to nothing in a coma patient, someone the best medical minds totally gave up on, and then suddenly they're up and around as if nothing has happened. That's one of the mysteries of medicine—we have to have standard definitions of when death has occurred, because in truth, *no one really knows when it's happened.* What's to say you didn't go into a deep, deep state of unconsciousness only to wake up when you got to the cemetery?"

It was a hard thing to hear, and she wasn't sure if she could take it in. Yes, the idea had occurred to her, especially after that horrible letter Monica and Dave had put on Facebook suggesting she'd faked her own death on purpose, just for the sake of getting some undeserved attention. But she'd never allowed herself to really consider it, that she *was* in fact a live, living, breathing, *normal* woman who'd miraculously been given another chance to start over.

It would mean that maybe, just maybe, the tickle of

attraction she felt toward Malcolm was something she could afford to consider, to explore, and even to attempt to foster. There was the opportunity to see if he felt anything for her, if his kindness was anything more than what was apparently his immense and slightly intimidating good will towards all of humanity.

She ran her hand over the collection of zombie lit on the counter. "If I *am* alive…"

He waited.

What did she want to say? What about the things that *didn't* fit? Why was her skin cold, much colder than she'd ever been before? Why couldn't she stomach fresh things? Why were her eyes so strange, with the pupils locked in place and the irises flat, like someone had somehow removed all their depth with some crazy real-world Photoshop filter?

"Am I alive?" she said finally, in a very small voice.

"I think you are," he replied, and a wave of warmth and happiness swept through her that threatened to dislodge her from the stool and right off her feet onto the floor.

"Okay, okay," she said, thoughts tumbling too fast through her head. "I… have to think, have to think about this, okay? I'll come home later…" *home, she'd called his place home…* "I just have to… you know, get used to the idea… will you… can you leave the door…"

She was already halfway to the door of the comic book store, turning the deadbolt and almost sliding down the stoop in a haze. He was following her, but she was barely aware, scooping up his keys, calling out for her to take care and watch herself, and *just wait a moment while I lock up…*

And then, she saw *him*. The boy, the one who'd been following her, the pretty little chimney sweep with the delicate face. He saw her looking at him, but she knew, she *knew* he'd been watching her all along, spying on her while she talked to Malcolm in Kensy Comics, trailing her from the cemetery, even stalking her movements when she'd gone out to the Beaches for her make-over then to the Royal York for the insane and oh-so-unsatisfying zombie speed dating event.

She was hardly aware of Malcolm calling out to her as she yelled at the boy, "HEY! You! Yeah, you, you little sneak!" and took off after him.

The boy was fleet-footed, and she was in the stupid goddamned fuchsia heels, but desperation and anger made her both fast and furious. She thundered after him, closing the distance between them with murderous intensity. "I— am going—to beat your—scrawny—butt!" she panted, still making up time and getting closer until she could actually reach out and grab at his collar with one cold white hand. He dodged her the first time, but she was far too committed to let him get away.

She brought him down on a grassy curb and engaged both hands and one hip to keep him down. When he struggled and tried to break free, she started to tickle him until he was crying with tears of frustration and suddenly, without a word, went limp in her hands.

Then, at last, she was able to pull him to a sitting position and take him by the shoulders. "Why have you been stalking me?" she shouted. "Who are you? What do you want?"

Distressingly, her stalker burst into tears.

The Rising

57.

He unlocked the back door of the very normal looking house, and turned to her with his finger near his lips. "Be quiet—I don't want to wake up my family."

"How old *are* you?" she whispered. "Should you be out this late anyhow?"

"I'm fourteen," he said indignantly, and it made her laugh, but she managed to do it quietly.

He led her inside and down the stairs into a finished basement with half-buried windows. The Redhead waited while he felt around for the light switch, and covered her eyes as he flipped it on. She forgot, almost every time, that her frozen pupils had just that much more trouble adjusting to changes than before the cemetery. Before she… but then, if Malcolm was right, there was no real before and after. There was no Sharon-live and Redhead-undead, just her, just a girl who'd cheated death in favour of a totally new life.

There was a soft whickering near her elbow, and the Redhead, eyes still blossoming with dark splotches, jumped away.

"Sorry," he said, "that's just Sharon II."

She let that go for a moment, instead asking, "And you are? I forgot to ask that."

"Waglet," he said. "Don't laugh. It's a perfectly common Haitian name. Only sounds stupid up here."

"I don't think it sounds stupid," she said, oddly affected by his pouting tone. "I think it's cool."

He didn't answer, but instead held out his hand. Understanding what he wanted, the Redhead reached into her pocket and pulled out the odd assortment of bones and feathers tied together with hemp twine and decorated with beads that had fallen out of his garments when she was tickling him.

"Okay," she said. "Explain."

He motioned toward the low single bed with pillows heaped on it, and the Redhead sat, thinking all the time that this was a comfortable room, a room in a home where people lived together and loved each other. It was like the bed she remembered from her distant, long-ago childhood, before she realized that her parents were slowly learning to hate each other, before she had to grown up too quickly. It was also a lot like the bed she'd tried to create for herself in her old apartment, in the low-rise she'd revisited just after her reawakening. Each of those pillows represented an expenditure she could hardly afford at the time (who knew that pillows could be so expensive?) and a few had been laboriously stitched by hand from patches of fabric and stuffed with batting purchased at Walmart.

But somehow, Waglet's bed was the real thing, and hers was a pale imitation. She'd never thought of her little haven as a mockery until she'd come here. What a sad thing, to find out that your mainstay of comfort was just a hoax perpetrated on you *by* you, a bit of self-deception that couldn't outlast a confrontation with the room of a little boy called Waglet from Haiti who'd been your stalker for the last few weeks.

"Here's Sharon II," he said, interrupting her chain of sorrowful reflections. She looked up at him, and held out her hands for the whickering, furry Kleenex box he was passing to her.

"What…" she started, and then realized it was a guinea pig. A furry, stinky…

"She's undead," he said. "I needed to make sure I could do it, you know, before I brought you back."

The Redhead held her namesake up to the light. Yes, the guinea pig eyes were fixed and button-like, not limpid like the eyes of a living creature. Much like her own, in fact. Its teeth emerged from the furry face and nibbled softly at her fingers but made no effort to bite. He handed her a rotten carrot which the pig took from her and worked its way along, chomping quietly.

"See? When I knew she was still a vegetarian, I figured it was safe to bring you back. I knew you were Vegan, so I didn't think you would try to—you know. Eat anyone."

She stared, bemused and a little conflicted. "How did you know I was Vegan? How long were you stalking me?"

"Not stalking," he said indignantly. "I *loved* you. That's different."

"Still sounds kind of stalkerish," said the Redhead, trying to sound severe, but Waglet's earnestness was defeating her best attempts to be censorious.

"I just wanted what was best for you. So when Sharon II died, I thought, if I can bring her back, then I can help you as well. It was for you."

She indicated the beads and bones. "And you did it…"

"My grand-père told me all the old stories, about the voodoo priests and their servants. I knew that zombis were supposed to be just mindless slaves, but then… that's not how they are in the movies! That's not what Sharon II was like. She remembered me; she knew her cage and my room. I thought, if I could bring you back, why would you not be able to move on your own, maybe even think, maybe just *be* exactly who you were before…"

"…only dead."

"*UN*dead," he stressed. "You're not really dead. You have a mind, and thoughts, and your memories. I knew that as soon as I saw you go home to your apartment. I was so sad when I saw that they'd thrown away your things."

He moved away from her then, digging through some boxes and clothing piled near the small desk under one of the windows. From the clutter, he extracted…

"My pillow!" she exclaimed, truly surprised.

He brought it to her, the tiny pillow that had started her collection. It was a Hello Kitty miniature cushion, less than a foot wide or high, pink and glittery. The Redhead felt tears collecting in the corners of her eyes. "This stupid, ridiculous… thank you, Waglet." She took it from him, and hugged it to Sharon II and to her own chest. "Thank you."

He gently took Sharon II from her, letting the guinea pig finish munching on the rotten vegetable.

"Do you…" the Redhead said suddenly. "I mean, that carrot looks great."

Silently, he handed her a bag of gooey miniature carrots, and she extracted one, careful to avoid getting any slop on the pillow.

It was a lot to take in. Really, a heck of a lot. A whole, holy, horrible heck.

"What you're telling me is that I died in a ridiculous wedding bouquet toss accident. I was pronounced dead presumably by some doctor or other at some hospital, none of which I remember because I was, well…"

"…dead," he supplied.

"I was getting there!" she protested. He needed to let her do this in her own time. It wasn't like she was being told her grades were down, or she couldn't get that coat she liked in the colour she wanted. "I was transported to some mortuary, put in a coffin, driven in the back of a hearse to a cemetery…"

And then.

"And then, or sometime in the meantime, you were out killing a chicken—killing a chicken?"

"Lots of people eat chicken. It's only ethical and honest to know how they are killed if you're going to put them on your plate."

"I'm a Vegan," she reminded him. "It's things like that I became Vegan to avoid."

Earnestly, he nodded, petting Sharon II a little harder. "Yes, and it's that kind of goodness that made me care so much about you!"

"Hold your horses, Wag-Lothario. Let me get through this. You did the thing with the chicken, and shook the bones and the feathers and burned the… stuff you burned, the burny stuff you burned, and then—and then you brought me back to life."

"Exactly," he confirmed. "It's an old family tradition. My people are houngan, mambo. That's like priests. Mostly Rada voodoo, but some Petro—that's the kind that makes zombi. My grand-père was a very famous houngan, very powerful, and my Auntie Cecilia too, powerful mambo."

"Okay, losing me a little," she admitted. "But how… I mean, Malcolm—he's the one…"

"I know," said Waglet, and she detected a dark note in his voice. Jealousy?

"Well, he kind of walked me through the zombie thing…"

"Not real zombis."

She took another carrot. "I never thought in my life—or whatever—that I'd be trying to sort out what a *real* zombie is opposed to the other kind. What's a real zombie?"

"Voodoo zombis. No 'e.' Voodoo has a darker side called Petro, practiced by very few. It was used to make servants for the houngan, mindless and obedient. But I thought I could maybe make some improvement on that, make it so you wouldn't be anyone's slave. I wanted you to be free, Sharon. Alive, and free from everything that oppressed you."

"I wasn't exactly oppressed," she said, but it didn't feel like the whole truth. Maybe Waglet *had* given her a new kind of freedom. She wasn't trailing around after Dorri trying to get with the in crowd; she didn't still spend her nights hoping that Dave would appreciate her instead of trying to change her (and obviously seeking some of his entertainment entirely outside their arrangement). She'd even given a bit of that new sense of liberty to Deanna and maybe helped her kick Sylvia to the curb.

Waglet smiled, with a disturbing kind of maturity that she thought pretty unnerving in a fourteen year old boy, no matter how exotic his upbringing.

"So you just… brought me back," she confirmed. "From the dead. Why?"

He blinked a couple of times, then looked down into Sharon II's fur. "Because I love you, Sharon."

"Ulp," she said.

58.

It was midnight. Jason unlocked the door, balancing the tray of coffee on a hip as he did so.

As promised, Malcolm was sitting behind the counter, back to the wall.

"Coffee?" said Jason, and brought it over. "And not made by the evil machine either."

Malcolm reached up, but didn't get up, so Jason joined him. "I got donuts too," he said, and unpacked a bag from a big pocket in his coat.

They ate in silence for a few minutes before Malcolm said, "I think I broke her, man."

Jason raised an eyebrow. "Just let me get this straight. This is the zombie girl with the backpack, the one who thought *The Zombie Survival Guide* would give her some insight on how to live in Toronto."

"Yep. I looked all over for her. She just vanished. I mean, it's not like she has any stuff but what's in the backpack, right, and that's with her. There's no reason for her to come back here."

"You told her she got the room at Teeny's?"

"Yeah, but man, I think the comics really freaked her out. I thought if I could show her what a zombie's supposed to be, she'd either admit it was some kind of weird playacting, or that she, I don't know, had a skin thing and this was just an easier way to deal. Or she'd realize she's been stuck in this delusion about being dead when really, it's impossible when you look at what that would mean."

Jason took a sip of coffee and considered it. Finally he said, "What would you do if it was true?"

"If what was true?" Malcolm said. "That she's a card-carrying member of the walking dead?"

"Yeah, what if?" Malcolm turned to look at him, but Jason

seemed serious. He continued. "Seriously, just entertain the notion. You like this girl, right?"

Malcolm didn't say anything, so Jason went on. "I'll take your silence as that usual faboo male reticence to talk feelings. But here's the thing. Just say for a moment, she's a zombie. She died; she came back to life. Could you accept that?"

"I don't know," said Malcolm, but it was a little quick.

"Just think about all the other kinds of hurdles relationships face. Seriously. Cancer. Car accidents. Diabetes. Fuck: herpes, gangrene, necrotizing fasciitis. We don't get to be healthy and whole just because we're in love. And then there's Alzheimer's, depression, bipolar…"

"Okay, okay, I get it. Yeah, you don't always get to be the young immortal you're fooled sometimes into believing you are."

"So—just think about it. That's all. You threw her for a loop tonight, obviously. It's only fair you should get a mind-fuck too."

Malcolm laughed wryly. "And you're just the asshole to do it."

"Hey—what are bosses for?" He gripped Malcolm's shoulder. "She'll come back, man. I know it."

"Because?" Malcolm asked.

"Come on, guy. Girls can't resist your employee discount."

59.

NECROMATCH / BOARDS / EVENTS & RUMORS / CANADA / TORONTO

THREAD: / UDRH???

ZOMBREE Moderator *superuser* *1845 posts, active since 05/08*	Hey guys, yes it's true, she's coming to town. Just confirmed deets w MOCKLIN's producer. ALL communiques need to go through this board or they WILL NOT BE RESPONDED TO
UNDEAD BUMBLEBEE *majoruser* *341 posts, active since 11/10*	Can't WAIT!!! Any update on location?
ZOMBREE Moderator *superuser* *1845 posts, active since 05/08*	Nothing but date will definitely between the 4th and 16th, since MOCKLIN is touring after that with <u>Rodeo Greenspan</u>
MARY MARY QUITE CORPSARY *newbieuser* *4 posts, active since 03/13*	Woo hoo! I've been following her since the first virals. Does anyone have pics of her pre-zombification?? I heard someone has a grad pic from her high school!!
LE MORTICIA *majoruser*	Loving the zombie rights angle.

535 posts, active since 06/11	
ZOMBREE Moderator *superuser* *1845 posts, active since 05/08*	Just in: GARVY BARKER (no relation to CLIVE before you ask) is promising photo ops for price TBA with UDRH after the rally. If anyone is interested, I will be setting up another thread, with Paypal links.
MARY MARY QUITE CORPSARY *newbieuser* *4 posts, active since 03/13*	Sign me up please!!!
ZOMBREE Moderator *superuser* *1845 posts, active since 05/08*	[see above post]

60.

It didn't go like he thought it would. Sharon had left, and there was a big hug but that didn't mean that she was really, truly open to his love. She had said as much, but it was an idea so crushing he didn't think he could afford to process it. Not yet, not now.

He though it might just have been the last part of the conversation that had disturbed her too much to see just how much he loved her, how devoted he'd be.

She was holding Sharon II when it happened, stroking the

smelly tuffs sticking up from the pig's back. Suddenly, she'd said, "Waglet—I don't know if I really believe it. I mean, maybe I really *did* just get lucky after going into a coma. Malcolm said…"

And this time, because he was feeling so much love toward her, he lashed out with a little of his frustration as well. "You see Sharon II? You see how she's starting to decay a little? Hold her up—look at her paws. She's rotting, Sharon! You know why you're not? Look at the scar on your…" He couldn't say "chest." Or "cleavage" for that matter. "Your— you know." He waved instead, averting his eyes as he did. "That's an autopsy scar! I can see the needle marks where they inserted the pump to remove all your blood! Do you see the little pink dots on your hairline? That's because the mortician did a poor job. The fluid wasn't circulated properly."

She stared, eyes even more fixed than… well, than they always were. But she didn't respond, so he *went there,* finished it off.

"You were *embalmed,* Sharon. That's why you're not rotting except around your injuries. That's why you'll be fine. It's proof. You are exactly what I say."

Her mouth had been falling open, super slowly, as if caught in a miniature localized time warp. The look on her face broke his heart, and he saw that he'd been far too cruel, far too direct.

Then, she shook her head, and handed him the guinea pig with slow gentle hands. "Waglet," she said slowly, "I believe you. I know you're telling me the truth. I'm not mad. You've given me a second chance at a lot of things, but I don't think love is one of them."

She stood, and put her coat back on, slung her cute backpack over her shoulder. "There's something else you have to know, and it's not going to be easy for you to hear, but if I can get used to what you just told me, you know you can deal with this. Okay?"

He handed her the bag of carrots, trying to delay whatever she was about to say, but she folded them up calmly, putting them in her pocket, and went right on.

"I'm not a teenage girl, Waglet. I can't have a relationship with you, alive or dead. It would be so, so wrong. It could never be right. When people are older, age difference matters less, but it could never be right between us without it being so very wrong. But you are a magical, amazing person. Somewhere out there, there's a magical, amazing girl just waiting for you. It's just that it's not me. But if you keep trying to be in love with me, she'll be all alone, and you'll be sad too."

"I *AM* in love with you," he insisted.

"I believe you about that too," she said. "But there's a beautiful girl out there who is your soulmate, someone who'll love you as much as you love her, and not someone like me who can't. I want you to be happy, Waglet. You gave me a new life. I can't ever repay you."

Then, he was crying, which was *incredibly* embarrassing, but she didn't seem to mind. And then, because he was suddenly feeling more mature and grownup than he'd ever even wanted to, he said, "You should go find Malcolm. He's probably worried about you."

She kissed him gently on the cheek while Sharon II made comforting little whickery noises, and then she was gone.

He put on some music and sat on his bed with the guinea pig until he heard a gruff voice calling from upstairs. "Boy! Waglet-boy! Come give your old Papa Georges a cup of tea if you're going to be up all night!"

61.

From the case files of V. X. Morgoni, cryptoparapsychocriminologist

Unbelievable. It's official.

I have gone over that piece of footage every way known to man, and there is NO other explanation. Special effects, makeup, I mean, if I had NOT been there when it was shot, I would be able to poke a million holes in it. But there is NO way I can put what I saw with my own eyes together with what that creature who stole my camera shot without believing that THIS IS THE REAL, UNDENIABLE TRUTH.

1) No breath. In the alley shot, the zombie clearly is breathing in and out, but while the breath of the *bitch thief* is clearly visible despite her being all the way behind the camera, the zombie's DOES NOT SHOW UP AT ALL. Only explanation: that her breath and the air temperature are too close for exhaled vapour to become visible.

2) The eyes. While contacts seem like a viable explanation, again the footage presents a real problem. Contacts reflect because they are lubricated by the wearer's tear ducts just like the actual irises on which they sit. While the zombie showed a certain amount of moisture in the CORNERS of the eyes, there appeared to be little or

no active wetting of the eyeball through the action of blinking. In a normal person, this would be an EXTREMELY UNCOMFORTABLE situation.

3) Scarring and tearing of flesh. Despite all the enhancements I can make, the flesh of the zombie's chin remains inexplicable except as a deep cut, right to the bone, which nevertheless shows no sign of either healing or bleeding. Cosmetic effects applied with latex or makeup etc are always ADDITIVE, but this wound DESCENDS INTO the flesh. From certain angles, you can see RIGHT THROUGH THE WOUND to the room beyond. Since I know there was no greenscreen etc, the only explanation is that this is a REAL WOUND AND NOT AN ARTIFICIAL ONE and a wound such as this would either a) bleed profusely if it was as fresh as it appears to be or b) have started to heal if it was older.

I have with almost not doubt identified this zombie-girl with the woman who accosted me at the bus stop in the ridiculous party dress, and Juan Carla, Dibber, and Fawn are spread out around the area on active zombie watch, working in shifts to cover as much time and ground as possible.

I, Victoire Xandria Morgoni, have WITHOUT A SINGLE DOUBT positively identified the world's first actual, documented zombie, living here in Toronto and in all probability in the Kensington Market area. THE WORLD NEEDS TO KNOW.

62.

Well after midnight. Jason had left (and took the rest of the donuts, the bastard) but Malcolm lingered in Kensy Comics, not wanting to go home when there was a chance she might return.

She could of course show up at his place just as easily—but he knew if he went home, he'd probably fall asleep and might just miss the knock on his door. Losing her because his buzzer was broken and he couldn't stay awake would be the most shameful kind of dumb.

He slipped out for a cigarette into the back alley, a ridiculous amount of nostalgia welling through him at the sight of the dumpster. *Who'da thought I'd go mushy over trash?* he mocked himself, then didn't light up after all. He could hear Sharon saying like she had, leaving one of the apartments they'd viewed, as he reached for his lighter, "You shouldn't smoke! It'll kill you!"

"And coming from you…?" he'd laughed, and she burst out giggling too.

So, no smoke. Back inside, he picked up the latest issues of all the books he followed, but after turning a few pages, realized that there was no way he was going to be able to concentrate enough to read. His mind was on one thing and one thing only, and she wasn't here.

So, he did the only thing he could think of that wasn't just sitting and waiting, and called Teeny. She made it down in less than five minutes, and brought cookies. He made coffee (never his or Jason's first choice, since the ancient coffeemaker that lived in the shop's basement was as likely to produce sludge or water as something in between and drinkable) but neither he nor his sister wanted to leave the shop to see where was still open for take-out.

When they were armed with one of the better attempts at coffee the machine had yet produced, and had broken out the cookies, Teeny broached the main question.

"Okay, idiot brother. What did you say to her?"

"Hey!" he protested. "Nothing. I just suggested, you know. That she might be alive after all."

Teeny sighed. "I suppose that's fair, but do you know for sure?"

"You sound like Jason," he said.

"Look," she said. "I know you're a good guy, Malcolm, but a girl like Sharon, she doesn't necessarily need your help to fix her problems. Not if what she really needs is for you to shut up and listen."

"Just believe she's a zombie?"

"Look," she repeated. "What do you like about Sharon?"

He considered for a moment. "She's happy. Like, crazy no-reason-at-all happy. Not like someone who doesn't experience the bad as well as the good, but like someone who knows there's always still good to come. Does that make sense?"

"Yeah," Teeny said quietly. "That's nice. And a bit like someone else I know. What else?"

He thought for a moment. "I don't know. It's… you can tell that she hasn't had a lot of people in her corner during her life. Like she's gotten kicked or ignored or used more often than not. And she used to put up with it."

"Before…"

"Before whatever," he agreed. "And now, she's found this way to be… just as nice and positive, but she's not taking any shit either. *And* she rubs off on people in this amazing way too. It's like she… *nices* away her conflicts. Like no one can resist her goodness."

Her *Vegan goodness* he almost said, but that would be too cornball even for this very cheesy conversation… Except that everything he had just said was true, and saying it made it feel even more so. Sharon was just an amazing, magical person, and he was lucky to know her. So why was he so determined to convince her that she was wrong about what had happened to her?

He'd started off thinking exactly the opposite way, or had at least led Sharon to believe that he was okay with whatever she wanted to believe. Had he just been humouring her and not really being the good guy he liked to see himself as? Was he really trying to impose his viewpoint on her, without considering what she needed?

Teeny had apparently got to that exact thought before him. "You always know what's good for everyone else, bro. And sometimes you're wrong. I'm totally glad to be back at school now, but for all your pushing, I wasn't going to go back a day sooner than I did. Some days, when you'd get out your 'I believe in your potential' lecture, it was all I could do to resist either hitting you or vowing never to *ever* set foot on a campus again. What I needed was someone to help me talk it through, not someone to keep treating me like some kind of child who just needed a push to figure it out."

"That's not what I…" he protested, but she cut in.

"I know you, Malcolm. You have this way of making people want to please you, to keep your good will. It almost killed me to take the time off I needed because I was so terrified of disappointing you. Don't do that to Sharon. You have to let her work this through, and figure out if she's alive or dead or just deluded. But *help* her, don't try to pattern her the way you think she should be. And that goes double if you wanna date her."

"Who said I…" he said, suddenly indignant.

"You gotta go," said Teeny suddenly.

"Whu…" he began. At that moment, there was a tapping at the window, cluing him into what Teeny had already seen. Expecting to see Jason back again for another kick at his ego (but potentially with more food), he stopped dead. Well, *dead* was probably a bad way to put it. *Cold* was more her thing than his too.

"Or *we* gotta go," said Teeny behind him.

Because there she was, waving through the glass, red hair gleaming in the glow of the streetlamps, framed between a giant Hugh-Jackman-as-Wolverine figuring and a tower of vintage tin robots.

He rushed to the door and unlocked it for her. "Come in— you've got to be freezing," he said.

She laughed. "Always," and put her fingers on his cheek. Yup, just as cold as ever.

"Where did you go?" he said, and she bounced a little, as if trying to figure out what and how much to tell him. Teeny had faded into the shadows in the store, and he was glad.

"That boy—the one I was chasing?" He nodded for her to

go on. "His name is Waglet. He grew up in Haiti, and his family does Voodoo. He brought me back from the dead. I know—it's a little hard to believe, but hey, not like much of this makes sense, right?"

"He brought you back, with a Voodoo something or other," said Malcolm. "Sharon…"

She bounced again. "It's cute. Really. When I was alive, you know, he had this big crush on me. He used to come into the office where I worked, I guess, because his mom was our caterer for meetings and he sometimes helped her out with the trays. And he saw me a couple of times when I was volunteering at the library. I used to read to the little kids, fairy tales and stuff."

He smiled a little, in spite of himself. Sharon, sitting surrounded by children, reading about dragons and princesses. Way too perfect.

She returned the smile, but looked uneasy. Whatever this part of it was, this was what she was unsure about telling him. "I know. Fairy tales are kind of my comic books, you know. Anyhow, he had this big, massive crush on me, so when I died it kind of killed him. Not killed, you know, but…"

"Yeah, I get it." He waved to Jason's stool and she sat, taking a bag of desiccating mini carrots out of her pocket. She started to offer him one, realized what she was doing, and laughed.

"Sorry—they don't look nearly as good to you as they do to me, I guess."

She turned her face away, and Malcolm got the distinct impression she was about to lie to him, or at least to skimp on the truth. "It's really kind of sweet. He really liked me, he brought me back, only even then he was too shy to talk to me until I knocked him over and tickled him."

"You tickled…"

"Hey, Sharon," said Teeny suddenly, stepping right in beside her brother.

"Hi!" said the Redhead, genuinely pleased.

"Sharon, why don't you come back to my place tonight," Teeny said, shooting a look at Malcolm to shut him up. It did *not* sound like a question.

"Okay…" said Sharon slowly.

"It's good," said Teeny. "Jackie left a bed and I just did a load of linens, so you'll be all warm and comfy. Malcolm says you're hardly leaking any more."

"Not since the makeover," said the Redhead proudly.

"Okay then. 'Night, Malcolm." She grabbed the Redhead by the hand and all but pushed her out the door. "Just—out in a second."

She closed the shop door, shutting Sharon outside, and turned to her brother, hissing in a whisper, "You think about what I said. I know you want to do what's best for her, but make sure you know what that is before you impose your ideas on her, okay?"

"That's not fair…" he began, but Teeny put a finger to her lips, hauled the door open, and was gone.

218 - undead redhead

Gather, Darkness

63.

Geary met her at the airport check-in counter with the electronic boarding pass.

"You could have emailed it," she said crossly. She was running on three hours of sleep, and had just realized she would need to repack half of her carry-on into her checked luggage because of the insane restrictions on items in flight. Like she was going to hijack the plane with her hand cream.

"No, I couldn't," he said, "because then I couldn't have given you this."

He reached into the pocket of his bomber jacket (*always trying to look like the coolest guy in the 80s,* she thought disapprovingly) and brought out a thumb-drive and a small velvet box. "Your press kit. If you thought I was uploading this to the government's user-sucking spy-cloud, you have another think coming. And there's this."

She pocketed the drive and flipped open the box. "Geary! Really."

"I thought you could use it."

She lifted out the necklace with the fat, cylindrical pendant. "I thought you said this was entirely and excessively illegal, not to mention proprietary military technology.

"But of course," he said, affecting a French lilt. "Only the best for Madame. Just remember, it's strictly one use only, and it's going to fuck you up too, so only use it if you have no other choice. Consider it your 'get out of shit free' card."

He took out a square parcel wrapped in tape, then lowered his voice to a bare whisper, hardly moving his lips as he spoke. Of course, worried about audio and video surveillance. "This one you can only use if you can get your hands on some black powder. I left instructions inside about cannibalizing consumer-grade fireworks, but you probably won't have much luck getting your hands on any at this time of year."

"You'd be surprised," she said. She had fans in Toronto too.

"I'm not taking the chance of putting any explosives through customs."

She smiled, with only one side of her mouth. Geary loved that sly, child-eater look. Went really nice with the boobs.

"Now," he said, handing her the slim folder he'd removed the boarding pass from. "You'll have to cab it from the airport, because we don't want any record you came in from out of town. Hotel's on the Mocklin McLaughlin show, because he thinks you're from someplace called… uh, Scarborough, and it's better if you're staying in town before and after the rally. They're going to send you room service, and you're all set up to order a bunch of bloody raw things that you can cook in the microwave; just make sure you flush any leftovers. We figured salad and stuff like that you can get away with, as long as you do enough raw meat for the image. And yes, we swung you a car to and from the rally, *and* there's going to be a fully catered after-party paid for by, if you'll believe it, the Toronto League of Extraordinary Undead Ladies and Gentlemen."

He helped her with the clasp of the necklace, enjoying being able to touch her hair but not lingering long enough for her to laugh at him. She was pretty damn good at catching him at stuff like that.

When the necklace was on, she took out a makeup mirror and admired it. Amazing how much technology you could pack into one small gadget. Satisfied, she gave him another of those sexy, crooked grins.

"Thank you, Geary. Now, should I check it through, or can I get away with wearing it on the plane?"

64.

"Anyhow, he'd already made his guinea pig into a zombie…"

"He *what?*" Teeny handed Sharon a cup of Oolong. It had smelled the closest of all her teas to something rotten, so that seemed to be the one to try.

They were in the Redhead's new room, which so far featured nothing but a bed, a folding chair of the summer barbeque variety, and a slightly rickety TV stand which would work for a table, as long as you didn't put anything too heavy on it.

Teeny slid onto the bed where Sharon already sat, legs curled under her, high heels a blessedly fading memory for her poor toes. The Redhead held her tea in both hands, and had a pink Hello Kitty pillow tucked on her lap.

"He calls her Sharon II, after me. She's really cute, and sweet, but I don't think she's going to live much longer than a live pig. I mean, she's not immortal, I don't think, and she's even kind of decaying. But me…"

She stopped.

"You?"

"I didn't tell Malcolm everything. He wants me to be alive so much…"

Teeny waited. If Sharon wanted to go on, she would.

"It's about the scar. This one." The Redhead indicated the pair of incisions starting at each shoulder and joining to form a Y with one rising from the center of her cleavage. "Teeny, I'm scared. Until tonight, I think I really could believe that maybe, just maybe I was really alive after all."

"What changed?"

"Proof," she said, and her voice held a little bit of sadness. "I don't mind—not really, but Malcolm… He doesn't want to know. But this scar… It's from an *autopsy*. Someone cut me open, and stitched me back up after they removed all my organs. I thought that might be why I can't eat the same stuff any more, because they put my stomach and everything back wrong… I know, but that's the kind of thing you think when you're a freak."

"You're not a freak," said Teeny, firmly. "You are *Sharon*. You're a great person, and Malcolm thinks a lot of you."

"But he's never going to be able to accept that this is me. That I'm really, really, truly undead. Zombified. That I really died and came back. He wants me to just say, *okay*

Malcolm, it's all in my head. I accept that what I believe is impossible. You're right."

"He's not like that," protested Teeny, but hadn't she said exactly the same thing to him?

"If I tell him, *show him,* I'm going to lose him and I don't think I even have him yet!"

The Redhead slumped, and dribbled a bit of tea out of her cup onto the coverlet. "Sorry," she said. "I'm making a mess."

"Sharon," said Teeny. "I think you're biggest problem probably is worrying about our mutual roommate."

The Redhead looked up. "Because…?"

"Well, she has a little bit of a thing about zombies right now. Like she's a little obsessed."

The Redhead sighed. "Really? Teeny, I'm just so exhausted by all this. It's too much. I feel like I just started out when I woke up in that coffin, and nothing before that even mattered. All I have is the people I've met since then, and one stupid backpack with a couple of dumb keepsakes and a pair of shoes that are killing me one blister at a time. I'm scared of losing *any of it,* but especially I'm scared of losing Malcolm. He's the best friend I've ever had."

Teeny sat for a moment in silence. Then, she reached out and touched the Redhead's knee with gentle fingers. "What do you want?"

The Redhead's eyes opened a little wider, showing the odd matte eyes off in the light from the overhead bulb. "What do

I want? I want to keep feeling this good about being me, and I want to be even *more* me if that's possible. If there's one thing that's really changed since I came back to life that has *nothing* to do with my circulation or anything else physical, it's my… confidence? You might not believe it, but I think I've really been myself, my own real self, twenty-four hours a day, seven days a week, for the first time ever, just since some kid from Haiti decided to kill a chicken and resurrect me. Is that crazy?"

"Totally," said Teeny, "but it also sounds kind of wonderful."

"I don't want to go back to being who I was before, dating a guy I didn't really like who didn't really like me, putting up with terrible treatment from people who said they were my friends but didn't act like it, trying to keep up with a family that never seemed to want me. I'm *me* now, and if that's some kind of undead zombie Redhead, that's okay. No one's going to take this new thing away from me, and I'm going to enjoy every gosh-darned minute of my life-after-death."

Teeny sat up, and made a quiet whooping noise. "Battle cry of the Redhead!"

"You're darned tootin'!" the Redhead laughed.

They giggled for a moment, then Teeny said, "Don't ever change. I for one don't care if you're dead. In fact, knowing you, I wish more of my friends were."

The Redhead snorted. "Don't say that too loud."

Teeny shrugged, then changed the subject. "So this Wagger kid…"

"Waglet. It's apparently a very common name for boys in

Haiti."

"This Waglet then. He's not going to be a problem. Because he's got a crush on you, I mean."

"I told him that there's a wonderful girl out there just for him, but I'm not her."

"Wow, that's beautiful."

She nodded, satisfied and only slightly embarrassed. "Yup. Best kiss-off line I ever came up with."

65.

The plane landed at midnight and the cab got her to the hotel by one thirty, which meant she had enough time for a solid night's sleep before tomorrow's festivities. Just enough time, as well, to do a final video blog to entice a few more of her "local" fans.

She'd been in makeup since getting the cab driver to drop her at an entrance to the hotel that went through the bar instead of at the main entrance. Wearing a hat and glasses, she rolled her suitcase into the bathroom, and put on her makeup and costume before heading out to the lobby to check in.

She'd made a sensation at the desk, which was a rush and, she knew, just a taste of the fun to come. Room service had sent up an uncooked hamburger patty on a separate plate from the bun and toppings, so it was easy (if not exactly gourmet) to zap it in the microwave for dinner. Leftovers were not an issue.

After checking her numbers (three hundred new followers on Twitter, almost eight hundred new likes on her Facebook page, not to mention more people claiming they were coming to the rally tomorrow than the venue could hold), she logged into her streaming account, checked her makeup one last time, and turned on her webcam.

"Hi, everyone," she said. "Your friend and warrior for undead rights here, your very own Undead Redhead. Made it in from Scarborough—ain't the Don Valley Parkway hell?" A little regional flavour never hurt, did it? She'd boned up on the geography and as many of the local hot spots as she could research. Geary had added a few choice bits for her to throw into her appearance tomorrow, and he'd be watching to catch any mistakes so she could explain them away in a future blog.

It was just sad he couldn't be on headset with her, but it would be hard to do it remotely. Next time, she'd have to make sure they brought Geary in to run her tech. She'd think of some way to justify and explain it.

"I hope you're all as pumped about tomorrow as I am. Just think—for the first time ever in a public place, we shall come together with one great purpose in mind—to show the world that zombies are people too! You're going to love my friend Mocklin McLaughlin, if you haven't already watched him…" as if *she* was the famous one, not him "…and I've got some surprises up my slightly bloodstained sleeves for you as well."

And she did; her Toronto contact was as good as his word and there was a nice box of fireworks waiting in her room, just ready to be taken apart and reengineered.

"So, until tomorrow, my beautiful undead children. Your hearts may not beat, your blood may not flow, but you are people too!"

With that, she signed off and sat back, satisfied. Now to get this damn latex off, and soak in a bath. Ooh, and raid the mini bar.

And tomorrow, fame and fortune awaited.

66.

In the morning, the Redhead found the pair of old sneakers Teeny had promised to lend her in the hall near the door along with a pair of wooly socks and some bandaids. She kicked off the heels gratefully, bandaged and socked herself, and put on the much more comfortable shoes. It was heaven.

She heard some low muttering from the far corner of the living room, the part that Teeny had explained was the exclusive purview of her new as-yet unseen roommate Morgoni. Up already, and already working. Teeny had said that Morgoni *did* sleep in her room, but you'd have to be pretty quick to catch her moving between places. And it was like winning the lottery or getting struck by lightning if you actually saw her leave the apartment, especially lately. She'd also called her "Morgoniarty" which the Redhead found hilarious.

Quietly as possible, she disengaged the multiple deadbolts and chain, and slipped into the hall where she relocked the door with the set of keys Teeny had presented to her ceremoniously before they'd both gone to bed. Before falling asleep, the Redhead had transferred them to her Mewtoo keychain, and threw away the ones belonging to her old life. It felt good.

Outside, she savoured the warming air and light wind which brought a smell of sewage and decay which, probably logically, was very appealing. She took her time walking to the grocery store where she gave the produce manager half an hour of instruction and came away with a whole bag of slobbery tomatoes, a very soft eggplant, and two bananas that not even banana bread could redeem. Not for a *living* person, anyhow. To the Redhead, they looked just fine.

She checked her email at the library, and bought a bag of peanuts in the shell to feed to the squirrels while she ate her own breakfast.

In the park near the library, she saw a familiar figure.

"Hey!" she called. "Got any change?"

The cracklady turned to see who was hailing her, and a smile creased her face. "Honey! You look good. Found a place to live?"

"I *did!*" said the Redhead, joyful. "No money yet, but things have definitely looked up. Also, I've got peanuts!" The squirrels in the area had already figured that out, apparently, and a couple were edging in closer in those zigzags squirrels ran in to pretend they really weren't interested.

"Good for you," said the cracklady. "You seem like such a nice girl."

"Thanks," said the Redhead. "How about you?"

"Ah, still doing crack." She shrugged. "I really can't get off it. Tried everything, but you know. I figure you can only do what you can do with your life, and anything more is impossible anyhow, so why sweat it?"

The Redhead considered this, feeling sad but not sure what to do or say. The cracklady reached over and put her hand on the Redhead's knee, much as Teeny had the night before. "Don't worry about me, hon. I knew what I was doing when I got into this life. It's not great, but I'm managing. And hell, as long as there's life, right?"

That made the Redhead grin, then start to giggle. The cracklady cracked a smile too (*Get it? Crack?*) and they both giggled and giggled while the squirrels came up and chattered, reminding them that they still had peanuts they hadn't distributed.

"As long as there's life," laughed the Redhead.

When the peanuts were gone and the Redhead's sides ached (another of those odd times when something physical seemed to affect her—but much nicer than a headache or the old hunger pains!), she gave the cracklady a hug and walked back to Augusta.

As she passed Vegan Goodness, she made a mental note to see if she could work some kind of similar deal with them as she had with the produce manager, maybe see if she could score some prepared meals she could leave out in her room to get tasty. She turned the corner, and stopped. If she kept going this way, she'd pass right in front of Kensy Comics, and there was a pretty good chance that Malcolm would be working.

Did she want him to see her? Did she want to see him? It had all gotten so confused so quickly. Yesterday, when she wasn't sure one way or another about her state of animation, she'd been ready to admit she had pretty powerful feelings growing for him.

And today, with the absolute assurance that she was, in fact, a dead girl reanimated by the power of a fourteen year old boy's crush and some crazy Haitian voodoo?

Today she wasn't sure if she could even face him.

She crossed the street, and went into a fruit market that smelled deliciously of rot. This was the one that Dave had always complained had the worst produce in Toronto, and she agreed.

She browsed, all the time checking out the open front door to the sliver she could see of the Kensy Comics window display. It was probably good there wasn't much room to look in or out, or even with the vegetable and fruit stands partially blocking her, Malcolm might have seen her.

As it was, she saw him first, and darted back into a display of watermelons. A little Asian man, possibly the owner, caught her and steadied the pile.

"Watch, watch," he said.

"I'm so sorry," said the Redhead reflexively, but still tried to peek out enough to see… yes, there he was. Malcolm, moving something around in the window, looking back over his shoulder as if talking to Jason as he did so. Her heart leapt—or whatever part of her undead body that mimicked that live-person function leapt, at least.

"You dead?" said the little Asian man, and the Redhead turned to him in surprise.

"Dead girl," he said again, but it didn't seem to bother him. "Dead?"

The Redhead nodded.

He copied her nod, and gave her a slight bow, satisfied. Then he said, "Dead on TV, yes?"

That was a little harder to understand. "Dead on TV?" she repeated, wondering if it would make a different kind of sense if she said it back.

"Dead," he said firmly. "On TV, yes?"

He waved inside the shop, and she found her feet (her very comfortable sneakered feet) taking her inside. Above the counter, a television hung, showing a countdown and a view of a street in Toronto with police barricades blocking off traffic, and a huge crowd gathered.

"Thank you, thank you, thank you," said the little man, and the Redhead pulled her eyes away from the screen. What was he talking about now? "Not you, not you, but thank you too."

She stared. What on earth?

He gestured to the small Asian woman standing behind the counter, and she, apparently much better at this game than the Redhead, turned up the volume of the TV in response.

A familiar voice filled the shop. "…down the very last hour, and my goodness, my goodness indeed. You will *not* believe the turnout. The studio is *packed to the gills* with the ragin' undead, my friends. I haven't seen so many corpses since the last Christmas party at the CBC. I kid, because I love…"

The little man gestured again and the woman lowered the volume again. "Mocklin McLaughlin," he said. "With Dead Girl." He pointed to her again, then at the TV.

"Mocklin McLaughlin…" she tried to put it together. "The talk show guy who has all the crazy celebrities?" She hadn't been a fan, but Dorri was, so she'd watched it a few times. Of course, she'd usually ended up listening more to Dorri talking about all the connections she had to various celebs or their entourages than to the show itself.

That was apparently all she was getting out of the little couple who ran the shop—until the woman held up a hand to warn the Redhead to stay put, and rushed off to the back of the store. The Redhead stood awkwardly with the man until she returned a moment later with something wrapped in brown butchers' paper.

"Brains, good," she said, handing the packet to the Redhead, then made motions toward her mouth. "Good, yes?"

"Thank you," said the Redhead, and walked out into the sunlight in a daze.

She crossed the street without looking either for traffic or to watch for the curb, but made it all the same. Malcolm wasn't in the window anymore, but Kensy Comics loomed large and friendly in a world that had, again, turned on its side.

67.

"Is she here?" Mocklin barked. Garvey and the makeup artist were the only ones in the room—he insisted on that. And since no one had entered or left or texted or called since the *last* time he had asked, Garvey put it down to nerves. Which Mocklin had more often in the singular than the plural, as he had generally demonstrated throughout his years in steely pre-show attitude.

"Relax," Garvey began, but Mocklin wasn't having any of it.

"She's going to screw us, isn't she? We pull out all our favours for the last seven generations and she's a freakin', freakish no-show."

"It's only the half," Garvey soothed. There was no use trying to talk sense to him in this mood; the best he could do was distract him with minutiae. "The band wanted a final sound check but I said it was up to the big boss. Also…"

Mocklin shot him a look to freeze water in the Caribbean. "The band has three minutes. Up the music in the main hall to preshow levels and run the promo. Then the six minute zombie doc with all that cheeseball voiceover and the— what was it? Ten second Christopher Lee cameo? Start the laser show on stage at the three, and bring out the dancing girls right on the hour, just as planned. That gives me what? thirteen and a half minutes to not have to listen to or look at you, and to pull something *spectacular* out of my ass so that you remember *JUST WHO THE DAMN BOSS IS.*"

Garvey shot out of his chair, already on the walkie. Mocklin was on. At least as far as that went, they had nothing to worry about.

A moment later, he stuck his head back in. "She's on her way. And you're gonna *love* it!"

68.

Jerry had pulled in a favour from a connection at a movie

stock car company, and had exceeded even her extremely high expectations.

Geary called the location to make sure there'd be a camera outside to capture her arrival. They were scrambling to get a live feed for the interior of the venue. When he asked for numbers, the P.A. was able to give the best response possible: "SRO. We've got 'em lined up in the halls."

This was going to be *mad*.

At Zombie Central, way back in Pennsylvania, Geary sent his Undead Redhead a text. They were a go.

69.

Morgoni reared upright at the desk. This was not happening. A ridiculous, lowest common denominator low-brow *talk show* was going to scoop her on the story?

The message from Juan Carla was clear. The Baldwin Street Irregulars would zombie up (entirely unrecognizably, judging by the sample pictures Fawn had Instagrammed) and get in line. The announcement of venue and time had been calculated to give zombie aficionados lots of time to arrive and line up on a busy Toronto street, to heighten the intensity even more, Morgoni knew. *Bastards, playing their Mein Kampf Albert Speer mind games.*

This was not a position Morgoni had ever been in before: she felt truly, entirely *helpless.* Someone else had not only found the zombie, they'd secured an interview. Presumably, this would shake the foundations of the whole paranormal investigative world.

Everyone and their lame, blind, ninety year old mother would be joining the field now. You wouldn't be able to get *into* the woods for an alien abduction or lycanthrope sighting without tripping over a million wannabes with cameras and gadgets. Instead of the profession being a profession, it would overflow with glory-seekers, halfwits, and the opportunistic mentally unstable. Even more than it did now.

This was the lowest point of her *life*. Her entire body of work was as good as worthless if she had missed out on a story like this evolving right under her own nose. And it wasn't like she'd been totally clueless. She'd been on the trail—but she'd lost. Mocklin Freakin' McLaughlin, the laughing ape, had scooped V.X. Morgoni, and it was all as good as over for her.

Still, she was a professional—and she owed it to herself to stay that way to the bitter end. She'd watch the live broadcast, and then she'd unplug her hard drive, tear down the wall of research, and even erase the white board.

If she had any less self-respect, she'd put that video from the cafe up, just out of spite—but it would hardly have the impact of a live interview. The best she might have done would be to have sold it in advance of the event to the network in question, or to a rival, but that wasn't her way.

She had, after all, her integrity.

Sighing, head starting to throb with the onset of a powerful headache, Morgoni called up the trailer from the network and the cafe footage, which now seemed less like an amazing opportunity and more like a cruel joke.

And she stopped, cold. Her fingers froze above the rounded

oval of her mouse. *What the…?*

She leaned in closer to the screen, then used control+ to zoom in on the browser screen. Hit play. Hit pause. *Really? No…*

She brought up the window in her editor with the cafe footage, and ran it to the best angle on the Redhead's face. Paused. Pulled up the enhanced screen capture she'd run through the Photoshop filters to remove noise and up the contrast.

Whirled in the chair, ripped the hard copy of the capture off the wall, pressed it to the side of the monitor. Rushed to the other side of the room and—for the first time in months that it had been used—flipped on the overhead light.

Returned to her seat. Stared. Compared. Stared again.

From her room, where she'd been napping, a sleepy Teeny called out, "Morgoni? Everything okay?"

No, it wasn't. And yes, it was. Everything had changed. Again.

Teeny emerged, rubbing her eyes. "Are you all right?"

"Look at this," cawed Morgoni, her voice harsh and stressed. "Come here!"

Actually invited in for the first time ever, Teeny circled the whiteboard barrier. "What's up?"

"Look!" Morgoni said again, urgent. "This isn't the same person, is it?"

"Where did you get this?" Teeny breathed, going cold, and

it wasn't just from the lowered metabolism of the untimely-awoken.

"That redhead is NOT this redhead. Right? There's absolutely no way."

"You're right," said Teeny. The redhead on the right had a longer face, different eyes, a slightly different hairstyle, even though the colour was remarkably similar. The redhead on the left was Sharon.

"I need the Irregulars," Morgoni said, sounding decisive for the first time since Teeny had stumbled out of her bedroom, but still more flustered than she'd ever heard her roommate since they'd tried to live with a guy who played Pong—through his stereo—at all hours of the day and night.

"The…" Teeny asked, not having been acquainted with Morgoni's youthful helpers.

Morgoni tensed like a feral cat ready to pounce—Teeny backed up with alarm as her roommate threw herself from her chair, drawing her cellphone like a pistol. "Fawn," she barked into it as Teeny grabbed the chair before it tipped over. "My place. Now!… Well, plans have changed… I know you've never been here but don't pretend you don't know exactly where it is and how to get here. I trained you too well for that. Grab the other two and get here *stat!*"

Teeny felt as out of breath as if she'd run blocks for a streetcar that refused to stop—and she wasn't even the one having the fit. She'd *never* seen Morgoni like this. And over a picture of Sharon!

Sharon! The focus of Morgoni's zombie hunt, and possibly on her way home *right now.* The fun of hiding Sharon under

Morgoni's nose seemed like a willing invitation to disaster now. She had to get to Malcolm, tell him to *keep Sharon away at all costs,* at least until Morgoni was either out of the apartment or off the warpath.

Then, as she tried to remember where she'd left her own phone, she realized a deadly silence had fallen in the room. She came around the white board partition, and saw Morgoni, standing near the door with a furious, cold look in her eyes. And in her hand…

A bright fuchsia high heel. Sharon must have borrowed Teeny's sneakers after all, but she'd left her own shoes by the door. But really, how could they have known that Morgoni had a clue what Sharon was wearing? Morgoni's mouth pinched into a thin line. "Whose are these, Teeny?"

Final Fantasy

70.

Waglet brought the tea on a tray, with a couple of the thin ginger biscuits his grand-père preferred. He waited while the old man dipped one in his cup and took a slow bite, wiggling the cookie up and down against his two front false teeth until it broke.

"Papa Georges," he said at last. "I did it, just like you used to. I brought someone back from the dead."

"Good, good," said the old man, and picked up the television remote.

"Papa Georges," Waglet tried again. "Did you hear what I said? I made a zombi, just like you told me about back in Haiti."

The old man turned to him, as a rerun of CSI: Miami began to blare from the box in the corner. "Don't be smart with me, boy. We left all that in the old country. No Voodoo here. Your Auntie Cecilia works at the hospital now. They don't like to hear that kind of talk."

It was because Auntie Cecilia worked at the hospital that the news had come to Waglet about Sharon's death, so of course he knew what she did and where. "I know, Papa Georges.

But I am telling you—I brought my friend Sharon back from the dead after she… You don't believe I have the power too? You were a great houngan! Don't you believe your grandson could do the same kind of magic?"

Papa Georges silenced the TV with a flick of his finger against the remote. "Waglet boy, I know you loved those stories. But that's all they were—just stories. Your Auntie Cecilia knows medicine, and because of that many people called her 'mambo.' But we were spinning tales for a young boy, not speaking literally."

Waglet stared. How could the old man say such things? It was as bizarre as having a parent tell you there was no Santa, but only after you returned from a visit to his workshop at the North Pole. "I'll show you!" he said, passionately, and without waiting for a response, he flew down the stairs to his room.

Sharon II was tucked into her hollow log, making the soft, comforting noises she did when she was content. "I am sorry, Sharon II," said Waglet, as he opened the top of the cage. "I need to show my grandfather the truth."

Something in his tone or the roughness of his touch must have startled her; the pig shied, suddenly becoming a wiggling, slightly damp ball of fur with small claws scrabbling at his fingers. She wriggled herself right out of his hands, and darted with surprising guinea pig speed up the stairs.

At least she was going in the right direction. Waglet thought as he chased her, pausing only to grab some wilted celery in case he needed to lure her out of a hiding place.

But as he ascended, the worst possible thing happened: back from her shift as an RN at the hospital, Auntie Cecilia opened the front door and came in with a hearty, "What are you still up for, old man?"

Sharon II, sensing freedom, darted between her legs and out into the little front yard, Waglet in pursuit. "I'll be back, Auntie!" he shouted over his shoulder. "I need to show you something!"

If he could catch her.

71.

She put the final touches on her cheeks—just a bit more shadow into the bones to really make them pop, and then enough powder to make sure she stayed matte under the lights. Good thing she was more likely to be too cool than nervous. She'd have to remember to seem excited to be there: wouldn't do to insult Mocklin's ego by acting like she was doing *him* a favour. Credit where credit was due, after all. If today came off, she'd be set for life if she played it right. Merchandising. Appearances. Talks. Cons. A book deal. Oh, yeah. It was *all* within her beautifully undead grasp.

And wouldn't Sharon be proud, that her name was carrying on, that her story wouldn't be forgotten?

The Undead Redhead, stiletto-pumped, primped, hair so shiny it would gleam on stage, put her retied package under her arm, centered that very special pendant between her breasts (oh so stunningly displayed by her very expensive push-up bra) and left her hotel room.

72.

Waglet ran until he got to the park, the little pig surprisingly fleet leading him on. Every time he got close to her she'd run again. It was crazy—he was chasing an undead guinea pig through Kensington Market, and no one, no one at all was paying attention to him.

Finally, he saw her nestled in the grass by the foot of a tree, munching on what looked like a rotten apple core. Good—now was his chance to trap her. He took off his jacket and snuck closer, trying to stay out of her line of sight. He had no idea how good her eyesight was, but Sharon hadn't seemed to have any problems except with changing light levels.

"Good Sharon II," he crooned. "Don't worry about me; I'm just in the park to enjoy myself, just like you…"

He tossed, and the coat went perfectly over the pig's stubby body. He scooped her up, jacket and all, and uncovered her head just enough to feed her a piece of slightly slimy celery from his pocket. Now *that* was going to leave a nasty stain!

Sharon II wiggled a little bit, but seemed content to sit in his arms and nibble instead of actively trying to escape. Waglet breathed slower, calming himself. Now to return home and prove to his family…

But something took his attention. A zombie? Really?

The girl had a cut across her forehead, a flap of skin hanging from its side. Her clothing was ragged and she carried a large, obviously rubber machete.

As Waglet watched, she was joined by three other girls, also dressed as zombies, and a boy done up the same.

What was going on?

Looking around at Augusta Street, he could see a few other people in zombie gear as well. It wasn't the right time of year for Toronto's Zombie Walk, and he hadn't heard about any conventions that might attract costumed attendees.

"Excuse me!" he called out to the nearest zombie group. It looked like everyone was headed in the same direction—north toward College. There had to be something major going on. Or some kind of crazy stunt—would a bunch of zombies suddenly start to dance in the middle of the street?

A zombie couple paused and let him catch up.

"What's going on?" said Waglet, feeling like he was going to lose his breath all over again.

"Oh my God," said the girl. "Is that supposed to be a zombie guinea pig? So *cute!*"

73.

"Hey," said Jason as the Redhead came in.

"I have to talk to Malcolm," she said, dazed, dropping a mushy-looking brown parcel on the counter followed by her backpack.

Jason waved her to the rear of the shop. "He… stepped out."

"Smoking is terrible for your health," she said absently,

hardly looking at him, and made her way to the back door and out into the alley.

"Sharon!" Malcolm said when she came out. He was leaning against the wall, shredding a cigarette with his fingers. A pile at his feet attested to the fact this wasn't his first.

"I…" she said. "There's another me. Not me. A woman with red hair who looks a bit like me, I guess. But she's going to be on some kind of special live Mocklin McLaughlin today, to tell people what it's like to be a real zombie."

His brows furrowed. "You're not the only one?"

She shook her head emphatically. "I am, or I think I am. She's an impostor. She's *pretending to be me.*"

He was silent for a moment. "Okay. So, that's good, right?"

"Good?" she said, a little sharply. "No! I mean, here I am stuck as an undead and slightly rotting person, all my old friends running like rats off the Titanic, and all because— well, if you forget the zombie thing—mostly because I'm standing up for myself for the first time. Everyone who's out of my life now obviously never liked the real me, even without the dying thing. I was trying so hard to please everyone and fit in, and I never had to because you like me, Teeny likes me… Waglet liked the real me even if I never showed her off much. Deanna likes me, and I like her too, especially now neither of us are bending over like crazy trying to please people who only want something from us, not who want to be around us…"

She ground to a halt. He waited, not sure what to say. Finally, she said, "I can't let someone *else* take away who I am and make me into some kind of… undead nonentity."

Expectantly, unsure, she extended her hands in a gesture of near-helplessness. Malcolm found Teeny's advice going through his head. "Sharon," he began slowly. "Teeny says I put a lot of pressure on people to, well, to live up to my own high expectations. Maybe that's true. But I do like you for who and what you are. I guess I don't totally believe you're really dead, but that's my problem, not yours. When we met, I said you need to have self-respect. Well, I have to respect you to, for exactly what you think you are not what I think you should be. Okay? So if you want to find some way to contact this person and tell her to stop pretending she's you, I'm there. Right beside you, all the way. Everything else is my shit to deal with."

She smiled, but there was more she needed to say, and it was *urgent*. "Thank you," the Redhead said, with fire in her crazy flat eyes. "But right now, it's not about writing a polite email or two. I'm going down to that TV station and call that bitch out."

74.

"Where did you get a *crossbow?*" Teeny was running after Morgoni whose longer legs ate up the pavement far faster. Talking had done no good; explanations sounded pretty weak when you thought about it. *Sorry, roommie. Yeah, I asked a zombie to live with us. Yeah, I know it's kind of your thing, but hey! I'm sure we'd all have had guacamole together sooner or later.*

Then, Teeny had tried to distract Morgoni with other roommate stuff, like if there *was* going to be a zombie living with them, would she want money for produce that went bad, or could Sharon just have it because she'd be throwing it out anyhow.

All in all, she'd held the other woman up maybe ten minutes, but it hadn't cooled Morgoni down one bit. Instead, Morgoni had used the time to oil and otherwise check out the pair of crossbows that apparently lived in her closet in the bedroom she hardly ever entered. By the time the knock sounded on the door announcing the arrival of Morgoni's crew (Morgoni had *staff?*) Teeny had almost run out of ideas of how to divert her from what apparently was her new and unshakeable plan.

Teeny hung back, but stayed in sight as Morgoni went to the door and opened it to three pint-sized zombies of indeterminate sex. "Fawn," Morgoni said to one, handing the smallest her precious video camera. "You're on point. Record everything, and we'll edit it down if it's too gory for broadcast."

To the tallest, she gave one crossbow and a package of quarrels. "Juan Carla, I hope you're up for this." The child, a girl Teeny thought, nodded, and took it solemnly. Morgoni went on, to the third, probably a boy. "Dibber, I need you to watch my 6… My back, idiot. Weren't you listening when we went through this?"

And with that, she took the second crossbow, shouldered it, and lead the way out of the apartment at fast speed, Baldwin Street Irregulars at her heels. Teeny grabbed her keys and followed as fast as she could. *My God, they were going to KILL Sharon!*

75.

The hearse pulled up outside the Mocklin McLaughlin Show, and the crowd of zombies, vampires, and other undead creatures erupted in applause, not to mention howls and moans. Mocklin's obviously overwhelmed security cleared a path, but it was clear almost immediately that this was one guest who didn't have any interest in arriving either incognito or without chaos.

A pair of women in chauffeur uniforms emerged from the front of the vehicle and circled it. One opened up the rear door of the hearse, and the other slid out a flat panel on which rested, of course, a coffin.

Much more easily than Sharon had escaped from her untimely interment, the Undead Redhead lifted the lid smoothly on well-oiled hinges, and stepped out onto the sidewalk, aided by her chauffeurs. The crowd erupted again, straining against the security guards who obviously had not expected this kind of crazy reaction from this kind of new and supposedly minor celebrity.

Walking between the two chauffeurs, the Undead Redhead started toward the studio doors, waving, mouth quirked in her best sexy moue. And dammit, the heels were *hot.*

76.

Waglet saw the unlikely fivesome coming toward him at speed—the crazy woman with dreads who seemed to end up in the same place as Sharon a little too often, the pretty girl in her early twenties, and the three pipsqueak zombies. He hugged Sharon II to his chest where she sat comfortably enough inside his jacket.

But instead of continuing toward him, the crazy one (*was she carrying a CROSSBOW?*) diverted toward Kensy Comics where he'd seen Sharon a few times now, talking mostly with Malcolm or the owner. Shockingly, Waglet could see one of the small ones also carried a crossbow. Their leader waved for Crossbow Kid and the one with the camera to go down the alley (*setting a trap?*) and for the other to follow her into the comic shop. The pretty twenty-something seemed agitated, nearly frantic, and desperate to stop the other woman.

As they vanished inside, Waglet picked up the pace. *Sharon was in danger, he could almost feel it!* Either he was very connected to her, or he'd watched just a few too many episodes of The Walking Dead.

Deciding the pretty girl was already on Crossbow Woman's tail, he elected to follow the other two down the alley. *I'm coming, Sharon!*

77.

It wasn't so much that Mocklin had run out of material, but he was too old a hand at this to not notice when a crowd was getting restless. It took everything he had not to call attention to the fact and dig himself a serious hole: *So what next, kids? If she doesn't show in the next five minutes, do you all rush the stage and bite me a new one?* That's the way comics died. Mostly not literally, but dying on stage was a million times more scary than that. There was only one kind of immortality Mocklin respected, and that required the undying attention and interest of *fans*.

Suddenly, the music changed. Mocklin took the hint instantly, raising his hands in the air like it was his instruction to the booth to put on the new cue. As subtly as he could, he shot a look to Garvey in the wings, who gave him a big thumbs up. Yes, his Undead Redhead had arrived.

78.

Jason tried to greet Morgoni as she came in, heading furiously for the back of the shop, trailed closely by Dibber and Malcolm's sister. "Teeny?" he said. Something was very wrong.

Morgoni zeroed in, laser sharp, on Sharon's backpack sitting on the counter. Without a word, she unzipped it, and the bouquet fell out. She shook it in Jason's direction, and without thinking about what he was saying, told her, "She's out back with Malcolm."

That was enough for Morgoni. She didn't wait for permission but went straight through the back room like a freight train, then motioned for Dibber to freeze while she put an ear to the door.

Behind them, Teeny wasn't sure whether she should follow or find some weapon of her own. "Call the cops!" she said to Jason, then, "no, forget I said that. Don't under any circumstances call the cops. Oh God, I hope we won't need an ambulance. How would you explain that one?"

Morgoni opened the door quietly and cautiously, just in time to hear the Redhead make her oath. She flung the door open the rest of the way, and lowered the crossbow at her adversary, saying "You're not going anywhere, freak."

The Redhead whirled toward the open end of the alley as Morgoni positioned herself beside Dibber who was watching her back maybe a little too literally. "Keep that door closed," she hissed at him. Idiot.

Fawn with her camera and Juan Carla with the other crossbow, levelled but shaky, had entered the alley, effectively blocking off the only other escape route.

Morgoni was irritated to see that yes, there was a young man standing with the zombie, the loser who worked for the loser inside. That could make for complications. But she was here to do a job, and she'd do it.

"Die, zombie," she said.

Her hands on the crossbow wavered. The trigger finger felt sluggish, wouldn't engage with the mechanism.

In front of her, the zombie she'd been chasing stared at her with what looked like sympathy. "It isn't that easy, is it?" she said kindly. "I know—same thing happened when I tried to eat you. And then I found out it would have just been a waste anyhow, in so many ways."

Morgoni gritted her teeth, and tried again. "Juan Carla!" she barked. "Take your shot!"

But out of the corner of her eye, she could see that the child had already lowered her crossbow and was staring in amazement at the Redhead. A small smile was on her face. "Awesome," she breathed.

The Redhead turned her head to look at the little girl. "Thanks," she said. "Although I think the colour does *not* suit me at all."

The girl laughed shyly, and her companion emerged from behind the camera long enough to smile as well at the Redhead.

"Fawn!" spat Morgoni, and the camera came back up. The

crossbow did not.

"It's okay," said the Redhead. "I would probably be a little freaked out if I knew about me. But—here's what you've got to know. I don't eat people; I'm not infectious; and I know you've been looking for me."

Morgoni eyed her suspiciously. The crossbow dropped an inch but still stayed on vital areas of the Redhead's anatomy. Or areas that would be vital in a live person.

Malcolm put a hand on the Redhead's shoulder, and said, "Morgoni, she's not dangerous."

"Says you," said Morgoni. "What was it? Bio-infection? Toxic waste? Government experiments?"

"Voodoo," said the Redhead, genuinely amused. "I was dead, and then I wasn't." Then, with pleasure, she called out, "Waglet!"

Morgoni turned, and saw a young boy had joined Dibber, probably in his early teens to Dibber's twelve. In the newcomer's jacket, something moved, and a guinea pig head poked out from the V of the zipper. "Sharon!" he exclaimed. "Are you in trouble?"

"I don't think so," said the Redhead, fixing Morgoni with a steady gaze. "Morgoni, right? I think we're roommates," she said. "Sorry this is the way we're meeting."

Morgoni tried once more. "Get your hands up!" she barked, but the Redhead shook her head.

"No, it's not like that at all. There's something more important going on, for you *and* for me, right at this very minute."

Morgoni stared, then said, "Mocklin McLaughlin?"

"There's someone who's pretending to be me about to go live on national television. She stole my identity! And without you, I don't think I have a hope to prove it."

Malcolm moved in closer. "Sharon, do you really…?"

The Redhead put her arm around him. "I think Morgoni wants to prove I exist as much as I do. And I think she's got as little patience with liars and bullies. Or for misinformation being spread by the media."

Teeny, trying to keep quiet near the doorway, smiled into her hand. Sharon had just hit at least a couple of Morgoni's biggest buttons.

Now the crossbow in Morgoni's hands drooped and took aim at the pavement in front of her feet. With a little bit of crossness in her voice as if unable to allow herself to sound enthusiastic about anything, she said, "Where is this thing and how do we get there?"

"Not too far," said Malcolm, "but I'll see if we can all pile into Jason's car." He squeezed Sharon, then disengaged, giving her a quick look to see if she thought she had the situation under control. When she nodded, he went back toward the door to Kensy. "Okay. I'll get the keys."

The Redhead looked around at the crowd that had ended up gathered in the alley. "Will there be enough room?"

She felt a small pressure on her fingers, and a little warm hand slipped into hers. At her side now, little Fawn said, "I can sit on your lap."

79.

"Zombies, vampires, and other members of Toronto's Undead elite: the one, the only, the miraculous—Undead Redhead!" Mocklin thundered. This was it, this was TV gold.

The lights came down, the spots swung together on a single piece of stage, and into it walked…

He was glad to see they'd miked her properly. He could see the glimmer of the mic wire in her hairline. And what a hairline! That colour was all Hollywood. Couldn't possibly be natural. He wasn't sure the tits were either, but the attitude, now that was pristine. The girl was either a natural, or the slickest pro this side of Oprah.

"Hello," she said, so quietly it was almost a whisper. The big room fell silence.

She smiled. "Thank you all so much for coming, and thank you to Mocklin as well for letting me stand here in front of you today."

Yeah, all Hollywood. Now she was trying to cut him out of his own show. Time to reassert…

"The Undead Redhead!" he shouted, a little miffed that so little light had been left on him. In the booth, the engineers scrambled to refocus at least a couple of the spots on him. Good. They could keep their jobs.

She obviously didn't want to cede any control back to Mocklin, but at least allowed him to lead her over to a couple of stools set out for the interview. She waited until he was seated, then made a big show of getting onto hers and settling her short skirt over her thighs. "Mocklin!" she said, pretending to be more upset than she was. "You want everyone to see my netherworld parts?"

The crowd roiled in hilarity. This was good, and not good. It was great to have a fab guest, but only as long as she remembered whose show it was!

"Darlin'," he said, shooting the audience one of his patented ironic looks. "Even with all the dead folks here today, I'm sure any part of you would be enough to cause an instant resurrection."

More waves of laughter, and this time he smiled. *Yeah, they could eat out of her hand for a bit, but only if they knew who their daddy was.*

80.

Garvey grinned into his headset. Usually he didn't like the technicians to see how happy he was, but this was already a triumph. He never figured the only thing better than a dead celebrity would be an undead one, live on the show. They never taught you that one in journalism school.

Suddenly, he felt a tug on the elbow of his jacket. He looked around, then way, way down to see a tiny zombie-girl holding a crossbow. She handed him a folded piece of paper, and he took it, perplexed. Unfolding it, he read the brief message, written in square letters in thick Sharpie: *YOUR ZOMBIE IS A FAKE, AND WE CAN PROVE IT LIVE.*

Really.

The tiny girl raised the crossbow, not enough to threaten but maybe enough to show she meant business. Behind her, Garvey now saw an odd group of people—two more kids dressed as zombies, a slim black boy, an older guy in a comic book shirt, and a couple of good-looking kids in their twenties, also of African heritage but more mocha-skinned than the younger boy. And now moving into sight were an androgynous woman with a watchcap and dreads, and…

"Holy crap," said Garvey. He recognized the dress and the shoes, not to mention the bouquet, from the viral video their guest had claimed as the proof of her demise. But suddenly, Garvey found himself reconsidering at speed: yes, this new young woman had that same unlikely brilliant red hair and the zombie-pale skin. But she—she *looked* far more like the girl in the video. And she looked pissed.

"Ladies and gentlemen," he whispered into his headset. "I need another couple more lavalier mics down to the right wing. *NOW*."

81.

She was in her glory. She gave Mocklin pert and flirty answers to his questions, and matched him laugh for laugh. Maybe managed a few more actually: she could ask him after they wrapped, because for *sure* he was counting. It was delicious, watching him pretend he didn't care how much the audience was loving her.

And they *did* love her. She'd sent one of the 'chauffeurs' to set the explosive package at the front of the stage where it would make the most impact (and not cause any bodily harm; that was the last thing she wanted, although it wouldn't be the end of the world she figured), but it was looking like pyrotechnics were all but redundant. Who needed fireworks when you *were* a bloody spectacle?

"Folks," Mocklin was saying, then put his hand to his earbud headset. *What was this?* He listened for a moment, then went on, shooting her a glance that abruptly seemed to have cooled.

Holding her face very still in the same sly grin she'd perfected for the Undead Redhead character in front of the mirror, she said, "One more thing, Mocklin," but he cut her off.

"Hang on, just one second. We've got a surprise guest, and I think you're going to want to stand to welcome her along with me."

Well, that didn't give her much of an option, did it? Pretending not to mind, pretending in fact to be *enthusiastic* about giving up the full attention of the audience, she stood. Daring a little contact, she snuggled herself into Mocklin's shoulder. "I hope it's not a justice of the peace—or an exorcist. I don't roll that way."

But she was losing them—and a moment later, she was as stunned as the crowd (more stunned—after all, they *came* here to be shocked and surprised) as a lone figure emerged from the wings, teetering on a pair of fuchsia high heels.

She took it all in: the hair, the dress, the bouquet, and the face. The face of… "Sharon!" she gasped, despite herself.

"Zombies, vampires, and all that spooky jazz," boomed Mocklin, clearly loving it, "I give you… *another* Undead Redhead. Now, ladies, can either of you prove to me which one of you is in fact a zombie, and which of you is just a fake?"

The Redhead came forward, not quite the polished presence as the woman already on stage. She looked a little frail even, teetering on the fuchsia heels as if she either wasn't particularly good on them or had the mother of all blisters. It looked like makeup had maybe tried to give her a bit of colour on her cheeks and lips, but really, all that did was heighten the unnatural palour of her skin.

Mocklin felt an odd unease—not something he was used to, not for years and years. There *was* something troubling about this new girl, with her bluish veining creating a subtle lace on her face and arms. He shivered, quite beside himself suddenly. He'd had no particular reaction to the first "Undead Redhead," but this new young woman…

A hush fell over the crowd. Sharon Backovic, reanimated corpse and former bridesmaid, stepped right up to the front of the stage.

"Hi," she said. "My name is Sharon, and I was killed—well, it was an accident, but I hit my head trying to keep a hold on this stupid thing." She shook the bouquet, and some camellia petals drifted down into the crowd. One zombie girl reached out and caught a couple on her palm, and pressed them to her cheek.

The Redhead smiled. "I woke up a few days after my death, in a coffin, in a hearse, on my way to my own burial. Fortunately, before they put me in the ground. I don't think I would have been digging my way out anytime soon."

Behind her, the impostor—Undead Redhead Mark II— vibrated with barely suppressed rage. No one, not even the real Sharon Backovic, was going to steal her thunder.

And just how was this even possible? *She'd* invented the reanimated Sharon idea. *She'd* done the social network marketing. If this—whoever she was thought she could walk in at the last moment and take all the credit… well, she didn't know what she was up against.

The Redhead was still talking, her audience rapt and attentive. "You know what's funny? It wasn't as hard to be dead as it was to deal with how… inconvenient my presence seemed to be to people. I would have probably been okay with people running in terror—and yes, a few did. But people I really thought I could count on, people I thought were my friends, acted like it was just too much trouble to be around me any more, and that's what really hurt. But the good thing is, if they didn't like who I am, if I had to be pretend to be someone else to get along with them, well, that hurt me a *lot* and couldn't really have done them any good either. Right?"

Mocklin found himself fixated on the Redhead's cleavage, and not for the usual reason. He could *see* into her deep incision, could see the slightly ham-handed stitches used to close up the ugly gash, done by someone who knew that cosmetically, it was really irrelevant to do a good job.

"Mocklin! Mocklin!" came Garvey's voice, buzzing through his earbud. "This is good, but don't lose it, bud. Get her to give you proof—she's got some kind of expert here; we're wiring her up right now."

Mocklin shook his head, making a bit of a show of it. If you had a lapse of any kind, bring the audience in on it, and make it a joke. "Sweetheart, sweetheart, just hang on a moment." He joined the Redhead at the stage edge, and put an arm around her. "We have two zombie-claimants on the show all of a sudden, and—to borrow a bit from another show—*there can be only one.* So what about it, little dead lady? I hear you have some proof for us."

"I do, Mocklin," said the Redhead.

The Undead Redhead, her Southern Flame glowing under the lights almost as brightly as the other woman's, tried to get comfortable on her stool again. If there was one thing she understood, it was timing, and this interruption had to run its course before she could do anything about the disaster. *How was this happening?* She'd kill to be able to run off stage and call Geary, but even a single mistake at this time would complete her fall. No, she had to stick it out and wait for her chance. And seriously—proof? Of being something that didn't exist?

Not that this girl didn't look even more like the late Sharon Backovic than she did…

From the wings, an awkward, androgynous figure emerged, even more hesitant than the Redhead had been. She carried a laptop which she carried to the center of the stage and set on the stool Mocklin had previously occupied.

"And who is this?" said Mocklin to her, amused but with fairly low hopes of another great discovery personality-wise. She could barely bring herself to face the crowd.

"This is Morgoni," said the Redhead, jumping to the rescue. *Good,* thought Mocklin, *at least she got that dead air can kill a show.* "We started off as enemies, but Morgoni knows who I am better than anyone—as much of a surprise to me as to anyone."

Mocklin gave her some room as Morgoni tapped keys. On

the monitors above and around the stage, a video started to play. Mocklin recognized it, vaguely, some video that had gone viral a few months before.

Morgoni's voice was shaky, and not quite loud enough to reach the microphone. "You may remember this video…" she began, and Mocklin leaned in to adjust the mic towards her mouth. She jumped, almost knocking the laptop off the stool. Then, giving him a dirty look, she rallied and began again with more confidence. "This is a viral video that racked up millions of hits on YouTube…"

82.

In the wings, Malcolm watched with his arm around Teeny. The three Irregulars had been convinced to lower their weapons (Dibber was especially hard to convince, since he'd been in possession of Morgoni's crossbow for the least amount of time) and a P.A. had led them over to the craft table where they were happily huddled over a laptop they'd somehow borrowed, munching cookies and drinking probably way too much pop.

A little ways from Malcolm and his sister, Waglet sat on a stool near the wall, eyeing Malcolm with suspicion.

When he was sure that Sharon was doing just fine on stage, Malcolm motioned to Teeny that he was going to go and speak with the younger boy. She gave him a quick squeeze and a look that communicated just fine without words: "Be careful, moron!" *Sisterly love is strong in this one,* Malcolm thought, and braced himself to talk to Waglet.

The younger boy pretended as long as he could that Malcolm wasn't actually walking toward him, focusing instead on the zombie guinea pig still tucked into his jacket. "Hey," said Malcolm, and Waglet looked up. Malcolm saw a certain amount of jealousy there, for certain, but also fear. What did the kid think—he was coming over to *fight* him for Sharon?

Waglet nodded in acknowledgement of his greeting, but was clearly planning on let Malcolm do all the work.

Malcolm cleared his throat as quietly as he could, still garnering a bit of a dirty look from a stage hand. Awkwardly, he moved in closer and put his mouth near Waglet's ear. "She did great out there, huh?" he said.

Waglet waved at his ear as if to tell the other young man that he was tickling his ear with his proximity, but Malcolm took that as bravado as much as a serious complaint. Now, though, Waglet did answer.

"She is great," he said.

Malcolm nodded, and, inspired by Teeny's advice from the night before, waited.

From the stage came Morgoni's voice, gaining in confidence with every sentence. She'd apparently given her footage to someone to run up to the booth, and was screening some scene she had with Sharon in it, explaining step by step how she'd come to realize that Sharon was in fact a zombie and not just a girl who looked like one.

Waglet listened for a moment, then said softly, without looking at Malcolm, "If you hurt her, I will kill you. And *not* bring you back."

Malcolm tried to hide his smile. "Fair enough," he said.

Then, another inspiration, "Can I hold your guinea pig?"

Despite his attempt to keep a stern face, Waglet now smiled a bit too, and gently removed the softly snorting pig from his pocket. Malcolm smelled the same slightly rotten scent that Sharon had, a little stronger than on her, and without the hint of formaldehyde that he was now starting to find oddly enticing on her… "Cute pig," he said.

Waglet watched Malcolm's hands, as if expecting him to mistreat the animal, but started to relax before long. Then abruptly, the boy said, "Do you think Sharon will come and show to my grandfather how I succeeded? He used to tell me about voodoo, but he was lying I think. I brought her back, and he doesn't believe me."

"I'm sure she'd love to," Malcolm said, and Waglet nodded, a little happier. "She's good out there, isn't she?" he said.

"Awesome," agreed Malcolm. "And I don't think this is going to be the last time she does it, either."

83.

Morgoni wrapped up her presentation with a flourish—an unexpected one. Just as she neared the end of her evidence, the P.A. who'd been wrangling the Irregulars lost track of them, and all three ran out onto stage, surrounding their "boss," all chattering at once.

Morgoni hardly missed a beat, and the kids could apparently care less that they were in front of a crowd of people *and* the cameras shooting a live television broadcast. Fawn had reclaimed the video camera and was trying to do her job, shooting everything of interest in case it could be used in the podcast. The other two had the crossbows (unloaded, the Redhead saw thankfully).

Behind her, just to the left of center stage, the Undead Redhead was indecisive probably for the first time ever in front of an audience. She was *not* used to being upstaged, and her options for getting back on top were fading fast. All she had left were the necklace and the explosives. At least, so far the evidence was in favour of the other Sharon being a real zombie, but nothing had been said about her being a fake. She could still salvage things.

While Morgoni was distracted, she jumped up and went to the power position the Redhead had previously claimed at the front of the stage. She beamed out at the audience, who was now viewing her with what she could only describe as suspicion. Waves of it came off them. It was Hail Mary time—now or never.

"Sharon Backovic," she said loudly, over the chatter of the Irregulars and Morgoni's failing attempts to either rein them in or introduce them, "You are my hero. But no matter what your friend says, you know you're not really a zombie."

It was breaking all the rules of the stage: never admit to an illusion; never let them see behind the curtain. But it was literally all she could think of.

"Mocklin McLaughlin," she said, pulling him by his arm to her side of the stage, "may I introduce to you a true medical marvel. Sharon Backovic, an amazing woman who survived death, survived nearly being *buried alive in her own coffin,* and who has come here today with me to talk about this very real, very scary issue. We talk a lot in the media about when life begins, but the truth is, we know just as little about *when it ends.*"

She could almost see the wheels turning in Mocklin's head. Someone was apparently also communicating with him through his headset as well, and he was calculating and recalculating the angles. Follow her lead? Call her out? It was a presenter's nightmare: getting answers to a question you never asked.

A laugh cut in to her frantic spinning, the repositioning of her appearance that she was trying to make so calmly, as if it was all part of the show. The other Redhead, the one she was now absolutely sure was in fact the same Sharon Backovic whose memorial page she'd created and maintained, the inspiration for her trip to Toronto…

Sharon Backovic, the Redhead, the one and only original Undead Redhead, was laughing.

The sound cut through the room, and the crowd of dressed-up zombie fans—joined in.

Suddenly Morgoni, who had calmed the Irregulars and finally got out of them what they were trying to tell her, tapped Mocklin on the shoulder, and handed him a note. *"YOUR ZOMBIE IS A FAKE, AND WE CAN PROVE IT LIVE?"* he read.

Irritated, she motioned for him to turn it over. "HER REAL NAME IS PHYLLIS HOEGSWANKER AND SHE'S AN UNSUCCESSFUL ACTRESS FROM PHILADELPHIA."

The Undead Redhead gasped. Sharon stopped laughing, and looked at her with sympathy, maybe even pity.

"Is it true?" asked Mocklin in his best "here's the real scoop" voice.

She didn't answer, frozen, feeling ridiculed and, for the first time in her life, unhappy to be in the spotlight.

"Well, *Phyllis?"* Mocklin said, and something in her just snapped, broken, cracked right in half.

It wasn't fair! It was *NOT FAIR.* She'd worked pretty damn hard at this identity, and to have someone, some *other fake dead person* saunter in and take it all away was *intolerable.* It was *NOT GOING TO HAPPEN.*

"You are a fake, a total fake!" she screamed. "I hate you! I hate you! I wish I'd never heard about you. Your death wasn't tragic, it was ridiculous! And coming back on live television is a *STUNT.* A stupid, attention-seeking *stunt!"*

And with that, she reached up to her neck and pressed the two ends of the cylindrical pendant hanging there together.

The Last Book In The Universe

84.

The ELF pulse swept through the auditorium, through backstage, and half a block in each direction. Although the infamous "brown note" had eluded researchers and myth-debunkers alike (a good thing for everyone present, and for the state of their underwear), a less caustic but no less debilitating "green note" had been found.

Instead of releasing the bowels of everyone within its range, the green note merely affected the central nervous system, sending wracking pains through the stomach and gut and a feeling of nausea that, while passing quickly, was nonetheless extremely intense for a good couple of seconds.

Every single living soul within that area of that Extremely Low Frequency pulse's effect—that lovely little device stolen from a military arms fair by a Philadelphian called Geary and smuggled into Canada on a chain by a woman called Phyllis Hoegswanker pretending to be a zombie—every single living soul doubled over in intense pain. Most fell to their knees or collapsed to the floor.

But not Sharon.

A moment after the pulse, the former and debunked Undead Redhead Phyllis Hoegswanker lifted her head enough to see

Sharon Backovic coming toward her. Except for what seemed to be a genetic unsteadiness on those high heels, she was just fine. Utterly, and totally unaffected by the ELF.

"You're real," she breathed, and accepted Sharon's hand to help her straighten.

"My plumbing wasn't put back in right after the autopsy," Sharon said, "I think."

It was too much for her to process. Now that she was closer, she could see what Mocklin had—the way the Y-incision from her postmortem examination had gone *into* her body, and how a little hint of bone could even be seen at its deepest point, how her eyes were definitely not the eyes of a living woman.

"It's okay," Sharon said softly, "I get it. It's hard to be yourself, to figure it out and live with it. I get it."

The niceness was almost worse than having her angry would have been. What right did this bitch have to be generous and accepting? She would have *killed* someone who stole her identity, even if it was just to rip off her credit card numbers. She would have *revenge,* not empathy.

Mocklin was straightening now too, and the rest of the auditorium was starting a slow recovery as well, and all apparently becoming aware faster or slower that Sharon, alone of everyone in range, had not suffered at all, whatever the cause of the debilitating, crippling pulse that had rendered everyone on the verge of puking up all over their ripped zombie costumes.

It was now or never to get away, to fade into the city. Somehow they knew her name, but she wasn't travelling under that. Geary helped her out with that one. All she had to do was get out of the building, and vanish.

Time for a little bang.

85.

Malcolm had just gotten to his feet and was helping Teeny up when the explosion bowled them back over. Terrified, only able to think about Sharon's safety, not sure if he'd heard a bomb or a gunshot, he barrelled onto stage.

The smoke was thick there; he crashed into a stool and then into Mocklin. "Sharon!" he yelled.

He put out his arms, and advanced slower, now unsure how close he was to the edge of the stage. Then, in the slowly dispersing fog, he heard her voice. "Malcolm!"

Gingerly, they worked their ways toward each other. Their fingers touched first, then Malcolm pull her into a full embrace. "You're okay?" he said, not caring that his voice was carried over the mic to the speakers around the hall.

She laughed. "What more can happen to me?" she said, then louder, not leaving his arms but speaking for the benefit of the crowd now, "Everyone—don't worry. It was a flash bomb. No one up here is hurt. Is there anyone down on the floor who needs help?"

Malcolm stepped back, and let her work. It was pretty inspiring, the way she just recognized the problem and went straight at it looking for a solution. He wondered how much dying had really changed her, and how much differently she would have handled things before. Was it possible for death to actually make life more worth living, and worth protecting?

He felt a hand on his shoulder. "Where's the other one?" said Mocklin, his voice a little hoarse from whatever had been expelled from the bomb. There was a taste of powder, like talcum maybe, in the air, and even though the worst of it had settled (making everything as white as Sharon's skin), Malcolm felt a tickle in his own throat.

"Gone, I think," Malcolm replied. He could see most of the stage now and into the crowd. Only one redhead, undead or otherwise, was on the stage, and it was the real, the authentic, *his* Sharon.

Mocklin whispered something, his voice apparently giving out a little or at least dried out from the dust. "What?" Malcolm asked.

He repeated himself, over the growing sound from the earbud—Garvey's voice shouting for instructions and for clarification on what had happened. "Great fucking night," said Mocklin McLauglin, and slumped onto the edge of the stage, grinning like a maniac.

86.

She knocked over a kid at a street corner. He was in the process of flipping up his board and hardly seemed to notice —probably well stoned. That was all for the better; she hardly needed *more* cops chasing her.

He probably wouldn't even notice she'd lifted his hat, or would figure he'd lost it on his own merits. She stuffed her red hair under the ball cap, pulled the brim down, and kept running.

When she thought she'd gone far enough to elude immediate pursuit, she slipped into what seemed to be a combination tattoo parlour and bar, and took a stool at one end.

Okay. They had her real name. But it wasn't like that was the one she'd used for a very, long time. It wasn't the one on her passport, for example, so at least she'd have no trouble getting out of the country, even it it meant abandoning her stuff at the hotel. No big loss.

While the bartender was bringing her a scotch, she felt a slight pressure on one of her shoulders, and looked up and into the mirror to see a trio of white-faced black-clad weirdos surrounding her.

Her kind of people.

They looked a little menacing, but when the tallest of them spoke, his voice was honey.

"What's your story, doll?"

And from the ashes of her last plan, a new one started to form…

87.

Three days later, in a park near a Kensington fruit market, a homeless man talked philosophy and current events with a cracklady of his acquaintance who had only one thing to say about Toronto's newest celebrity:

"She's not a zombie, though. She's on crack!"

88.

**From the case files of V. X. Morgoni,
cryptoparapsychocriminologist**

My first appearance on the Mocklin McLaughlin show aired
tonight, and barely had my image left the screen but who
should text? That little weasel of a bastard who still
laughingly calls himself ILLUMINATED_ SEEKER.
Except for the timing, I would have expected some kind of
message accusing me of calling the CRA to advise them of
exactly how much he's been cheating on his taxes (which of
course he can't prove), but no.

Believe it or not, the little prick (and I speak
euphemistically but with expectations that the term is a
literal truth as well) – the little prick was calling to
CONGRATULATE ME on my segment and see if I still
wanted his help getting into Beta Kappa to check out their
paranormal disturbances.

Un-fucking-believable. Last week, he was courting a liberal
arts major with an IQ barely north of her bra size, and now
he can't stop telling me how 'amazing' he thinks I am.

Well, moron, I've seen where that compliment *COMES*
from, so no fucking thanks. If you were *ANYWHERE* near
my level of intellect or integrity, you wouldn't have
followed your little pointer away from truth-seeking in the
first place, and you'd have known my quality without
waiting for some shlepping television pop culture preacher
to validate it.

I can't stand the mentality of someone that only loves what
other people value. And I *know* that's the case with him,
because I have it on good authority (from a joint

Dibber/Fawn investigation) that he only wanted the blue-haired girl in the first place because one of the Beta Kap boys was dating her.

Mocklin and his flunky Garvey are of course the lowest kind of scum—only interested in sensationalism, mass market appeal and the kind of yellow journalism that makes my blood boil. But Phyllis (who is now going by the name Stella Art Two and performing with some kind of horror cabaret troupe), surprisingly, came to my aid and negotiated what seemed to be a fairly bulletproof contract.

She's going to be a good manager/agent, I think, and apparently the fact she's American is incredibly good for ratings, although I don't understand why. If you ask me, the benefit is she has even more experience manipulating the media than they do and so far she has been ahead of them on all their dirty tricks.

She's also given me some surprising tips on how to make their vanity and insecurity actually work for me, not to mention how to tap into the resources of the station to get us into places I never had access to before. My Beta Kap ghost hunt is going to be *incredible*, and all without a lick of help from the Illuminated Weasel.

Sharon is actually a decent roommate, and she's letting me do a weekly vlog on her vitals (can you call it that when you're dealing with someone without a pulse or body temperature?). Teeny wanted me to make it about what apparently is an ongoing relationship between the zombie and her brother (Teeny's, not Sharon's of course) but that is ridiculous. Not to mention not the kind of journalism I choose to practice.

All in all, things have been far better in the world of the

paranormal exposé than they have been for years, maybe ever. I hope I will still be able to do my best work if I am not continually angry. I suppose I'll just have to give it a try.

Reminder: Do NOT under any circumstances say anything around Mocklin about a zombie love story segment.

89.

"A zombi pig?" Papa Georges said. "You made a zombi *pig?*"

Waglet couldn't quite figure out if his grandfather was angry or shocked, but he didn't seem pleased. Still, the old man's hands were gentle in the guinea pig's fur, and Auntie Cecilia seemed rather taken with having an undead rodent in the house.

In the door to the kitchen, his mother leaned against the frame, sipping her coffee. "Waglet, I have the feeling I should be punishing you, but I'm entirely unsure for what or how. They never really covered reanimation in the parent handbook."

Waglet looked down into his hands. His Mama could be stern, and she could definitely think up some imaginative punishments if she thought he deserved it.

"However," she began, and Waglet raised his head. There was a new tone in her voice that gave him a bit of hope. "However, it looks to me as if, although you have done something *very* dangerous without knowing the consequences, that girl is actually doing just fine, like your little pig there. If you promise *never* to do it again, I am willing to consider that what is done is done, and there's no reason to punish you for something you tried because some pair of old crones made you think you could."

"Hey!" said Auntie Cecilia. "Is it our fault the boy believed a fairy story?"

"Papa, Auntie," said Waglet's Mama, "maybe you've forgotten how houngan are respected back in our home. You knew when we lived there. And I seem to remember that both of you managed to do some pretty wonderful things in your time too."

Auntie Cecilia was silent, and looked at the old man, who looked down into his hands. "Mebbe," said Papa Georges, crossly.

"And I know a certain cousin of mine who could teach a talented boy a thing or two…"

"Oh, not him!" Auntie Cecilia was not so much dismissive as wary.

"Yes, him. Waglet deserves a change to see if he really can be a houngan. If he wants to, that is. What do you think, my sweet boy? Would you like to go back to Haiti for a while and become an apprentice to a *real* voodoo priest?"

"Mama, yes!" said Waglet, and although Sharon's face flashed quickly through his thoughts, he immediately found himself looking forward, to that beautiful, sad country of his birth with the poverty and stripped landscape where nonetheless you could find rare beauty, and of course magic. And maybe, even, that amazing, magical girl Sharon had promised was out there for him. Why not? If you can bring a girl back from the dead, love should be a piece of cake.

90.

There aren't many nicer places in town than the rooftop patio at Wayne Gretzky's, the restaurant owned by Ontario's favourite backhanding hockey son. Malcolm brought the drinks—wine for Sharon, and a beer for himself—and slipped under the awning of the cabana they'd reserved.

"Oooh, rotting grapes!" she said, clapping her hands.

"Cave Springs, actually, I think," he said. "But it should go down nicely."

Mocklin had sprung for a mini-shopping spree for Sharon when he'd heard how the contents of her apartment had been disposed of and how she'd been left with only one very bright and clashing bridesmaid's dress to wear. Tonight, she was wearing a soft green tunic and long patterned skirt that brought out the red of her hair instead of actively battling it.

"You look great," he said.

"Thanks," she said, reaching out for the wine he'd momentarily forgotten about. "So do you."

She patted the couch beside her, a little shyly, and he took the seat next to her.

Across the bar, a ruckus started between two guys who apparently had both arrived expecting to meet the same girl. Sharon took a sip of her wine and watched, waiting for the noise to die down. Malcolm watched her.

Finally, with the arrival of a couple of beefy security guys, the noise settled, and Sharon turned to her date. "Was that Mr. Get-It-On?" she said.

"Who?" he asked, but she just laughed.

"It doesn't matter. I'm just glad we're here, and that this—" and she indicated, broadly, her whole body "—is, you know, okay."

"More than okay," he confirmed.

They both turned their attention back to the other side of the bar where one of the guys who'd been escorted out (and yes, she thought, it was Mr. Get-It-On from the Zombie Speed Dating—small world!) had readmitted himself and was in the process of being ejected a second time.

Sharon used the distraction to inch her fingers towards Malcolm's only to find he'd done the same and met hers in the middle.

"So…" he said. "Do you know how this thing is going to work?"

"Nope." She shrugged, closing her hand around his. They laced their fingers together. "You?"

"Hey," he said. "I've dated *live* redheads before, but this is new territory for me."

"I guess we'll just have to figure it out for ourselves," she said, and despite having no blood in her veins, she could swear she was blushing.

"Okay," he said. "I can live with that."

"Right, rub it in," she said, mock-upset. "You live people are always so cocky about the whole… living thing." She might be dead, or undead, but she had the craziest feeling a new life, a whole new *creation,* had just begun.

"Let there be light," she said.

He laughed, although he couldn't know why she'd said it. And leaned toward her. And kissed her.

And it was good.

THE END

280 - undead redhead

about the author

Jen Frankel is the author of the "Blood & Magic" series about young heroine Maggie Stuart. The first two books in the series, The Last Rite and The Red Ring, deal with Maggie at ages 13 and 16 respectively. The third (and penultimate), Heaven & Hell, will feature Maggie at age 23, living in Montreal and still struggling with her powers.

Jen is also an avid screenwriter and an award-winning poet, as well as a great lover of fish, birds, cats, and all other living creatures. She even has a soft spot for human beings, provided they behave at least as well as their pets.

She lives and works in Toronto, Ontario, Canada, but you can count on her showing up all over North America (wherever there are comic book conventions) and online at www.jenfrankel.com.